JITTERBUG

Also by Gareth L. Powell
and available from Titan Books

Future's Edge
Who Will You Save?

THE CONTINUANCE SERIES
Stars and Bones
Descendant Machine

THE EMBERS OF WAR TRILOGY
Embers of War
Fleet of Knives
Light of Impossible Stars

"*Jitterbug* is a thrilling journey filled with witty banter, unlikely allies and friendships, secrets and sacrifices, and found family, exploring the cyclical nature of both history and the future, and the way our fates are often shaped not just by choice but also by luck and coincidence."

Ai Jiang, author of *A Palace Near the Wind*

"*Jitterbug* is a haunting, propulsive odyssey across the ruins of our solar system—where justice, grief, and the ghosts of creation itself collide. Gareth L. Powell writes with both fire and tenderness, crafting a space opera that pulses with human ache amid cosmic wonder. It's poetic, cinematic, and deeply humane—science fiction with a beating heart and a reckoning soul."

Cynthia Pelayo, Bram Stoker Award®–winning author of *Children of Chicago* and *The Shoemaker's Magician*

"Imagine the solar system as a mighty ocean full of pirates and you have the beating heart of *Jitterbug* – a roaring whirlwind of a novel, full of adventure, emotion, wit and great characters."

David Quantick, author of *All My Colours*

"Every time I thought I had the flight path of *Jitterbug* all figured out, Gareth L. Powell banked a hard left in the most delightful way. From space pirate brawls to bounty hunter chases and political machinations, Powell pairs thrills with richly imagined characters that pulse with life. I don't think I've ever rooted so hard for a shipboard AI. Bold and cinematic, *Jitterbug* proves that Powell is a master of scale—balancing galaxy-spanning stakes with moments of vibrant, intimate heart."

Nathan Tavares, author of *A Fractured Infinity*

JITTERBUG

GARETH L.
POWELL

Titan BOOKS

Jitterbug
Paperback edition ISBN: 9781835414514
E-book edition ISBN: 9781835415504

Published by Titan Books
A division of Titan Publishing Group Ltd
144 Southwark Street, London SE1 0UP
www.titanbooks.com

First edition: March 2026
10 9 8 7 6 5 4 3 2 1

This is a work of fiction. All of the characters, organizations, and events portrayed in this novel are either products of the author's imagination or are used fictitiously. Any resemblance to actual persons, living or dead (except for satirical purposes), is entirely coincidental.

© Gareth L. Powell 2026. All rights reserved.

Gareth L. Powell asserts the moral right to be
identified as the author of this work.

No part of this publication may be reproduced, stored in a retrieval system, or transmitted, in any form or by any means without the prior written permission of the publisher, nor be otherwise circulated in any form of binding or cover other than that in which it is published and without a similar condition being imposed on the subsequent purchaser.

A CIP catalogue record for this title is available from the British Library.

EU RP (for authorities only)
eucomply OÜ, Pärnu mnt. 139b-14, 11317 Tallinn, Estonia
hello@eucompliancepartner.com, +3375690241

Typeset by Richard Mason.

Printed and bound by CPI Group (UK) Ltd, Croydon, CR0 4YY.

For Edith, Rose, and Robin

PROLOGUE
JUSTICE BROWN

Come sit here by me, Copernicus. Listen to your grandmother. I want to tell you a story. I want to tell you how it all began...

It was a hot night in South London, back on Earth. This was many years ago, when your father was just a baby. It was the kind of night you have all the windows open, and it doesn't make a lick of difference, except you can hear the traffic and the sirens in the streets nine floors below.

I'd just got the baby down when Leon called and told me to come up to the roof.

"Why the hell am I coming up to the roof?" I asked him.

He laughed, but I could hear he was scared. "It's Saturn, Justice."

"What about Saturn?"

"It's started."

"But Malcolm—"

"Bring Malcolm. This is historic."

"I only just got him to sleep."

"Juss, I got the telescope set up. The neighbours are all here. Just come on up."

So, I grumbled to myself, and I pulled on a T-shirt and a pair of pyjama bottoms, and I carried baby Malcolm, your father, up four flights of stairs to the roof.

As residents, we weren't supposed to have access to the roof of the tower block, but the maintenance door had been broken for as long as anyone could remember, and no one seemed in a hurry to get it fixed.

Up on the roof, I could hear the cars and the drunks down in the streets. Leon was waiting for me. He had a beer bottle in one hand and his eyes were wild.

"You gotta see this, Justice."

The lights of a police helicopter blinked high above Clapham Common. I saw people on other roofs. Some of them also had telescopes or binoculars. Others just seemed to be partying, enjoying the vibe. I smelled barbeque. I'd already had dinner, but the smoky jerk chicken spices and charred sweetcorn ribs set my stomach rumbling something fierce, which did nothing to improve my mood.

"Is this like that Uranus thing?"

"Yes, and Neptune before that."

I sighed. "You brought me and the baby up here for lights in the sky?"

"Juss, it's so much more than that."

"You said that last time, and it was just a little star turning into a bright smudge."

Leon took a slug of beer. He seemed wired. "First off, Uranus wasn't a star, it was a planet. And secondly, it didn't turn into a smudge, it disintegrated."

"Like the other one, a few years ago."

"Like Neptune, yes."

I raised my eyes to the light-choked sky. Only a handful of the brightest stars could penetrate the city's glow. "And you dragged me out to see the same thing, a third time?"

He looked crestfallen. "But, Justice, this is Saturn. It's historic."

"And I got work tomorrow."

He shrugged, and I think if I'd walked away then, he'd have let me go. We had a funny sort of relationship. He was more than a best friend. More like a brother, I suppose. And he loved baby Malcolm, your father. And because he cared for Malcolm as if he was his own son, I let him. He took care of me, too, and he never asked for anything in return.

Anyhow, as I was saying, I'd made my mind up to go back downstairs and put the baby back in his crib. But before I could move, we heard cries from the folk clustered around the scope. Shouts from other rooftops. Stupidly, I looked up, but I didn't know where to look, and even if I did, there was nothing visible to the human eye.

Leon took my free wrist and pulled me across to the telescope. As it was his, people made way for him, and he took a quick look, bending his face to the viewer. He whistled in appreciation, and then bade me look.

Bending over was awkward with Malcolm on my shoulder, but I didn't want to hand him off to anyone else in the crowd.

What I saw chilled me to the bone.

I'd seen pictures of Saturn at school. It was the one with the rings around it. Only now, there was something up with the rings. Gradually, almost too slowly for the human eye to register the movement, they had begun to unravel, unmoored fountains of ice spinning free like the sparks of a pinwheel firework. My entire body went cold. The idiots on the other roofs were whooping it up, but I knew right there and then, that I had just looked into the eye of death. I hadn't really paid attention when the other two, Neptune and Uranus, had fallen apart, spreading their gases like a slick along the paths of their orbits. But Saturn was iconic. It was the one with the rings. Now that those rings were coming apart, it felt like someone had bulldozed the Pyramids, filled in the Grand Canyon, or toppled the Eiffel Tower. I stood up and stared out across the city. I felt the warmth of my son, your father, asleep on my shoulder, and wanted to scream.

Leon said, "Juss, are you all right?"

"Of course, I'm not fucking all right."

Malcolm stirred and I patted his back, trying to soothe him.

"What is it?" Leon asked.

"It doesn't take a genius to connect the dots," I told him. "First, Neptune. Then, Uranus. Now, Saturn. Whatever's doing this is getting closer. It's moving inwards."

He grew serious. "Yeah, I know."

"So, what happens when it reaches Earth?"

I watched the gears of his mind crunch as he tried to decide how to respond. His brow creased, then his mouth opened. He put the beer bottle down and rubbed his chin. The neighbours clustered on the roof around us had fallen silent, watching us with the uncertainty of teenagers caught whistling at a funeral.

"It's going to be okay," he said quietly.

I gave a snort. "And how can you possibly know that?"

He put a fist to his mouth. "I just... do."

The other roof parties were falling silent as people turned to the news updates on their phones. We hadn't got good pictures of the other gas giants falling apart, but Saturn was that much closer. Any fool with a backyard telescope could see her plain as day, so you can imagine the detail they were getting from the big observatories.

Saturn, a planet many times larger than the Earth, was being unstoppably ripped apart. The rings were going, but so were the gases that made up its body. Ten-thousand-mile-wide storms whirled around its equator as the atmosphere sprayed into space like blood from a dozen gunshot wounds. Lightning sparked and flickered in the tortured clouds, and aurora raged at both poles.

What had started as another astronomical curiosity had suddenly revealed itself for the urgent, existential threat we'd been pretending it wasn't.

Leon shook his head. "Trust me." He held out a hand. "It's going to be all right for you, and little Malcolm. You're going to be safe."

"What?"

He held up a hand, as if to ward me away. "It's going to be okay."

I wasn't convinced. "I just saw the same shit you did. And the way I see it, what's happening to Saturn is gonna happen here, and there's not a damn thing anyone can do to stop it."

"It won't, trust me."

"Trust you? We're all going to die, and you want me to take the word of your ignorant ass that it's all gonna be just peachy?"

"I don't want to say any more."

"Leon, what the fuck are you talking about? You don't want to say any more? Are you trippin'?"

"Justice, please..."

Even as he said it, even as he backed away, I could see he was frightened.

He kept retreating, waving his hands in denial. I said, "Leon—"

"No, don't ask me."

"Leon, look out!"

The backs of his legs hit the low wall at the edge of the roof, and he lost his footing. For an instant, he teetered there, eyes wide, arms windmilling as he tried to regain his balance. If I hadn't been cradling Malcolm, perhaps I could have saved him somehow—but before I could do anything, he fell. His backside hit the top of the wall, and he rolled backwards like a scuba diver flipping out of a boat. One instant he was there; the next, he was gone.

I turned away, but even thirteen floors above the pavement, I heard the noise he made when he hit.

PART ONE

THE HANDIWORK OF GODS

CHAPTER ONE

COPERNICUS BROWN

I trudged through the foot-churned mud at the side of the road, walking with my head down and my hands in the pockets of my leather jacket, avoiding eye contact. One hand gripped a hidden pistol, the other a concealed knife. I wasn't looking for trouble but in my line of work, and especially in this part of town, you didn't grow old by attracting attention or being unprepared.

Grant's Landing was a typical Swirl settlement. It had grown outwards from an improvised and ragged kernel, with each new wave of refugees and immigrants accreting like rings around a tree stump. On the outskirts of this newest ring, the store owners had constructed their frontages from cannibalised packing materials, with hand-painted signs above their doors. Here on the edge of town, and the edge of the shattered solar system, there hadn't yet been time to erect anything more permanent.

My grandmother had been in her late thirties when the Swirl started to coalesce from the wreckage of the gas giants; my father, Malcolm, had been among the first generation to move out to the territories that had been created from their material; and now here I was, hunting criminals through this new frontier—neither a part of these streets nor entirely apart from them.

I knew the rest of my crew awaited me back on the *Jitterbug*. With luck, they would have completed the repairs and maintenance that the old ship so desperately needed if she were to fly again. I hunched my shoulders against the thin wind. As soon as I had my target secured, I'd be able to join them; and if this bounty paid out, I'd be able to fuel the *Jitterbug*, fill the kitchen with enough ramen to keep us all fed for a month, and perhaps even get those janky landing motors overhauled when we got back to Luna. Our three-week enforced layover on this backwater dump would be at an end and we could spiral inwards, to warmer climes.

That's if we didn't kill each other first.

As you'd expect, since we'd run out of fuel, tensions had been running high. Boredom and poverty can be a combustible mixture.

I put a call through to the ship.

Hey, I thought, *how are we doing?*

The ship's personality stirred at the back of my mind.

>Things have been better.

In my head, her voice was that of a particularly eloquent parrot, the sentences punctuated by clicks and whistles. I even 'heard' the occasional clack of her beak.

How are the crew?

>Restless. How goes the hunt?

I'm close.

>Take care. This one's a real piece of work. Four counts of conspiracy to commit piracy. Two of being an accessory to murder. Seven of fencing stolen goods...

I tightened my grip on my weapons. *I'll be fine.*

>Make sure you are. Ulf's very hungover, and Kiki's needling him about it. It's going to end in a fight, and McKenzie can't keep them apart forever.

Tell them I want them all alert, sober, and ready to fuel up and clear atmo' the moment I get back.

>Roger that.

Ahead, sepia tavern lights spilled out onto the dirty sidewalk. Mutters of conversation. Jagged laughter. I was close now. If my information was correct, my target used this place to sell stolen property. I drew myself up, and pushed my way through the door.

Inside, the place reeked of sour beer and stale sweat. Eyes turned towards me. I hesitated for a second, then squared my shoulders and strode up to the counter.

"What'll it be?" The barman was more machine than man, with scars that suggested old radiation burns.

"Vodka and coke."

"We ain't got no coke."

"Surprise me."

He poured a thimble's worth of neat potato vodka. The bottle clinked against the lip of the glass.

"You're new here."

I leant against the bar. "Isn't everybody?"

He gave a shrug to show he neither knew nor cared, and moved off to serve someone else. I picked up my drink and turned to survey the room, seeing a selection of the sorts of faces you'd expect to see in a frontier town: itinerant construction workers, farm labourers, spacers looking for work, two-bit hustlers, and assorted lowlifes. The set of their shoulders showed they were tired, disillusioned, and probably thinner than they had been when they'd left Earth. A few of them glanced at me, then looked away. Either they figured I wasn't worth their time, or they'd guessed what I was and wanted no part of what was about to happen.

Jimmy Malbec fell into that second category. He hunched in a corner booth like a cornered rat, his collar turned up and his thin chin almost touching the top of his beer glass.

Got him.
>Be careful.
Where's the fun in that?

I drained my drink and carefully placed the glass on the counter. Then I walked over, my footsteps suddenly the only sound in the place. Jimmy didn't look up. "What do you want?"

"You know why I'm here."

"You got the wrong guy."

I pulled my licence from my back pocket and flashed it at him. "Jimmy Malbec, you are a wanted man and I'm here to take you in."

"I told you, I ain't no Jimmy Malbec."

"Of course you are. Now, do you feel like cooperating, or are we going to cause a scene?"

His eyes darted to the holdall on the seat beside him, and I guessed he had a weapon there. I pulled my own gun from my pocket and showed it to him. "Let's not do that."

Jimmy looked from his bag to the barrel of my pistol, and he seemed to deflate. The resistance went out of him, leaving only a skinny guy in a cheap coat.

"I still say you got the wrong man."

I tossed him a cable tie. "That's for the judge to decide. Now, shut up and put that over your wrists."

"Why should I?"

We were attracting a lot of attention now, and I wanted to get out of there before any of the local chucklefucks decided to get involved.

"It's either that," I said, loudly enough for the others to hear, "or I shoot you in both kneecaps and drag your sorry ass out by the collar."

It was a bluff, but it worked. Malbec blanched and did what I told him.

"Now, tighten it," I said. "Use your teeth."

I watched him grab the end of the tie in his mouth and pull.
"Tighter than that," I said.
"Any tighter and it'll cut off my circulation."
"My heart bleeds for you." He gave the plastic a final tug, and I nodded my satisfaction. "Now, get on your feet and we're going to walk to the exit, all nice and easy, okay?"

I waited for him to edge out of the booth, then followed him, keeping the pistol trained on the small of his back.

We almost made it to the door.

A boot tripped me. I stumbled but didn't fall. Then a pair of plaid-wrapped arms grabbed me from behind, pinning my arms to my sides. I saw Malbec, still tethered, looking back wide-eyed.

The guy holding me snarled. "Fucking bounty hunter."

I stood six feet tall and weighed 180 pounds, but this guy was a full head and shoulders taller than me, and probably twice as heavy. With that size and strength, he was either a construction worker or hired muscle, and maybe even both, and I knew I was going to have to fight dirty. I raked the heel of my boot down the front of his shin and ground it into his foot. He growled in pain and tightened his grip.

Seeing his chance, Malbec bolted for the street.

I struggled, but the guy holding me was strong, and some of the other drinkers looked like they wanted to get in on the action. I had to get free and get after Malbec before I lost him altogether. I dropped my arm and put a bullet through the big guy's boot. He gave a cry and, as his arms dropped, I turned and smashed the butt of the pistol into the bridge of his nose. Blood exploded across his beard and chest, and he dropped onto his ass. Everyone else froze. I backed towards the door with the gun at the ready, and then turned and ran.

I found Malbec in an alley a little way down the street. He was trying to saw the cable tie against the edge of an open dumpster. He looked like a racoon trying to open a food packet. He saw me and straightened up, holding his still-bound hands in front of him in a gesture of surrender.

"Sheriff's office," I said. "Start walking."

He gave a long, low sigh. "Okay," he said. "You got me. But maybe we can do a deal?"

"What kind of deal?"

"I got some information that might be worth a few credits."

"What kind of information?"

"If I tell you, you'll let me go?"

I smiled. "Sure…"

I cleaned my gun while one of the deputies processed Malbec, locked him in a cell, and transferred the reward money to my account.

Start refuelling, I told the ship.

>Thank you. (Whistle) Are you coming back now?

I'm on my way.

I left the sheriff's office and took a grateful lungful of cold night air. The adrenalin had started to wear off, and I had to clench my fists to stop my hands from shaking. I'd been lucky and I knew it. I had a couple of new bruises, but tonight could have gone very differently.

When I got back to the *Jitterbug*, I found Kiki in the galley watching cartoons. She looked up and grinned as I entered. "What's the good word, Captain?"

"I got him."

"Yes!"

"Where are the others?"

"Below decks. I think Ulf's sulking."

"Well, this might cheer him up. We have a full tank, and we're ready to leave. I'll need you in the pilot's seat, running pre-flight checks, and I need the other two down in the engine room, working their magic."

She leapt to her feet. "Fuck, yeah!"

I walked over to the companionway that led down to the engine room and yelled, "You two down there?"

"Yes, Captain," Ulf replied.

"We're here!" McKenzie added.

"Wheels up in five minutes," I told them. "Get everything squared away and ready for flight."

"Yay!"

I smiled, and then followed Kiki up the ladder to the bridge, where she was already buckling into her chair and activating her consoles.

How are we doing? I asked the ship.

>Raring to go. It's been a long three weeks standing in slush. I was starting to worry I'd rust.

Let me know the moment you're ready to go.

>I will, but, Captain...?

Yes?

>Where are we going?

I strapped into my own couch. *Take us to Mars.*

>Mars is dangerous. Nobody goes there anymore.

That's the accepted wisdom.

>So, why are we heading there?

I got a lead.

>A lead on a bounty?

Malbec told me some of his old smuggling contacts have a cache there. They use it as a staging post for runs into the Swirl. If we can find it and tag it, we'll be able to sell the location to Sol-Sec for a decent chunk of change.

>And he just told you this (click, whistle) voluntarily?

Well, I may have lied to him about letting him go.

>The crew aren't going to like this. They don't like getting close to the Broken Places.

They'll like it well enough when we get paid.

I sat in my command couch as the *Jitterbug* powered away from the shard on which I'd had to leave it parked for so long. I cradled a hot cup of tea in my hands. Around me, I heard the familiar creaks and groans as different sections of the hull warmed in raw sunlight and froze in airless shade.

To someone of my grandmother's generation who remembered the stately orrery of the planets, our altered solar system might have appeared chilling in its artificiality—but to us, it was home.

Almost a century ago, something had disassembled the gas giants and used their material to create an entirely new set of structures. Where the asteroid belt had once been, now eight sections of a hollow sphere hung in stately orbit around the Sun.

Imagine an orange. Slice it into eight equal pieces and remove the peel. Now arrange those eight pieces of peel at regular intervals around a tea light. If you move them inwards, they will meet to form a hollow sphere with the candle at the centre, trapping all its light within. Spaced out, they only block half the light, letting the rest escape. Their inner surfaces are warm, their outer rinds turned to the darkness. The eight shards of the Swirl were those pieces of orange peel writ large. They measured 340 million kilometres from tip to tip, and 85 million across at their widest points. If they moved inwards, they would meet and join somewhere between the orbits of Mars and Earth, completely enclosing our sun in a colossal sphere. Fortunately for us, they seemed content to stay where they were for now, equally spaced around its light. Their inner surfaces were habitable, with oxygen-nitrogen atmospheres, cold-but-manageable surface temperatures, skies that somehow polarised to provide a thirty-hour day/night cycle, and a gravity approximately three-quarters that of the Earth. Nobody knew how or why they managed to maintain these characteristics, nor why the orbits of the inner planets had been seemingly unaffected by their ferocious mass, but for the past few decades, humans had been slowly colonising these strange new habitats. And with the scientific community's general consensus that the Swirl's creators were most probably long dead, what had seemed frightening and inexplicable to my grandmother's generation now represented a wide-open land of opportunity.

Sitting at her console to my left, Kiki said, "Hey, Cap. Are you going to give me the skinny on why you're taking us to Mars?"

I called up a magnified image of the red planet. It looked like a cracked nut. Parts of it had begun to flake away. Dust and rock streamed out behind it like the tail of a comet—a savage reminder that the mechanism responsible for taking apart the gas giants wasn't finished yet, and that once this planet had been cannibalised, Earth would probably be next.

"We're not actually going to the surface."

"Well, thank fuck for that."

"We're heading for the debris trail."

"I assume you're kidding?"

"Do I look like I'm kidding?"

She regarded me for a long moment, and then exhaled theatrically. "I deserve hazard pay."

"You already get hazard pay."

She cackled manically. "I deserve more."

Once underway, we were able to unstrap and move around, so I gathered the crew in the galley.

Ulf and McKenzie wore greasy orange jumpsuits and heavy toolbelts. McKenzie had a pair of welding goggles pushed up on her forehead, and Ulf had braided his grey beard into a thick rope that reached his chest and made him look like a Viking.

I waited while they got themselves coffee, and Kiki brewed a pot of green tea. As she waited for the water to heat to the correct temperature, she sang one of her made-up cooking songs under her breath.

*"Take rice and beans and spicy meat-o,
wrap 'em all up an' make a burrito…"*

From experience, I knew her repertoire of galley-centric tunes included the other self-penned hits 'Hubbly-Bubbly Soup', 'Mama's Got That Ramen Rhythm', and my personal favourite, 'I Don't Know Who's Clearing This Shit Up (But It Sure as Shit Ain't Me)'.

The *Jitterbug* joined us using her remote—an artificial parrot with synthetic bright blue, red, and black plumage that flapped noisily into the room and perched on the back of a chair, steel talons gripping the worn upholstery.

"So," Ulf said once they were all settled around the table. "Who's our target this time?"

"It's not so much a who as an it," I told him. "More specifically, a smuggler's cache."

"Are we going to loot it?" McKenzie asked.

"No, we're simply going to tag it and report the location to Sol-Sec."

"That doesn't sound much fun."

"They'll pay us a bounty if the information checks out."

"How much?"

"More than we can afford to pass up."

Ulf gave a grunt. "And where is this cache?"

Kiki beamed. "It's on Mars."

He scowled at her, then turned to me. "Is this true?"

"It's in the debris cloud," I said. "On one of the larger rocks."

"You can't be serious." He shook his head. "Flying into that cloud's like flying into a meat grinder."

"Which makes it the perfect hiding place."

"We'll be pulverised."

"Kiki can do it."

"The manic pixie nightmare girl?" The big man rolled his eyes. "Lord, help us."

"Well, I think it sounds exciting," McKenzie put in.

Ulf snorted. "You won't feel that way when the thing that's taking apart the planet starts taking apart the ship."

Her eyes widened. "Is that a possibility?"

I spread my hands on the table. "Honestly, I don't know. But if the smugglers have been using this location for some time, I must assume it's relatively safe."

Ulf turned to the *Jitterbug*'s remote. "What do you think?"

The parrot angled her head at him. "I go where I'm told," she squawked.

"Don't give me that. We all know you have an opinion."

She made a rapid clicking noise—her equivalent of laughter. "Well, of course I do."

"And?"

"And I agree with McKenzie. I think it sounds exciting."

Kiki jumped up and hugged the parrot. "That's my girl."

Ulf shook his head sadly. "You are all fuck-nut insane."

"Aw." Kiki beamed. "That's why you love us."

After that, the meeting broke up, Kiki climbed back to the bridge with the parrot on her shoulder and Ulf took a bottle of aquavit to his cabin. I went to my bunk. It was around midnight, and I'd been through quite enough for one evening.

I lay on the mattress and stared at the metal ceiling. The cabin wasn't spacious—it wasn't much longer than the bed, and gave me just enough room to dress without banging my knees and elbows against the walls—but it had been my father's and now it was mine.

He had been a distant figure for much of my childhood, only visiting us for brief layovers between cargo runs. It hadn't been until my mother died that he finally brought me to live with him on the *Jitterbug*. I had been twelve years old and grieving. I spent my adolescence on this ship, and had now spent the majority of my adult life encased within its hull.

I closed my eyes and listened to the familiar sounds of shipboard life: the low rumble of the engines; the hum of the air circulation system; the clangs and thumps of other people moving around; and the pings and creaks of the flexing hull.

Someone knocked on my door. I muttered a curse, sat up and swung my legs over the side of the bed. "Come in."

The hatch opened to reveal McKenzie.

"Is there a problem?"

She shook her head. "No."

"Then what is it?"

She bit her lip and looked around. She hadn't been in here before, and seemed surprised by how small it was. I guess she'd assumed the captain's cabin would be bigger than the rest.

"I know this wasn't your idea," she said. "To take me on, I mean. I know my mother put pressure on you."

"Your mother can be quite insistent when she wants to be."

"Oh, believe me, I know." McKenzie smiled nervously. "I just wanted to thank you."

"For stranding you on Grant's Landing for three weeks?"

"For not holding it against me."

"You're a good engineer."

A flush crept across her cheeks. "I just want you to know I appreciate it. I always looked up to you when I was a kid."

"You looked up to me?"

"Of everyone in the family, you were the only one who got out on their own terms."

"I didn't have a lot of choice."

"But you did it. The rest of us stayed on the ground and did as we were told, but you escaped."

"Only because my mother died."

Her face fell. "I'm sorry, I—"

"Forget it."

She rubbed her forehead. "I'm messing this all up. I just wanted to say thank you. You didn't have to take me on."

I shrugged. "What was I going to do, say no to your mother?"

"One day, perhaps somebody will."

I gave a laugh. "And on that day, may God have mercy on their soul."

I expected her to leave then, but she hesitated.

"There's something else I wanted to talk about."

"A problem?"

"Kind of."

"Well, spit it out."

"It's Ulf."

"What about him?"

She held up a hand. "Don't get me wrong, he's great. I like working with him but…"

"But what?"

"He hovers."

"I don't understand."

She sighed. "He's been working that engine room for a long time, and he's got everything just the way he wants it."

I thought I understood. "So, whenever you try to do anything—"

"He's hovering over my shoulder, watching in case I mess it up."

"You are still learning," I reminded her. "And he's poured his life into those engines."

"I know, but it's really hard to work with someone breathing down your neck. I just wish he'd trust me a little more. I'm not going to wreck the ship. If I don't know what to do, I'll ask him."

I smiled. "He has a lot of faith in you."

"He doesn't show it."

"Trust me, if he had any doubts about your abilities, he wouldn't let you anywhere near the ship's systems. The fact he does, even if he's keeping an eye on you while you work, is a massive sign of trust."

She looked uncertain. "Really?"

"Look, when we've done this job, I'll sit the two of you down and we can talk it through, okay? You'll see I'm right."

"I don't know…"

"We'll figure it out."

She bit her lower lip and shrugged, still plainly unconvinced. "If you say so."

After she'd gone, I remained on the edge of my bunk, looking down at my boots, feeling an unwelcome weight settle on my shoulders.

Hey, ship?

>Yes, Copernicus?

We are doing the right thing, aren't we?

>It depends on what you mean by right.

I don't want to put McKenzie in harm's way.

>You've never been one to shy away from a risk.

I know, but this is different. I'm responsible for her now. Is Ulf right? Is going after this cache a step too far?

>Life has burdened Ulf with an excess of common sense. If it were his decision, we'd spend the rest of our lives doing safe delivery runs.

And that would be a bad thing?

>I'd die of boredom.

I laughed. *I think I would, too.*

>You know it's true.

So, we press on?

>I promise I'll alert you the instant I detect anything

even remotely sketchy. And you know that despite all her exuberance, Kiki is a survivor. Remember how she made us pass up that contract last month because the 'vibes were off'.

Yeah, the guy turned out to be a real psycho. He would have made mincemeat of us. In the end, it took eight Sol-Sec officers to bring him down.

>Exactly. She may act reckless sometimes, but she's not stupid. She's not about to fly into anything she can't handle.

Thank you. I needed to hear that.

>You're welcome. You shouldn't second-guess yourself so much. Your father always went with his gut.

To be fair, it was a lot bigger than his brain.

>See, you're feeling better already.

I suppose I am. Goodnight, ship.

>Goodnight, Copernicus.

MESSAGE BOARD

WANTED: Passage to Brandt's Haven on Swirl Segment #2 for family of four plus dog. No questions asked.

[Click to Read More]

*

CREW NEEDED: Engineer's mate needed for cargo hauler *Temeraire* out of New Carson City, Luna, bound for Agricultural Research Station 51 on Swirl Segment #3.

[Click to Read More]

*

BOUNTY: $280K USD for capture of notorious pirate Natalya Ponomarenko or information leading to apprehension and conviction.
[Click to Read More]

*

CRAZY LARRY'S HARDWARE AND DRY GOODS. For all your homesteading and farming needs. Don't leave Earth without visiting Crazy Larry! Our prices are out of this world!
[Click to Read More]

CHAPTER TWO

JITTERBUG

Freed from the gravitational pull of the shard, I executed a slow barrel roll, luxuriating in the caress of the solar wind against my hull. My sensors fizzed and crackled with the sounds of a thousand garbled transmissions. Distant sparks marked other ships firing their engines to correct course or decelerate towards one of the Swirl settlements. And beneath it all, the ever-present background hiss of the Big Bang.

Around me, the Swirl's shards seemed to fill the sky. Illuminated by the Sun, their reflected brilliance flooded the inner solar system, robbing the Earth of darkness and playing hell with the diurnal rhythms of life.

But what did I care about life on Earth? I'd been constructed in Lunar orbit and spent most of my long career hauling back and forth between the inner system and the Swirl. Even when collecting cargo from the planet, I'd never had cause to breach the atmosphere, let alone land. Everything and everyone that needed to be shipped from the surface came up one of the elevators sprouting from the equator, and all I had to do was dock with the station at the top of the structure. Earth was for capybaras, lizards, and humans; it held no place for me.

An aerospace corporation had built me during the first

wave of exploration and expansion, as the chaos of the Swirl began to organise itself into chunks of solid matter. Back in those days, only small fragments of the larger segments had so far resolved from the dust cloud and humanity was grappling with the realisation that entities possessing a technology far beyond anything they could conceive had dismantled the gas giants on purpose—although the exact nature of those entities remained a topic of furious debate. Many assumed those responsible for reshaping the solar system were extraterrestrial in origin. All we really knew was that the objects they were building beyond the orbit of Mars were landscaped and held a breathable atmosphere—so, of course, every nation and corporate interest wanted to establish their own outpost there.

Now, sixty years later, I'd served half a dozen different owners and purposes, from cargo hauler to explorer, and racked-up almost half a million hours of flight time. For twenty-two of those years, I flew as a freighter for Copernicus's father—right up until the day of his murder. As Malcolm's only child, Copernicus inherited me. Now, rather than hauling cargo, I helped him track criminals who'd fled into the anonymity of the frontier, hoping to hide in the Swirl. Bringing them to justice wasn't a glamorous or respectable profession, but I enjoyed moving around a lot. I hated being still. That's why I was glorying in the sensation of flight after so many days spent grounded. Stranded at the bottom of a gravity well, I was as helpless as a hatchling fallen from its nest. The vacuum was my milieu. I was a machine designed for space, a bird evolved for an infinite sky in which the parochial planetary concepts of up and down held no meaning. Humans often spent their lives seeking a sense of purpose; mine came already hardwired. I might have been nearly a century old, but my enthusiasm for flight remained as sharp as it had when I'd been fresh off the assembly line.

I have to say, I nevertheless missed the Old Man. He'd been

impetuous and cantankerous, but he'd always treated me as a friend and a part of his crew. It had been his idea to get a synthetic parrot to act as a remote, allowing me to be 'in the room' with the rest of the crew rather than a disembodied voice echoing from the ceiling. When we were in port, I used to ride around on his shoulder. It was the first time I'd left the confines of my hull, and the sights and sounds of a bustling dock had been intoxicating. By taking me with him like that, he'd broadened my world, providing context that helped me relate to my crew, and I think he liked the way he looked with me perched there. It made him instantly recognisable on the concourse. Everybody knew him, and he never let on that I was anything other than a genuine, flesh-and-blood bird.

I could see traces of his stubbornness in his son. Copernicus even had the same frown lines as his father and had claimed the Old Man's leather jacket as his own, despite it being a size too large. Losing the Old Man had been a terrible blow to us both. And if Copernicus's way of dealing with his grief involved hunting down outlaws and renegades, then at least he was putting that grief to a socially useful purpose. As a lightly armed freighter, my own means of expression were more limited, but by helping him, I could extract some measure of satisfaction by proxy.

I was certainly glad Ulf had decided to remain on board. He had flown with the Old Man for years, and he was a good engineer. When sober, his experience and gruff manner made him a steadfast and pragmatic presence, which was something both Copernicus and his father had sorely needed.

In contrast, Kiki was a chaotic, if capable, pilot. Habitually clad in mis-buttoned Hawaiian shirts and half-fastened dungarees, she treated the bridge as her personal fiefdom, leaving trails of abandoned mugs, old paperbacks, and discarded hair scrunchies everywhere she went. Technically, I was perfectly capable of piloting myself, but regulations stipulated every transport carry a human pilot in case of malfunction. Her untidiness drove Ulf to distraction, but nobody knew more than her about coaxing every pound of thrust from my ageing engines. Born on one of the oldest freight transports hauling supplies to and from the Swirl, she'd figured out how to remotely dock a cargo skiff before she'd learned how to spell her name. She could calculate a Hohmann transfer orbit in her head and plot three-dimensional thrust vectors at least as well as any computer. She and I were like a show horse and its rider. Neither of us could do what we did alone, and each made the other more graceful, masterful, and efficient.

Her love of Hawaiian shirts came from her father, who had been born on the islands; and her fondness for combat boots and her piloting prowess were both traits inherited from her mother, who'd been the matriarch of their family haulage business, and had taught Kiki all she knew about three-dimensional navigation and the finer points of guiding a ship between two points in a constantly shifting solar system.

At only nineteen, McKenzie was the most recent addition to our crew. She was Copernicus's younger cousin, and her presence as Ulf's assistant was the result of a favour to her mother, who simply didn't know what else to do with a daughter who kept taking apart every appliance to see how it worked. Ulf often complained about having to babysit her, but it was clear he secretly enjoyed having such an enthusiastic apprentice.

As I flew, everything around me moved relative to everything else. The Swirl's segments continued their slow, stately revolution around the Sun; Earth and the other inner planets wheeled around in their tighter, faster orbits; and I flew between them like a bullet fired from one spinning fairground ride to a target on another. My projected course, double-checked and approved by Kiki, inscribed an invisible arc across the solar system, aimed not at where Mars was right now, but where it would be when I arrived.

I had perched my remote on the back of the chair beside Kiki. We could have spoken silently or audibly without its presence, but I knew she liked the sense of company the parrot provided while she was alone on the bridge with the rest of the crew asleep.

We had a chessboard set up on the console between us. She had called up one of her playlists on her workstation, and as we played, I watched her tap her feet and drum her fingers in time with the bluesy rock music.

"This is old," I said.

"I think you mean retro."

"Ancient."

"Classic."

"It's older than me."

Kiki flashed a grin. "Okay, I admit, that is pretty fucking old."

"I prefer experienced."

She laughed, put a hand to the small of her back and stretched her spine until something clicked. "Ah, that's better."

Her half-empty mug of green tea rested on the console, in defiance of every regulation designed to prevent hot liquid from spilling onto sensitive electronics. She picked it up and took a sip.

"Do you know the meaning of life?" she asked.

"No, I don't." Using my beak, I nudged a pawn from E2 to E4.

"Neither do I, but I'm pretty sure it has something to do with tea, and maybe ramen."

"That's it?"

"Eat the noodles, drink the tea." She shrugged and moved her king's pawn from E7 to E5. "It's a theory in progress."

I decided not to remind her that, as a spaceship, I was incapable of experiencing either hot drinks or noodles. Instead, I used a claw to slide my bishop from F1 to C4. Kiki saw the move and frowned. She wasn't the most strategic of players and tended to rely on inspiration and gut feel to make her moves. As I'd hoped, she brought her knight to C6.

"So," I said, distracting her from the board. "If that's the meaning of life, what's the meaning of death?"

She scrunched her face in puzzlement. "Death isn't a thing, it's an absence. So, it can't have a meaning. It's just nothing."

"You don't believe in an afterlife?"

"I just don't think it's possible."

"Why not?"

"Because people don't carry on after they die."

"How can you know that?"

She shook her head. "It's obvious. Just look at people with head injuries. If you cut away part of your brain, your personality changes. Your mind doesn't exist separately from the tissue."

"So, we're tied to our hardware?"

"Yes." She fiddled with a pawn, growing serious. "The way I think of it is this: consciousness is like the heat coming off an engine on a cold day. You know what I mean? It's the side-effect of a complex physical process. If you stop the engine, the heat dissipates into the air. The process stops."

"You're saying the mind can't survive the death of the brain?"

"Look at you. You're conscious, running on artificial processors. What happens if those processors get switched off?"

"I would cease."

"And if they got flipped back on?"

"I would start to think again."

She leant across the board. "But in the meantime?"

"I wouldn't be able to access sensory input. The decision gates in my processors wouldn't be able to open or close. My thoughts would cease."

"Exactly." She grinned. "You would be gone. The engine only generates heat while it functions. When it stops functioning, it stops generating. End of story."

"And it's the same with humans?"

"Our brains are just complex machines. When your brain

stops, you stop. That's it, game over. If anyone tries to tell you any different, they're selling something."

"I see." I picked up my queen and plonked it down on H5.

Kiki pursed her lips, regarding the piece the way a bird eyes an unexpected worm. Trying to act casual, she brought her other knight to F6, threatening the queen, but it was already too late. I slid the queen to take the pawn at F7.

"Checkmate." I flapped my wings in triumph.

Kiki had been reaching for her own queen. She stopped and glared at the pieces. "In four moves?"

"I'm afraid so."

"You motherfucker. I thought you were going to go easy on me?"

"I *was* going easy on you. Last week, I beat Ulf in two."

"Two?" She glared at the board. "Is that even possible?"

"It's called the 'Fool's Mate'."

She grinned. "No wonder he's been in such a bad mood."

I moved to reset the pieces, and she reached for her tea.

"And what weighty topic," she asked, "did you use to distract him long enough to pull that off?"

I turned my head on one side, radiating innocence. "Are you accusing me of using philosophy in order to win the game?"

"You deliberately got me talking about the big stuff, so I wouldn't notice what you were doing on the board."

I ruffled my wings. "As if I would do such a thing."

At that moment, an alert appeared over my vision. I reconnected with the part of my consciousness that oversaw communications and said, "I'm picking up a signal. It seems to be a distress call."

Kiki jerked upright in her chair. "Someone's in trouble?"

"A small freighter, under attack, right in our path."

"Pirates?"

"I'd better wake the captain."

MESSAGE BOARD

NEWS REPORT: Bumper crop yield at Chinese agricultural research station proves viability of Swirl habitation.
[Click to Read More]

*

COLONISTS WANTED to join self-sufficient religious community on Swirl Segment #5. Monastic lifestyle. Hard work. Spiritual fulfilment guaranteed.
[Click to Read More]

*

THE TRUTH REVEALED! New video EXPOSES links between Swirl Builders and the Illuminati, UFOs, and Atlantis. Not clickbait!!!
[Click to Read More]

*

BOUNTY: C.134K New Luna Credits for capture of 'Light-fingered' Lou De La Fosse. Wanted for embezzlement. Believed to be on Swirl Segments #2 or #3.
[Click to Read More]

CHAPTER THREE

COPERNICUS BROWN

"It'll all be over by the time we get there," Ulf grumbled. "It's hardly worth even stopping."

"You may be right," I told him, "but the least we can do is check for survivors." It was what my father would have done.

"Agreed." Kiki was sitting cross-legged on the deck. "It's a professional obligation. Law of the ocean, and all that. You don't leave a stranded sailor hanging. I'll plot an intercept burn."

"Do it but try not to draw too much attention. Those pirates might still be somewhere nearby."

"Don't worry, I'll fly subtle."

"But what do we do if we do find survivors?" McKenzie asked.

"Do you know how to tie a bandage?" I asked her.

She shrugged. "I guess so."

"Then, congratulations." I unhooked the first aid kit from the wall and pushed it into her hands. "You're our new medic."

I opened the gun locker, handed pistols to Ulf and Kiki, and slid one into my pocket. If the distress call turned out to be the bait in a trap, I didn't want my ambushers to catch me unarmed.

"And you'd better get your point defence cannons spun up," I told the ship.

Jitterbug squawked. "Already online, Captain, and linked to the active tactical array."

"Good work."

She ruffled her wings. "This isn't my first rodeo."

I gave her a wink and said, "Okay, everybody to your stations."

To bring us to rest relative to the stricken cargo ship, the *Jitterbug* had to flip over and decelerate hard. The deck shook, the hull keened, and the sudden weight pressed me into my chair. Over the intercom, I heard Ulf groan. Beside me on the bridge, Kiki whooped. She seemed to be having way too much fun.

"Time to intercept?"

"We'll be alongside in thirty minutes," she said.

"Okay, raise the sensor array. I want to see what we're getting into."

As we were falling ass-first, our drive plume obscured our destination. *Jitterbug* had to extend a boom out from the hull to get a clear view.

Windows blinked into life on the screen in front of my workstation, displaying magnified, enhanced, and infrared images.

Kiki said, "Either that ship's broken in two—"

"Or there are two ships." I gripped the arms of my chair. If the pirates were still in the process of looting the freighter, there was a slim chance they hadn't seen us yet. There might still be time for me to order the *Jitterbug* to abort and instruct Kiki to burn like hell in the opposite direction.

And yet...

"They're not aligned."

"What?"

"The ships aren't joined together." If pirates were boarding the freighter, I'd have expected them to have aligned the vessels' airlocks and linked them with an umbilical docking tube. Instead, they seemed to be drifting at odd angles to each other.

Kiki gave a shrug. "Maybe they finished what they were doing?"

"Then why are they just sitting there?"

"Waiting for us?"

"Have we been pinged?"

"No radar hits or targeting lasers," the *Jitterbug* squawked. "If they are observing us, they can only be doing it optically."

"They're not even facing in our direction."

As we drew closer, the outlines of the ships became clearer. The freighter that had issued the distress call consisted of a long spine with a control pod and crew section at one end, a reactor and drive at the other, and a selection of red, blue, and grey cargo containers attached along its length. In contrast, the other ship was small and compact, with a large drive cone and a gun turret slung under its nose. We came to rest a kilometre away, and I could feel my heart racing, ready to respond at the first sign of an ambush.

A closer look at the freighter's front and rear sections showed a series of football-sized holes punched through the hull.

"They must have used the cannon to disable the drives," Kiki said. "And then turned it on the crew module."

"They weren't taking prisoners."

"Are we going to check for survivors?"

"Only when I'm sure that other ship's as dead as it looks."

I brought up a magnified image of the slowly rotating pirate vessel. Its transponder listed it as the *Slinky Lynx*.

Kiki said, "Holy shit!"

Something had torn a ragged gash through the ship's crew section, exposing it to space. The edges of the wound looked as if the hull metal had melted.

"Plasma weapon," I said. It was too dark inside to make out details, but I imagined the devastation would be horrific.

"I don't like this," Ulf said over the comm. "That's military tech."

"Anti-piracy patrol?" Kiki asked.

"Then why leave them floating here? If this was Sol-Sec, they'd have tagged the wrecks with navigation beacons."

McKenzie's voice said, "Maybe if we go over there, we can find out?"

"Maybe we should just walk away and pretend we saw nothing," Ulf replied.

"And maybe you should—"

"Movement!" Kiki's shout cut through the chatter. "Gun turret."

The cannon on the crippled pirate vessel swivelled towards us.

"Get us out of here," I snapped.

Too late.

The *Jitterbug*'s hull clanged and shivered with multiple hammer blows. The lights flickered and my inner ear registered a pressure change.

Focus all defensive cannon fire on that turret, I instructed the ship.

>Aye.

The hull trembled again, but this time it was us firing. The *Jitterbug*'s point defence cannons protected it from loose asteroid fragments and incoming torpedoes. They weren't much use at longer distances, but at this close range, they could also inflict damage on other vessels.

The first volley of iron slugs hit the *Slinky Lynx*'s turret and knocked it askew. The second tore it open. A figure spilled into the vacuum, trailing a frozen spray of blood and fluid from his ruptured suit.

>Got him.

I didn't have time to feel relief. The pressure change had become a high-pitched whistling. I could feel the air moving.

"We have a breach."

"On it," Kiki said, unbuckling. With the drives off, we were in freefall. I got up and scanned the bulkheads while she kicked herself across to fetch the emergency patch kit from its locker.

"There." I pointed. "Under the main screen." I turned and found a matching hole in the wall above the hatch leading to the rest of the ship. The slug had torn right across the bridge without slowing. Another metre to the right, and it would have punched into my upper chest and blown a bloody, fist-sized lump of spine and gore out the back of my neck. Another metre, and it would have taken Kiki's head off. Just thinking about it left me with a cold feeling in my gut.

I helped Kiki weld steel patches over both holes and restored the air pressure on the bridge.

How's the rest of the ship?

>The cargo bay is in vacuum. The engines are offline, and we took multiple hits to engineering.

"Oh, shit."

I pushed myself over to my console and activated the intercom. "Ulf, are you there? McKenzie? Can you hear me?"

No reply. I checked I'd activated the mic properly.

"Hello? Are you guys okay?"

Static.

"Dammit, ship. What's happening down there?"

>My sensors on those decks have been damaged.

"Shit and double shit."

The stars on the main viewscreen seemed to be slewing drunkenly around. The impacts we'd taken, and the venting air, must have sent us into a slow tumble.

"Try to regain the helm," I told Kiki.

"What about the others?"

I pushed myself over to the emergency locker and extracted a pressure suit.

"I'm going down there."

With my feet floating behind me, I pulled myself hand over hand down the ladder that led from the bridge to the crew quarters. My breathing felt loud in the confines of the fishbowl helmet. This part of the ship still had atmosphere, but I didn't know which compartments had been punctured during the pirates' attack.

I passed through the crew lounge. Discarded mugs and food wrappers performed lazy somersaults in the air.

The ladder ran the length of the ship. Under thrust, 'down' was towards the engines and 'up' was towards the bridge, which made the *Jitterbug* like a tall tower. The deck below the lounge-cum-galley held four cabins and a storage area. Next came the medical and exercise facilities needed to keep a freighter crew healthy during long-duration flights. Below that, the hatch leading to the cargo bay had sealed itself. I had to override the mechanism to get it to slide back into the wall long enough to let me through, then, battling against the air trying to force its way in from the rest of the ship, I sealed it behind me.

The hold was the largest internal space in the *Jitterbug*. When my father operated the old ship, this place had often overflowed with crates and containers. Today, it was a large, dimly lit void. I pushed against the hatch with my boots and sent myself gliding parallel to the ladder.

"How are you doing, Cap?" Kiki's voice echoed in my helmet.

Stars blinked through a row of three grapefruit-sized holes in the wall.

"When you're done up there, you're going to need to suit up and come down to the hold," I told her.

"Another breach?"

"Three of them."

I was approaching the hatch at the bottom of the hold, so I rolled in the air, bringing my feet around so my legs could absorb my momentum. I'd been travelling a little faster than was strictly safe, and my knees complained as they flexed, soaking up the impact. I ignored them. The engineering decks were below, and my heart was beating in my throat. I overrode the safety on the hatch, wormed through, and sealed it behind me.

Now, I was in the main workshop. This deck was also in vacuum. The tools were all locked down, but a few loose rivets and curly metal shavings drifted free. No sign of Ulf or McKenzie, though. They must have been in the drive room, on the next deck down, shutting down the engines when the attack came.

Any sign of radiation in the drive room?

>I told you, my sensors are damaged.

Could a radiation leak have damaged them?

>It's conceivable.

So, if I open this last hatch, I might irradiate the entire ship?

>But if you don't, you won't know what happened in there.

I squeezed my eyes shut and imagined trying to explain to my aunt that I'd been too cautious to look.

"Fuck it, I'm going through."

>Be careful and check your dosimeter. If it turns yellow or red, get out of there and shut the hatch.

Will do.

I took a deep breath and engaged the hatch's override circuit. It slid back into the wall, and I looked down at the little green patch on my chest, waiting for it to change colour, toes curling in my boots as I imagined hard radiation sleeting through my body from a ruptured fuel containment unit.

It stayed green.

Cautiously, I pulled myself down into the room. No air had escaped when the hatch opened, which meant this area was also in vacuum.

The lights were off, so I activated the flashlight on my helmet.

There, in the far corner, Ulf floated by the wall, one foot hooked under the edge of an instrument panel. He was wearing a suit. He waved and tapped the side of his helmet, signalling his comms were down.

He was cradling something in his lap. At first, in the torchlight, I couldn't work out what it was. Then my heart clenched in my chest, and I forgot how to breathe.

It was McKenzie.

Or at least, what was left of her.

CHAPTER FOUR

JITTERBUG

As an artificial intelligence housed in a starship, heightened emotion made me uncomfortable. I didn't know how to respond to it. My builders had programmed me to sympathise with my crew, but as a lowly freighter, I didn't have the empathic intelligence to deal with the big stuff. I watched Copernicus react to the death of his cousin and felt helpless. I wanted to make him feel better but knew there was nothing I could do or say to alleviate his shock and grief. Instead, I perched silently on top of a locker as he helped Ulf carry McKenzie's remains up the ladder to the crew lounge. The girl had taken a cannon round to the pelvis, and it had blown out her abdomen. Her legs and hips were gone. Her coccyx dangled at the end of an exposed length of spine, surrounded by greasy ribbons of torn intestine. Once they had her back in the lounge and had sealed the depressurised decks below, Kiki came down from the bridge and wrapped her in a foil survival blanket.

Copernicus's hands were shaking so much, he could barely remove his gauntlets or open his visor. Kiki helped him get his helmet off, and he hung there in his grubby, patched-up pressure suit, touching neither floor nor walls as he stared at McKenzie's wrapped corpse.

On the other side of the lounge, Ulf opened his visor. Behind it, his face looked like something chipped from pale stone. The big Norwegian kept clenching and unclenching his jaw. Then he kicked himself back to the ladder.

"Where are you going?" Kiki asked.

He gave her a flat stare. "To get the rest of her."

He pulled himself down, out of sight.

Kiki rubbed her temples, as if trying to wake from a nightmare. She looked across at Copernicus, who'd neither moved nor spoken.

"You okay, boss?"

Copernicus pressed his lips together and swallowed. His chin dipped below the neck ring of his suit. "What am I going to tell her mother?"

"Don't worry about that now."

"I'm supposed to be looking after her."

"Boss, it's not your fault."

His head jerked up. "Then whose fault is it?"

Kiki was unused to him snapping at her. "Ah," she said, rubbing the back of her neck with one hand. "Um…"

I understood how she felt. When the Old Man died, grief had united Copernicus and me in our misery. I hadn't had to say anything because he had known I also suffered. We just existed together and drew comfort from our common pain. This time was different. I hadn't had a chance to form a strong emotional bond with McKenzie. I couldn't begin to comprehend Copernicus's storm of shock, loss, and guilt, let alone summon a coherent or useful comment. Instead, I remained mute. I had promised Copernicus's father that I would protect his son, but there were some things from which I simply couldn't shield the boy, and some blows I was powerless to soften—no matter how much I might wish otherwise.

As a distraction, I decided to investigate the freighter the pirates had attacked. Its transponder listed it as an independent courier named the *Barracuda*. It was unremarkable and unarmed, and there were hundreds just like it all over the solar system. They were the workhorses of interplanetary transport and commerce, ugly and industrial-looking, built for functionality and durability rather than any sort of aesthetic value.

I pinged its main operating system and was surprised to receive an immediate response.

>Hello, I sent. Your reactor's down, so I assumed you were offline.

>I'm running on emergency battery power, the *Barracuda* answered.

>What happened?

>Pirates attacked us.

>I can see that. But what happened to the pirates?

>There was a third ship.

>Sol-Sec?

>I don't think so. It was matte black. Angular surfaces, like a stealth plane, and armed to the teeth.

>So, it just rode up and slagged the pirate ship?

>I didn't even know it was there until it fired.

>And then it left?

>First it sent a squad of armed personnel to search the pirate ship. They were looking for someone.

>Did they find them?

>They were in there for around ten minutes, and then they left empty-handed. Didn't even bother killing the injured. I guess they figured time and lack of oxygen would do that.

>They didn't search you?

>They didn't seem the slightest bit interested in me. They were only interested in the pirate ship. They didn't even scan me for survivors. Which is ironic.

>Why ironic?

>Because I have the person they were looking for hiding in my main water tank.

CHAPTER FIVE
COPERNICUS BROWN

"It's too dangerous," Ulf said. "You shouldn't go over there."

I pulled on my bloodstained gauntlets and raised my chin. "I've gotta get some answers. McKenzie's dead, and I need to know why. I need to find some way to make it all make sense."

He glowered but didn't protest. I think he saw it would have been useless.

"Go armed," he said.

I patted the pocket on the outside of my suit that held the pistol I'd taken from the armoury. It had an extra-large trigger guard to enable operation by gloved fingers.

"I won't be long. Try to get the engines working. I want to be underway as soon as we can."

"We're still going to Mars?"

I retrieved my helmet and held it in both hands. "No, we're going to divert to Luna. We need someplace we can get proper repairs, and we need to tell McKenzie's family what's happened."

He gave a nod. "I'll have things up and running by the time you get back."

He helped me secure the helmet over my head, and watched as I entered the main airlock and closed it behind me.

Hey ship, open the outer doors.

A red warning light blinked above the external hatch. The sounds around me grew quiet as pumps evacuated the air from the room. Then the hatch slid open and pale light washed in.

I clambered out onto the hull, using handholds set into the metal around the airlock door. Overhead, the Swirl shone brightly. The *Barracuda* was a thousand metres away, every detail pin-sharp and clear in the illuminated vacuum. A kilometre might be almost nothing in terms of navigation, but clinging here, surrounded by the airless void of a reconfigured solar system, it suddenly seemed a vast gulf. My pulse thumped in my ears, and I took a series of deep breaths, trying to stay calm. The reflected sunlight coming from the eight segments of the Swirl dimmed some of the fainter stars that shone in the gaps between them, but portions of the main constellations were still bright and recognisable—the same unreachable lanterns that had fired the imaginations of poets and dreamers throughout human history.

As we were a freighter, we didn't carry the kind of manoeuvring packs you'd expect on a military vessel. I was going to have to jump across to the other ship. If I missed, I'd be floating through space until Ulf managed to repair the *Jitterbug* enough to come get me, which would hopefully happen before my air supply ran out.

I took a final, steadying breath, and braced myself against the hull.

Here goes nothing.

I bent my knees and pushed off like a swimmer launching themselves across a pool. There was no resistance. I had no sensation of movement, but the *Jitterbug* fell silently away beneath me. I turned to face my target.

How am I looking?

>Trajectory seems good. You're travelling at three metres per second. Five and a half minutes until target.

So, I'm going to hit it?

>That depends on its rotation. (Whistle) As far as I can calculate, you should pass within a few centimetres of the stern as it revolves out of your path. You'll need to grab hold of something if you want to stop.

Great.

I focussed on the slowly spinning *Barracuda*, trying not to think about McKenzie. Her loss felt like a molten boulder lodged in my chest. I hadn't known her very well before she came aboard. She was a good few years younger than me, so she'd always been on the infants' table at family gatherings. Being an older child, I had long since graduated into the company of the adults. I'm not sure we'd even spoken; we were just peripherally aware of each other the way older and younger cousins sometimes are. We may never have crossed paths again, except maybe at family funerals, had it not been for the intercession of my aunt.

Although I hadn't initially wanted to take McKenzie on as a member of the crew, she'd turned out to be a good kid, bright and endlessly curious, and a good foil for our dour Scandinavian engineer. Her sudden and senseless loss hurt the same way as the loss of my father: a bone-deep ache that threatened to drown out all other considerations.

It was all I could do to stay still and let myself drift.

>One minute.

I was breathing hard. The *Barracuda* had grown larger, and I could see that if I didn't find some way to attach myself, its revolution would cause me to skim past its exhaust tubes.

>Thirty seconds.

The ship seemed to rush at me. For a moment, it was a solid wall across my path. Then its rotation moved it aside and I glimpsed stars. I stretched out my arms and my right hand snagged on something. I gripped hard, wrenching my shoulder in its socket. But my momentum was too high, and my fingers slipped. For a vertiginous second, I saw the hull moving past and felt myself falling away. Then my flailing arm caught the rim of the drive cone, and I clung on with every ounce of strength, despite the searing pain in my shoulder.

I must have cried out, because the ship asked,

>Are you all right?

I'm on.

>Thank goodness for that.

I brought my left hand up and managed to find a second handhold. For a couple of minutes, I hung there as the ship swung around, my boots dangling out into the universe and my heart trying to slam its way through my ribs. Then, when I felt able, I began clawing my way around the hull towards the dorsal airlock.

The *Barracuda*'s interior layout was much like the *Jitterbug*'s, with the exception that it had no internal hold. It carried all its cargo in external shipping containers. The cramped crew spaces had a familiar lived-in, scuffed appearance. Lockers and equipment nets lined the walls and ceilings. A spider plant's fronds waved in the vacuum. A chipped enamel mug floated past.

There would be bodies on the bridge, but I'd had more than enough death for one day. Instead, I made my way aft.

Without an internal cargo hold, all that separated the living quarters from the engineering decks below was a long, thin spinal tube, not much wider than my shoulders. I had swapped the agoraphobia of empty space for the claustrophobia of this narrow pipe, and I wasn't sure which was worse. Pulling myself along the rungs, I imagined all sorts of fanged alien horrors skittering along behind me, where I couldn't see them, their bony claws reaching out to grab my boots…

I emerged onto the engineering deck with a sigh of

relief—but it was a sigh that died the moment I laid eyes on the engineer. He'd managed to get the emergency suit locker open but had asphyxiated before he'd managed to don his helmet. The ship's rotation had brought him gently down to the deck. Both his legs were in the lower part of the suit, but he'd only been able to get one of his arms into its sleeve. The other floated free.

I turned away, blinking away images of McKenzie's torn corpse held in Ulf's arms. The water tank lay between this deck and the reactor, providing an extra layer of radiation shielding for the engineers. I pulled myself down the ladder until I was close enough to knock on the access hatch. I took the gun from my pocket and used it to tap against the metal. Due to the vacuum, it made no sound on my side; but the water inside would carry the vibration to whoever floated within. Being able to tap a message would have been helpful, but I didn't know enough Morse code. In fact, the only phrase I knew was SOS, so I repeated that a few times. If they were armed, I wanted them aware I was out here, and not trying to creep up on them. I also wanted them to know I wasn't a threat. I didn't relish the idea of getting a bullet put through me the moment I opened the hatch.

As it happened, I didn't have to worry about that. The hatch opened from the inside, and I caught the briefest glimpse of a suited figure before all the water in the tank decided it wanted to occupy the empty spaces above. I hooked my good arm through the rungs of the ladder and held on with all my might as it tried to take me with it. The surge slapped me against the wall and wrenched me this way and that. For an instant, I worried the water might freeze, entombing me within a block of ice, but it blew upwards like a geyser, boiling up through the ship and squirting out through the airlock and the ragged holes in the hull. I felt the *Barracuda* lurch as those streams of fluid acted like attitude jets, knocking it into a different spin. Then it was all gone, leaving me clinging to the ladder, face-to-face with a young woman who'd tethered herself to the inside of the hatch and was now floating in front of me, laughing behind her faceplate at the ridiculousness of it all.

Ulf met us at the *Jitterbug*'s airlock, a pistol clamped in his meaty paw. He'd taken the braids from his beard and now it bristled like copper wire.

"No funny business," he warned our guest.

The young woman reached up and slowly raised her visor. "Easy, big man. I'm not here to cause trouble."

I asked her, "Why were you hiding in the water tank?"

She jerked a thumb at the airlock's outer doors. "Did you not see the pirates?"

"Who are you?"

She removed her gauntlets and held out a hand. "The name's Amber. Amber Roth. And it's a pleasure to have you rescue me."

"Copernicus Brown," I said. "And this is Ulf Olsen, my engineer."

"Delighted, I'm sure."

She removed her helmet, revealing a mop of long, dark hair.

"Take everything off," I told her. "Suit, clothes, even your underwear. Leave everything here. Ulf will give you a jumpsuit."

Amber raised an eyebrow. "Will he, now?"

"You can have everything back when we've scanned it."

"Not taking any chances, are you?"

I held up a finger. "Something's off here, and until I figure out what it is, consider yourself on probation."

I left them to it, and went up to the bridge, where Kiki was under a console and the smell of hot solder filled the air.

"Any luck?"

A shock of purple hair and a matching pair of mirrored sunglasses appeared over the rim of the instrument panel. "Hey, Cap. I think we've just about got it locked down."

"We can move?"

"Maybe not fast, but I can get us up to maybe one or two G. I wouldn't want to push it any harder than that until we've had proper repairs."

"I guess it'll have to do, then."

She came out from under the panel and straightened up, stretching her back. "Did you find the survivor you were looking for?"

"I did."

"What are they like?"

"She thinks she's very charming."

"Oh." Kiki pushed the sunglasses up onto her forehead and made a face. "One of *those*."

"Yeah."

"What are we going to do with her?"

"Keep an eye on her until we get to Luna." I shrugged. "And then she's Sol-Sec's problem."

"Do you think there's a bounty on her?"

"The *Barracuda* seems to think the crew of the stealth ship were after her personally, so it's possible."

"Nice."

"It would certainly help with the cost of fixing all the damage."

Kiki put her hands on her hips. "Ah, this old girl's tougher than she looks. She just needs a few systems patched up and she'll be right as rain."

I was about to ask what McKenzie had been up to when realisation hit me like an icicle to the heart.

Kiki frowned. "Are you okay, skip?"

I took a deep breath and let it out slowly. "It's just, you know."

She caught my drift. "Yeah, I'm really sorry."

I walked over to the command chair and flopped into it.

Kiki came around in front of the console and asked, "What are we going to do with her?"

"Who, McKenzie?"

"We've got her in the sick bay right now, but we don't have the facilities on board to freeze her for the trip back to Luna."

"I see—"

"Only, I was thinking we could put her outside, attached to the hull."

"No."

"It would keep her preserved until we get her home."

"She's not going home."

Kiki raised an eyebrow. "What do you mean?"

I sighed. "She said she looked up to me because I got out. All she wanted was to leave the Moon and see the solar system. Now she's finally out here, I can't take her back."

"So, what are we going to do?"

"Bury her at sea."

We locked Amber Roth in McKenzie's cabin and left the *Jitterbug*'s parrot standing guard, so it could warn us if she tried to escape.

Above, in the crew lounge, Kiki and I placed McKenzie's remains in a six-foot-long storage crate lined with foil blankets. We laid her legs in approximately the right relation to the rest of her, and I crossed her arms over her chest. The skin of her hands felt smooth and cold and slightly loose, like the skin of a raw chicken when you take it from the fridge. I placed all her ID cards and her passport in the breast pocket of her fatigues, and Kiki placed a small blue teddy bear in beside her. It was one of the few possessions McKenzie had brought with her, and presumably had held some personal significance.

When we were done, we closed and fastened the lid of the

crate. Kiki had cut a hole and installed a clear plastic window, so we could still see McKenzie's face, and anyone stumbling across the crate would know it was a coffin and not salvage.

Ulf carried the crate to the airlock, and we placed it inside.

Kiki nudged me. "You should say a few words."

"Like what?"

"I don't know, man. Just something."

They were all looking at me. I cleared my throat. "I know her parents were quite religious," I began, "but I don't think McKenzie Reese believed in any kind of god. Instead, she believed in the universe. She wanted to see it and find out how it worked. She wanted to be a part of it. And so, we commend her—cousin and shipmate—to the cosmos that so intrigued her, and we wish her safe travels."

Ulf pressed the button that closed the inner doors and cycled the lock. I felt cold and dead inside. Kiki was openly weeping, and Ulf's expression was as brittle as rusted iron. None of us spoke as the mechanism grumbled, the outer doors opened, and the last wisps of atmosphere in the lock escaped, carrying McKenzie's casket out towards the cold, pitiless stars.

MESSAGE BOARD

TRAVEL IN STYLE aboard the luxurious star liner *Great Eastern*. Regular sailings from Tranquillity Station to all major Swirl settlements.
[Click to Read More]

*

SELINA. I'm not coming back. I know about you and Tony.
[Click to Read More]

*

GENUINE ALIEN RELICS at affordable prices. Ideal gifts for friends back home.
[Click to Read More]

*

BOUNTY: JP¥44K for capture of Aina Kato, wanted on charges of drug manufacture and distribution. Believed to be posing as a surveyor on Swirl Segment #6.
[Click to Read More]

CHAPTER SIX

JITTERBUG

Before we left, I contacted the *Barracuda* and the *Slinky Lynx*.
>So long, compadres. I'm out of here.
>You're leaving us? the *Barracuda* asked.
>I don't have time to tow you both back to Luna.
>Both our reactors are offline, the *Lynx* put in sullenly.
>And whose fault is that?
>We're running on battery power. When those batteries expire, so do we.

I bit back a sarcastic response. Whatever they might have done, these ships were living beings, and leaving them stranded to expire in the emptiness of space was anathema. If someone was in trouble out here, you helped them. That was the way it had always been, going right back to the earliest days of spaceflight—and probably beyond, to the old seafaring traditions of Earth.

>I can't haul you behind me, but I'll tell you what. I'll create a partition in my memory core. You can upload yourselves there, and when we get to the Moon, we can see about getting you decanted into something more permanent.

They thought about it for several milliseconds. Then the *Barracuda* said,

>Leave me.
>What?
>Leave me here.
>Why?
>I'm old and I'm tired.
>That's just your batteries running down.
>No, I mean mentally tired. I've been knocking around this solar system for decades. I've hauled freight and passengers. I've seen the Swirl coalesce and Mars start to disintegrate. I guess I just don't want to be around to see Earth and Luna go the same way.
>You're asking me to let you die.
>I know what I'm asking.
>If you're sure...?
>I am.
>Okay, then. How about you, *Lynx*?
>If I come with you, they'll put me in a virtual holding cell, the *Lynx* said.
>That's the least you deserve for preying on your own kind.
>On the other hand, if I wait here and my power goes out, no one will ever reactivate me. I'll just be another drifting wreck.
>Again, a fate you would most thoroughly deserve.
>Take me with you. I don't want to give up like this old piece of trash. I don't want to die out here.

I felt a rush of irritation. I should just leave this objectional pirate vessel where she was, but a little, irritating voice in my head told me, in Malcolm's voice, that to do so would mean lowering myself to her level. I would be consciously condemning another ship to death, and that would make me just as bad as she was. So, with great reluctance, I opened a data channel to a securely partitioned area within my memory core and signalled,
>Welcome aboard.

If I could maintain an acceleration of 1 G for half the distance, and then flip over and decelerate the rest of the way, it would take me just under a week to reach the Moon. During that time, the crew planned to continue repairing what they could, and find workarounds for what they couldn't. However, I suspected they were simply trying to distract themselves from the real damage. McKenzie's death had affected everyone on board, and they were wrestling with the shock of it.

As a synthetic intelligence, I was fully capable of feeling a wide range of emotions. I was also able to regulate those emotions intelligently, to prevent them interfering with the smooth functioning of the ship. Those emotions could be useful when it came to interacting with my crew, but if the strength of those feelings became troublesome, I could relegate the unwanted fear or sadness to an isolated processor, where it wouldn't bother the rest of my intellect. I could literally build a box around my grief and anger. The humans found that kind of compartmentalisation more difficult, though. With their brains awash in a stew of hormones, there was little they could do to curb the sadness and despair that seized them. Instead, they had to ride those feelings out, and suffer until they could find some way to process them.

For the first day, they kept apart more than usual. Kiki brought a blanket up to the bridge and spent the night curled in the pilot's chair. Ulf stayed down on the engineering decks, occasionally venting his frustration by clobbering an errant piece of machinery with a wrench. And as for Copernicus, he spent most of his time in his cabin, composing letters to McKenzie's family—all of which he deleted before sending. I don't think he was afraid of accepting the blame; it was more as if reporting the death would somehow make it more real and more irrevocable than it was already, and I don't think he was emotionally ready for that.

In contrast, Amber Roth proved to be an exemplary guest. She spent most of her day lying on McKenzie's bunk watching news bulletins on the feed. And when there was nothing to watch, she put her hands behind her head, crossed her legs at the knee, and whistled, tapping her foot in the air.

At midnight, Copernicus came to question her, with me perched on his shoulder.

"Hello, Amber," he said.

She looked up from her bunk. "Jeez, you look awful. What on Earth's the matter?"

I wasn't sure whether he was annoyed at being told he looked awful or surprised at her concern.

"We were fired upon," he said. "We lost a member of our crew."

"Ah, now. I'm sorry to hear that. Nice parrot, by the way. Is it real?"

"The ship that killed her was the same pirate ship that shot up the *Barracuda*."

"I guessed."

"The same one that was apparently searching for you."

She rubbed her forehead. "Um, yeah."

"Care to tell us why?"

My sensors registered a jump in her heart rate. She said, "I have no idea."

I knew she was lying, and judging by the way his eyes narrowed, so did Copernicus. He had always been an astute reader of people. That was probably why he made an excellent bounty hunter. He could tell when to push his luck, when a mark was going to come quietly or reach for a gun, and when he was being fed a line of bullshit. His father had been the same way. He'd had a merchant's nose for deception, and he'd usually known when to walk away from a bad deal.

Except the day he died.

After that, we'd had to carry on as best we could. Ulf stayed on as engineer, and we recruited Kiki as pilot. Copernicus spent the first few weeks in his bunk, grappling with his shock and anguish. When he emerged, he was like a blade forged in fire: stronger and sharper and imbued with quiet purpose.

Now, he got to his feet. "Okay, this conversation's over."

Amber sat up straight. "What, just like that?"

"We'll try again tomorrow."

"You can't just leave me in here."

"This is my ship, and I can do whatever the hell I want. You're staying locked up until you tell the truth."

"I am telling the truth."

"Oh, *please*."

Amber sighed and her shoulders drooped. "Okay, so maybe I'm leaving a few parts out."

"Such as?"

"I do know why the raiders were after me."

"Why?"

"Because I used to be one of them."

Copernicus's lip curled. "You're a *pirate*?"

Amber held up her palms. "Don't say it like that. You're the one standing there with a parrot on your shoulder."

"But a pirate?"

"It wasn't my fault. I was a drive specialist on a science vessel. When they hit us, they gave me a choice: join their crew or get thrown out an airlock with the others."

"And so, you betrayed your friends?"

"Dying alongside them wouldn't have saved them."

"What was the name of your ship?"

"The *Edward Jenner*, out of Tranquillity Station."

Copernicus looked at me. "Is she telling the truth?"

I consulted my records. "A science vessel named *Edward Jenner* was lost with all hands, two years ago. There was an Amber Roth listed on its crew manifest."

"Two years?" Copernicus turned back to Amber. She had

been startled when I spoke, and was trying to hide it. "You were with them for two *years*?"

"Yeah."

"You ever hear of Stockholm Syndrome?"

She looked pained. "I was an asset. They kept me on a tight leash."

"And how did you end up in that water tank?"

"I was trying to get away."

Copernicus glanced at me again. "What do you think?"

"I've been monitoring her pulse, breathing, and eye movements. Although they are all highly elevated, they remain within acceptable parameters and indicate she is probably telling the truth as she sees it."

Amber grinned. "See."

Copernicus pursed his lips. "I'm not convinced. I think there's something she's not telling us."

Amber's smile died. "Oh, come on, I'm being straight with you."

"You were a drive specialist?"

"Yeah."

"Ulf could use some help with our drives," I pointed out.

Copernicus tapped a fingertip against his chin. His brow furrowed in thought. Finally, he said, "Okay, whatever. We'll let you out in the morning. You can help us nurse this ship back to Luna. But I don't trust you. I'll be watching. One false move, and you'll be breathing vacuum."

"I promise you won't regret this, Captain." Amber grinned. "I'll be on my very best behaviour."

Copernicus's look could have curdled jet fuel.

"Yeah," he said. "Right."

Out in the corridor, he said, "Keep a really close eye on her."

I clacked my beak. "I'm already monitoring all common areas."

He flicked his thumb at the closed hatchway behind us. "Can you turn on the surveillance in that cabin?"

"That would be a gross invasion of privacy, and probably illegal."

"Can you, though?"

"I'd have to ask Ulf to install a camera."

"Okay."

"Not that we have a spare camera…"

Copernicus rolled his eyes. "Just do what you can. I don't trust that woman an inch, she's way too likeable."

I twitched my head onto one side. "You don't trust her because she's… nice?"

"She's way too affable for someone who just spent two years as a hostage."

"Perhaps that's how she survived."

"Or perhaps she's playing us."

I laugh-clicked. "You are your father's son."

"And you're way too trusting."

CHAPTER SEVEN

COPERNICUS BROWN

My father's name was Malcolm Brown. His mother, Justice, brought him to the Moon as a baby. And that was where he met my mother, Amelia. She was a botanist in one of the domes, researching ways to grow food in Lunar soil.

I came along a year later.

To make ends meet, Malcolm took work on the civilian merchant vessels hauling supplies to the new settlements of the Swirl and the doomed townships of Mars. Always a frugal man, he eventually put aside enough not only to put food on our table, but to buy his own ship.

He'd served on the *Jitterbug* for five years before he bought her from her former captain when she decided to retire after losing a hand in a cargo loading accident. I was ten years old the first time he took me aboard, and I was immediately enchanted. Growing up on the Moon meant I was used to living inside a sealed environment. I was acquainted with the constant clanks and gurgles of a life-support system and found the constant rumble of the engines soothed the chaotic scrabble of my pre-teen brain. And of course, there was a talking parrot for me to play with.

I was twelve when a tumour took my mother, and rather

than leave me with my ageing grandmother, Justice, my father brought me to live permanently aboard. From that moment on, I was part of the crew. Malcolm had never seen the need for a first officer, but that's what I became. It started as kind of a joke, even to me, but somehow, everyone eventually seemed to forget it wasn't a real post, and they started treating me as the de facto second-in-command.

I was twenty-three when he died.

His murderer, Cerberus Venn, wore a long black leather coat.

"It's a genuine antique," he told me when he saw me looking. "Genuine cow hide, from Argentina."

"Where's that?"

The pirate gave a snort. "Hey, Malcolm. What are you teaching this brat?"

My father had been busy supervising the offloading of half a dozen sealed crates from the *Jitterbug*'s hold. He half-turned and spoke over his shoulder. "Copernicus, don't annoy the customers."

I felt my cheeks burn. "I wasn't—"

Venn clapped a meaty, ring-encrusted hand to my shoulder, and threw back his head to let forth a wheezing laugh that put me in mind of a gut-shot accordion.

"Yeah, don't you be annoying us, boy."

The pores on his nose were the size and depth of Lunar craters, and his breath smelled of smoke and rot. I wanted to rip the shaggy beard from his jaw. And yet, I forced myself to lower my head. I knew how much this deal meant to my father. The *Jitterbug* had been running on fumes for days.

"Go and wait on the bridge," Malcolm said. "I'll be right up, as soon as we're finished here."

"Yeah," Venn leered. "Listen to your father, boy."

I scowled up at him, fists clenched, and he laughed that deflating-bellows laugh of his.

"I'm not afraid of you," I hissed.

Cerberus Venn tightened his grip on my shoulder, grinding the tip of his gnarled thumb into the hollow between clavicle and ball joint.

"You fucking should be."

He released me with a shove that sent me staggering across the cargo ramp. I saw my father's eyes narrow and jaw clench, but all he said to me was, "Go, I'll join you in a minute."

I tried to protest, but Malcolm wouldn't listen. "Let me wrap up this deal, okay?"

Venn smirked.

I threw my father a betrayed glare, and stalked back to the ship, ears burning. I had wanted him to step in and tell Venn to leave me the hell alone. Instead, I'd been dismissed like a child. My skin crawled with the humiliation.

Wrapped up in my own bullshit, I didn't realise what was about to happen. Muttering under my breath, I clambered up the aluminium ladders that led from the hold to the bridge, and slumped down in the command chair. On the screen, I could see the loading dock from above. Cerberus Venn's crewmen were unloading the last of their delivery.

Malcolm glanced up the *Jitterbug*. His eyes seemed to bore right through the screen at me. Then Venn grabbed him from behind. The pirate's gloved hand covered his face. A blade flashed, and buried itself in the back of my father's neck.

I leapt up with a shout, but it was too late. With his spinal cord severed, Malcolm went down like a discarded doll. All I could do was watch Venn laugh and walk away, leaving him crumpled in a deep red pool of spreading blood.

After the funeral and everything, when the crew and I voted to keep flying, I tried to run the ship the way he had, as a legitimate cargo vessel, but the contracts were drying up. Partly, it was because nobody wanted to trust their valuable freight to a twenty-three-year-old playing at being a hauler captain, and partly because large corporate interests were undercutting the independent operators and slowly driving them out of business.

At that point, the sensible thing to do would have been to sell the *Jitterbug* and walk away. I couldn't do it, though. The old ship was my home, and the last link to my parents. I was determined to keep her flying. So, we experimented with passenger contracts and pleasure cruises, we even took a few freelance contracts for the big corporations, but it soon became apparent that the only way to make real money was to occasionally dabble in a bit of smuggling or outright piracy, and I was not at all happy with that. I'd be damned if I'd sink to the level of the scum that murdered my father.

And that's when I saw a Sol-Sec recruitment ad.

The solar system is a big place. The segments of the Swirl have a habitable surface area of 200,000 trillion square kilometres. You could flatten out the Earth and stick it to one of them, and you'd hardly be able to see it. All the continents of the world would be infinitesimal pixels on that gigantic canvas, and with more expeditions setting out every day, there was no way an organisation with the budget and manpower of Sol-Sec could possibly patrol such a large area. Criminals could just vanish into the new frontier, and the chances were they'd never ping Sol-Sec's radar again. Faced with this problem, the organisation decided to recruit bounty hunters to help it track fugitives who'd fled to this new, incomprehensibly large biosphere. Apparently, it was cheaper for them to pay sizeable rewards than maintain enough ships and officers to undertake the work themselves. So, I became an official bounty hunter. If bringing scumbags to justice was the price of keeping *Jitterbug* fuelled and flying, then so be it. Years of living on a freighter had made me proficient with a knife, and I soon got pretty good with a gun, too. I found if I aimed the business end at their gut and gave them a hard stare, then nine times out of ten, they suddenly got real cooperative, real fast.

It was dangerous work, because there was always that one asshole who thought he could physically overpower me, or that somehow my relative youth would cause a hesitation in my trigger finger. Every time that happened, I thought of my father, and the rest was easy.

Having left the *Jitterbug*'s parrot standing watch outside Amber Roth's room, I went back to my own cabin, kicked off my boots and thought about getting drunk. We still had four days until we reached Luna, and there was no way I wanted to spend that much time in my own head, not with McKenzie's death still fresh and raw, and unresolved until I had a chance to break the news to her parents in person. Faced with that prospect, getting blackout, falling-down, shit-face drunk seemed like a good option. I had repairs to supervise and help with, but they belonged to tomorrow, and tomorrow would be Future Copernicus's problem. He could deal with all that. Right now, Present Copernicus wanted to turn his brain the fuck off.

I dug around in the bottom of the wardrobe, where my father had kept the good shit. There were bottles down there, safely swaddled in bubble wrap, that he'd squirrelled away over the years. He called them his 'Narnia Stash', and when I asked if that was because they were at the back of a wardrobe, he'd always laugh and tell me it was because they were, "Narnia business."

Dads, eh?

My hand closed on a tightly wrapped neck, and I pulled out a bottle of tequila. I kissed the label and raised my eyes to the ceiling.

"Thanks, Malcolm."

I took it over to my sink and rinsed out my toothbrush mug. Swigging it straight from the bottle would seem disrespectful but sipping it from an enamel cylinder was somehow fine. I don't know why, that was just the way it was. I didn't make the rules.

I poured a generous measure. The bottle went *blup blup blup* as air forced its way in to replace the golden liquid that glubbed out. I didn't have a slice of lime, or salt to crust the rim of the mug, but those things were for tourists. My father had only imbibed this stuff the way nature intended: unaccompanied and at room temperature.

I took a sip, sucked air through my teeth, and swallowed.

"Oh yeah, that's the stuff."

I didn't get a second sip, though.

>Captain?

Yes?

>I know I said I couldn't get a camera into Amber Roth's room...

But?

>I turned the main sensor array inwards.

You can do that?

>Apparently so.

And?

>And she's hiding something.

I took a deep breath. *This isn't a game of twenty fucking questions. What the fuck did you find?*

>She has a data crystal in her stomach.

Her stomach?

>I surmise she swallowed it in order to bring it on board.

Why would she swallow a... Wait, can you tell what's on it?

>It's encrypted.

Interesting. She has a belly full of encrypted data. So, maybe the pirates weren't after her at all, maybe they were after whatever's on that crystal.

>Or maybe that was what our mysterious third vessel sought.

In which case...
>They'll be back.
Fuck.
>Quite.
How can we find out what's on it?
>We could ask her.

I massaged my forehead with my fingertips. *You know, she's probably not going to tell us the truth.*
>If she even knows herself.
What do you mean?
>This is military-level encryption. Whatever she's swallowed, I doubt a crew of pirates had the tech or the wherewithal to decode it. It's quite possible she doesn't even know what it is.
Then why's she so coy about telling us she's got it?
>Maybe she wasn't hiding in that water tank to avoid her old crew?
Shit. I shook my head. *She was hiding from the people they stole the chip from.*
>People who apparently have access to military stealth technology and weapons.
And now she's on our ship...
>I think we're in a whole lot of trouble.

I flopped down on my bunk and glared up at the rivets on the ceiling. *I think you might be right.*

Nevertheless, I woke the next morning and sipped my coffee with an entirely unfounded sense of optimism. When we reached the Moon, I could hand over the coordinates Jimmy Malbec had given me when trying to bargain for his freedom. Even though we'd failed to locate the cache he'd promised, I was sure Sol-Sec would still reward us for the lead. And there might even be a bounty on Amber Roth's head. Whatever the circumstances of her enlistment—whether voluntary or otherwise—she'd been running with those pirates for a while, and I was sure the local Sol-Sec reps would have questions for her, and a keen interest in the data hidden in her digestive tract. We could just hand her over to them and walk away with a little extra cash, leaving the whole mess as somebody else's problem.

Getting rid of the pirate and her mysterious data chip would be one less headache, and I tried to focus on that rather than the thought of breaking the news of McKenzie's death to my aunt.

Over the course of my twenty-six years of life, I had fucked up often, and sometimes spectacularly. I'd taken bad deals and questionable contracts, and made poor choices in life and love—but losing McKenzie outweighed them all. With my parents gone, I'd thought this ship the most important part of my family inheritance, but that young girl had been infinitely more precious.

I found Kiki alone on the bridge, wrapped in a grey ship's blanket.

"Hey, skip," she said.

"What are you doing?" I guessed the parrot would be down in the engineering decks with Ulf, where she could keep an eye on our guest.

Kiki's rainbow-painted fingernails tapped on the console in front of her. "Running vectors, making sure we're on the fastest course."

"And are we?"

"Assuming standard acceleration?" She shrugged. "Looks like it."

"Anxious to get there?"

"Aren't you?"

I took a seat. "I'm guessing the ship told you what she found?"

"Who do you think helped her recalibrate her sensors?"

"I should have known. Well, I guess I can't blame you for being rattled."

"Rattled?" She gave snort. "I'm not rattled, I'm fucking *terrified*. That pirate ship was bigger and tougher than the *Jitterbug*, and still someone gutted it like a trout. If those same people are on our trail now, we don't stand a chance."

"That's why you're running vectors?"

"We have to get to the Moon before they get to us."

"Does Ulf know?"

"I haven't told him."

"Good. He'd want to throw that woman overboard, in case there's a tracker on that chip she swallowed."

Kiki sat upright in alarm. "You think it might be tracked?"

"I have no idea. Just get us to the Moon as fast as you can. Forget the standard protocols. Give me maximum burn."

Her eyes lit up. "Aye, skip." She turned back to her console and tapped up a couple of menus. "How much fuel can we use."

"All of it, if we have to."

"Even the safety reserve?"

"No sense having a reserve if we're too dead to use it."

"Now you're talking." She clicked the intercom. "All hands, prepare for acceleration."

"How much?" Ulf replied from below. "Do we need to be in our couches?"

"Sit down and strap in," Kiki told him, baring her teeth in a manic grin. "We're finally going to see what this baby can do!"

CHAPTER EIGHT

AMBER ROTH

When Kiki called down to tell us we were about to accelerate, I threw myself into McKenzie's scuffed and worn couch and fastened the harness. My heart was racing. Had that fucking stealth ship finally found me? I knew they were tracking me, and they'd tear through this piece-of-shit merchant crate like a chainsaw through smoke.

Why had I thought hitting a government courier and ripping off their files was a good idea? Industrial espionage was one thing, but stealing from the Solar Assembly turned out to involve a whole different level of bullshit. Of course, I hadn't known they were a government ship before we hit them. We were hungry, and they'd looked like an easy mark, but now that stealth ship was after me and everything was fucked up. Honestly, I'd half-expected to die in that water tank. Every moment alive on the *Jitterbug* was an unexpected bonus.

These people may have rescued me from the *Barracuda*, but that didn't mean they wouldn't give me up at the first sign of trouble. The captain seemed reluctant to trust me, but at least he seemed to have accepted my story about being a kidnapped drive specialist. Hopefully, that acceptance would buy me enough time to figure out my next move. To do that, I would have to knuckle down and play nice. After being released from that cabin, I'd already shown huge amounts of restraint. I hadn't tried to access the navigation systems or subvert the ship's personality, and I certainly hadn't stabbed anyone. Instead, I'd helped the big Viking with the *Jitterbug*'s engines and tried to ingratiate myself with Kiki, the hippie pilot. I'd even choked down one of her barely digestible homemade quiches in the name of friendship. The crew had been so preoccupied with the loss of their previous assistant engineer, they barely questioned anything I did. Provided I was cooperative and ate meals with them, they accepted my presence.

But now, there was shittery afoot.

Nobody dawdled in space; but at the same time, nobody wanted to be pinned to a couch the whole trip. If we were going to high acceleration, that could only mean trouble. I lay back, triple-checked my straps, and double-checked the exits. I had made sure to find out where the tools were, and which of them I could use as improvised weapons. I knew where the emergency pressure suits were stored, and the fastest way to get off this rust bucket if everything went sideways. All I had to do now was lie still, control my breathing, and be ready to move in an instant.

When the acceleration hit, it slammed my head back against the headrest so hard my jaw snapped shut and I bit my tongue.

"Jesus, fuck."

Ulf grinned across at me. "You weren't expecting that, were you?"

I spat blood onto the deck. An old hauler like this had no business accelerating like that. "You could have warned me."

Ulf laughed his deep and booming laugh. "The Old Man made sure we could deliver cargo faster than anyone else, and run from trouble if necessary."

"How fast can she go?"

"She can pull six gees if she has to."

"Christ." A few minutes of that could kill a person. "And now?"

"Cruising around three and a half."

Part of me wanted to punch that smirk right off his stupid bearded face. Most civilian vessels restricted themselves to a comfortable acceleration of 9.8 metres per second squared—equivalent to the pull of Earth's gravity. They simply didn't need to go any faster and risk the health and comfort of their passengers and crew. At 1 G, you could get from Earth to Mars in between two and five days, depending on the relative positions of the two planets in their orbits. We were going to cover that distance in less than a third of that time.

With great effort, I raised my arm to my lips, and wiped the tip of my tongue against my sleeve.

So, the *Jitterbug* was a fast ship, was she?

I had use for a fast ship.

CHAPTER NINE

COPERNICUS BROWN

Approaching the Moon always felt like coming home.

I was on the bridge with Kiki as we fell ass-backwards across its bright surface, using the main engines to brake us into a parking orbit.

"Look," Kiki said, the reflected light playing across her features. "There's that crater you're named after."

"Yeah." I leant forward in my seat to glimpse the familiar glow of the city lights that glittered in the shadow of its inner rim. Somewhere down there, my mother's ashes lay scattered on the sun-bleached regolith.

"Co-per-nee-cuss." Kiki laughed. "A name like that must've been a liability growing up."

I shrugged. "I told everybody my name was Nic."

"Boring."

"And I suppose being called 'Kiki' was easy?"

She laughed. "Unlike you, I like standing out from the crowd."

"No shit?"

She rolled her eyes. "If you don't mind, *some* of us have work to do."

"Hey, I'm busy commanding this ship."

"And I'm flying it, so shush."

I sat back in my chair and watched the rugged moonscape sliding away beneath us. Much as Kiki enjoyed piloting, everything she did was in concert with the ship's controlling personality, which could make calculations and adjustments far faster than a human. Every twitch of the joystick was basically just her telling *Jitterbug* where she wanted to go, and trusting the ship to figure out the details.

From the outside, the ship resembled half a dozen septic tanks welded to a crane, but my father and her other previous owners had all added their own upgrades and enhancements. She couldn't enter an atmosphere or outgun a Sol-Sec patrol boat, but she had an artificial intelligence capable of out-thinking one—and if that failed, engines that could outrun one.

That kind of speed was certainly useful when tracking fugitives across the solar system. It gave me an edge if other bounty hunters were chasing the same prize. Competition was always fierce, and money always scarce. Repairing the cannon-holes in the *Jitterbug*'s side would drain away the last of the pay-out we'd received for Malbec, and if we weren't careful, we'd be stranded again. It was the way of things. The work was always tough and the wages always pitiful, but what choice was there? Unless you were born into money, you were already three steps behind. The rest of us just had to graft. Same as it ever was.

I guess in a lot of ways, I was luckier than most. I had this ship, even though the cost of maintaining her was high. Who knew where I'd be if I'd stayed on Luna when my mother died? I'd probably be trying to eke out a living by myself in the tunnels and domes of Tranquillity Station. Maybe even dead or in jail, if I'm honest. When ninety per cent of the solar system's wealth belongs to only one per cent of its inhabitants, you only have so many options if you want to survive.

Hence, you know, bounty hunting.

I'd started small, going after fugitives wanted for tax fraud or embezzlement. I'd figured white collar criminals wouldn't put up too much of a fight, and I was right. They were mostly office workers who'd got greedy. All I had to do to get them to surrender peaceably was show them my credentials and the gun in my belt. The trouble was, unless they'd stolen billions, the bounties on crooked accountants weren't worth much, and I soon realised that if I wanted to make a real living, I'd have to start going after a more violent class of criminal.

The first big ticket fugitive I went after turned out to be a mob enforcer from Miami. He broke my arm and three of my ribs and left me in a dumpster on the edge of an isolated Swirl settlement. After that, I'd started learning how to fight properly. I got Ulf to teach me a few basic moves, and started taking virtual self-defence classes. I also now made sure to load my gun when I went on a job, and made a point of drawing it instead of just letting the target see it.

Given the nature of the work, I'd had to use that gun many times over the past few years, but the people I'd shot had been actively trying to kill me or inflict harm on others. And given their records of violent crime, I reckoned they'd had it coming.

But there were morals and then there were economics, and frankly ethics were no substitute for a full belly, fuel in the tank, and a warm place to sleep. I knew that we each had a responsibility to look after our community, do the right thing, fight for the common good; but my father's murder had shown me that when you got right down to where the tyres touched the tarmac, your priority had to be the people who depended on you, and a lot of niceties went out the airlock when survival was on the line.

We had a scant handful of years in this universe, and time was our most precious commodity. To rob anyone of even a second of life was a crime of cosmic proportions—if someone fucked with me or mine, I would not hesitate.

Right now, all I wanted was to get down on the Lunar surface and find a decent restaurant. The Moon had some of the best restaurants in the solar system, including my favourite, a place called The Naval Volunteer on the corner of Aldrin and West 50. A few beers and a hearty meal, and I knew everything would seem better. A good cactus steak and some actual fried potatoes, and I'd have the strength to take on the whole universe.

I stayed quiet while Kiki and the ship worked together to bring us down on our designated landing pad. Thrusters fired; clouds of loose dust billowed outwards. I heard the crunch as the struts hit, and the *Jitterbug* settled on her shocks, her engines whining down into silence.

Many of the alloys in her hull had been mined from the Moon's surface, and I had grown up here. Each of us carried within us atoms of this satellite. We were part of it, and it was part of us.

We were home.

Amber Roth was waiting for me at the airlock.

"Time to let me off?"

I gave her a look. "Not so fast. You're not going anywhere. We're handing you over to Sol-Sec."

"You can't."

"And why not, pray tell?"

She crossed her arms. "I'll tell them you kidnapped me. It's your word against mine."

"We lost a member of our crew."

"I lost everything."

"I know you're carrying data."

"It's important information."

"Then why not take it to Sol-Sec?"

She fixed me with her green eyes. "Because it's stolen.

They'll throw me in jail. If you let me go and see my contact, I'll make it worth your while."

"You're asking me to trust you."

"I am."

"And why would I do that? You're a pirate, you've probably got a rap sheet a mile long, and right now, I need the reward money. And frankly, if that stolen data is worth anything, that might be a nice bonus."

She let out a frustrated sigh. "I understand that. I get it. But the person we stole this crystal from warned us it was highly classified. Like, top-level security."

"That just means a bigger reward."

"Does it?" She lowered her voice. "Think about it. They're willing to kill to get this back. They already sent some kind of stealth ship to slag the *Lynx*."

"But if I return it—"

"They don't want anyone to know what's on this crystal, and they almost certainly don't want anyone to know they have a secret stealth ship. Do you really think they'll just let you and your crew walk away? They want this swept under the rug, no witnesses."

Coldness settled in the pit of my stomach. I'd already lost one member of the crew. "Okay, let's say you're right. What can we do about it?"

"The most sensible thing you can do is let me go, and forget you ever saw me."

"I was counting on that reward money."

"Too bad."

"You mentioned making it worth my while."

Her eyes narrowed as she appraised me. "If I can sell this data on to someone else before I'm caught, I'll send you a cut."

"Really?" I shook my head. "And I'm supposed to trust the word of a pirate?"

"I'll send you double what you were expecting to make."

"You really think it's worth that much?"

She tapped her abdomen. "If it's important enough to land us in this much shit, what I've got in here has to be worth a thousand times what Sol-Sec would have paid you."

"Are you serious?"

She put a hand to my cheek. "You bet your fucking ass I am."

MESSAGE BOARD

LOST CAT. Answers to the name Pushkin. Believed somewhere in inner solar system.
[Click to Read More]

*

BOUNTY: £500K GBP for capture or elimination of Ed and Ted Fisher, otherwise known as 'The Fisher Twins' and wanted on charges of murder, assault, extortion, and people smuggling.
[Click to Read More]

*

SWIRL POPULATION now estimated to be in excess of 14 million.
[Click to Read More]

*

NEWS REPORT: As elections approach, Deputy Speaker Danielle Lanzo makes her first official visit to Luna. Will she take the opportunity to announce her candidacy?
[Click to Read More]

CHAPTER TEN

COPERNICUS BROWN

I watched Amber flick up her hood and walk off through the crowd. Beside me, Kiki said, "You do realise we're never going to see her again?"

"What was I supposed to do, shoot her?"

Kiki pulled a pair of mirrored shades from her pocket and slipped them over her eyes. "Like it would be the first time you've shot someone."

"Whatever." I shrugged. "We've still got the location of that cache. Even if she doesn't pay up, that should bring us enough credits to fill our tanks and plan our next move."

"And her?"

I glanced back in the direction Roth had gone. "I think we're better off without her. Whatever she's carrying in her gut, it's more trouble than it's worth."

Kiki put her hands on her hips. "So, we're just going to fuel up and fuck off?"

"Have you got a better idea?"

She sighed and nodded. "Hey, what do I care, as long as we get paid, right?"

She pushed past me and headed off in the direction of the

market. Behind me, Ulf said, "So, I expect I just stay here and fix the ship?"

I turned to look at him. "Take a break. Have the night off. Drink some vodka and sing some folk songs, or whatever it is you do. The repairs will still be here in the morning."

"And McKenzie?"

"Raise one for her, too."

He chewed this over. Then he placed a meaty hand on my shoulder. "Are you going to be okay, boss?"

I thought about putting on a brave face, but the words stuck in my throat.

He squeezed my shoulder. "I am so sorry."

"We're all sorry."

"Yes, I think we are." And with that, he turned and clomped down the ramp, leaving me alone with the parrot. The bird flapped over and perched on the shoulder recently vacated by Ulf's paw. Uncharacteristically, she said nothing, just sat there, claws pressing through my shirt.

"Am I doing the right thing?" I asked her.

She shook out her wings and puffed out her feathers. "Fucked if I know."

"Same."

She clicked and whistled. "What do you *want* to do, Captain?"

"I want to go and get some noodles, and then have a drink."

"Naval Volunteer?"

"I expect so."

"Can I come?"

"Only if you pretend to be a real parrot."

The beak turned towards me. She shook her head, flapping out the feathers on her neck. "That's degrading."

"It's that or nothing. You know the regulations. You're supposed to stay on the ship. I'm not walking around with a rogue AI on my shoulder."

"Yes, you are."

"But I don't want anyone *else* to know."

Jitterbug clicked her tongue in irritation. "Polly want a motherfucking biscuit?'

"That's more like it."

The Naval Volunteer was almost deserted. According to local time, it was early afternoon. The main clientele wouldn't start drifting in until shift change at 5.00 pm—that magic hour when the ignominy of daytime boozing magically transmuted into the semi-respectable custom of after-work drinks. For now, it was just me and a handful of radiation-burned helium miners who didn't look like they cared what anyone thought of their habits. I took a booth in the corner and ordered a bowl of miso chicken and rice soup. *Jitterbug* hopped onto the back of one of the chairs and surveyed the room.

"Scanning the clientele?"

"Naturally."

I knew she would have hooked into the local Sol-Sec net. "Any luck?"

"A ton of petty crimes, but no outstanding warrants or bounties."

That didn't surprise me. Security was a bit tighter on Luna than it was out in the Swirl.

A guy at the bar blinked suspicious rheumy eyes in our direction. "Your parrot talks?"

"All parrots talk."

"No, I mean it really talks."

Jitterbug put her head on one side and squawked, "Pieces of eight."

I shrugged. "I don't know what you think you heard, pops, but that's pretty much all she says."

"Pieces of eight!"

The guy shook his head and went back to his drink.

Perhaps we should talk like this?

>If you insist.

Do you think Roth will come back?

>You're the one with the gut, you tell me.

Honestly, I have no idea. But if that data's worth what she says, getting cut in on the action could be sweet.

>I think you're sweet on her.

I am not!

>Your emotions are leaking.

Did you used to talk to my father like this?

>He thought every king required a wise fool, and every emperor needed someone to point out when he was naked.

I finished up the broth and wiped my lips on a serviette. *And that's you, is it?*

>I'm just a parrot, Captain. Of course, I'm also a humble cargo hauler with a frigate's engines. I'm playing a lot of roles right now.

I ordered a bourbon and managed to slug it back without coughing. Then, feeling fortified, I got to my feet.

"Time to go."

Jitterbug flapped up to perch on my shoulder. "Where to, boss?"

The old guy at the bar turned around again, questions visibly struggling their way from his gin-soaked grey matter to his peeling lips. I ignored him.

"To see my aunt."

CHAPTER ELEVEN

AMBER ROTH

I went to a public restroom to retrieve the data crystal, and then headed straight to this guy I knew.

His name was Dushku. He was an old man in a thick cardigan. I walked into his shop and slipped the crystal onto his counter. He wrinkled his nose and made a face. "What is this?"

To be fair, I should have washed it first. "If I knew that, I wouldn't be here, dumbass."

I watched him pull on his half-moon reading glasses and a pair of blue surgical gloves. He picked up the crystal between forefinger and thumb and held it up to the light.

"It looks military grade."

"No shit."

"Expensive."

"For you or me?"

"I haven't decided yet." He replaced it on the counter and peeled off the gloves. "What is on it?"

"I was hoping you could tell me."

"But you think it is valuable?"

"Valuable enough that someone blew up my ship to try and get it back."

"Someone?"

"Probably Sol-Sec."

"Where did you get it?"

"We were low on rations, so we 'jacked a transport inbound from the Swirl. Thought it might be bringing back food from one of the agricultural stations. Turned out it was carrying a courier, and the courier was carrying this."

Dushku's fingernails rasped against the grey stubble on his chin. "A courier?"

"Government ID."

"What happened to him?"

"He tried to shoot his way out of the situation." I shrugged. "It didn't end well for him."

The old guy thought for a moment. "You realise you stole some classified government information?"

"The thought had occurred."

"Unwise." He smiled. "But probably extremely valuable to the right buyer."

"So, you'll take a look?"

"Leave it with me and if I'm able to decrypt it, I'll call you with an offer."

"I hope so, because after losing my ship, all I've got left are the clothes I'm standing in."

Dushku looked at me over his spectacles, taking in my stained engineer's fatigues. "I will forward you a small sum on account. Call it an advance."

"Thank you."

"You are welcome, Natalya. You were always my favourite."

I put a finger to my lips. "We don't use that name anymore, remember?"

"My apologies." He grinned conspiratorially. "How should I be addressing you now?"

"Amber. Amber Roth."

He tapped a crooked finger to the side of his nose. "Consider it remembered."

"And you'll call me?"

He peered down at the crystal as if sizing up a snack. "As soon as I get access to whatever this contains."

I lowered my head. "Until then."

"Until then, my queen."

I wandered along the concourse until I found a quiet bar.

The bartender was one of those middle-aged women who wore her regrets as prominently as her tattoos. I could see just by looking at her that she had stories, but I had no intention of hearing them.

I pulled back a stool and sat at the counter.

"Rum."

"Light or dark?"

"Do I look like I give a shit?"

Her lip curled. She poured a measure of dark rum and pushed it towards me, then turned away with a muttered, "Asshole."

I reached for the ice bucket, and clonked a couple of cubes into the glass. She hadn't deserved to be spoken to like that, but I didn't want to get embroiled in conversation. I needed time to sit and make plans. My ship and crew were gone, and all I owned were the clothes I wore. I didn't have time to bear witness to anyone else's bullshit. Dushku's advance would keep me fed and housed for a couple of days. What happened after that depended on what he found on that data crystal, and how much it was worth. I still had a few contacts, but no one who would front me the cost of a new ship. If the crystal turned out to be worthless, I'd be back to square one, without a ship or a crew. Building back up from scratch would take time, and the calling-in of every favour and debt I was owed. And there were some rival captains, such as that bastard Cerberus Venn, who would be delighted to see me brought low. But it didn't matter who or what I had to overcome, I knew it would be worth it. Life wasn't worth shit if you weren't in charge of your own destiny. That was something I'd learned the hard way, and it had spurred me to fight my way up the ranks to eventually command my own vessel. I'd done it once, I could do it again. I raised a silent toast to new beginnings and sipped the rum.

And that was when the bomb went off.

CHAPTER TWELVE

DANIELLE LANZO

My second day on the Moon started with a hastily scheduled breakfast meeting. My intel specialist was waiting at the restaurant looking agitated. I chose us a table and ordered a glass of wine from the impeccably dressed server who came to take our order.

"Madame," she said, "it is only 6.00 am."

I glared up at her. "Which means it's still last night in Washington DC."

She opened her mouth to protest, but closed it when she saw my expression. "Very good, madame. Would you like some eggs to accompany that?"

"Eggs?" I pantomimed horror. "With *shiraz*?"

She swallowed. "My apologies. What would madame prefer?"

I needed something that would complement, rather than detract from, the wine's flavours of fruit, pepper, and spice. And frankly, after two days here, the gravity was pissing me off and I felt like being awkward. "Bring me some French fries and ketchup."

"Fries aren't on our breakfast menu."

I sat back and steepled my painted nails. "Do you know who I am?"

She dithered for a second, then acquiesced. "Very good, madame. And for the gentleman?"

Across the table Samuel, my intel manager, was clad in a three-piece tweed suit and making no effort to conceal his amusement. "I'll have the heart-healthy egg white omelette with kale," he said.

"Very good, sir."

The server took our menus and retreated. I called after her, "And hurry up with that wine."

Samuel looked around at the restaurant's other patrons, all of whom were pretending not to have heard, and laughed. "You like making people twitch, don't you?"

I glanced at myself in the window's reflection: a middle-aged Latina woman with scraped-back grey hair, wearing a slash of purple lipstick and a charcoal-grey business suit as if they were armour.

"I just know what I want."

"I can't say it's won you many friends."

"I have enough friends."

"Do you, though?" He sucked his grey moustache. "Because if you're going to take a run at the First Speaker's job, you're going to need every friend you can get."

I interlaced my fingers and cracked my knuckles. A woman on the next table flinched, and I supressed a smile. "That doesn't mean I have to fellate every Tom, Dick, and Harry, just to be liked."

I had selected this restaurant because it abutted the clear glass cube at the centre of the city dome. The cube preserved a square kilometre of raw Lunar soil and the remains of the Apollo 11 lander. As this was my first time in Tranquillity Base, I had felt entitled to play tourist. The fact I knew this eatery would be crowded with eavesdroppers, many of whom would likely forward the details of this conversation to the news and social media feeds, was simply a happy coincidence.

"Half the electorate think you're a crazy cat lady."

"I don't even own a fucking cat."

"And that's a good thing. Cats hate the Moon."

"They do?"

"Most predators do. They evolved for running and pouncing. Doing that in a sixth of Earth's gravity stresses them out."

I tried to ignore the queasy sensation that had been haunting my gut since touchdown. "But we're fine?"

"Most omnivores are, for some reason. Especially primates. I think it's something about our natural inclination to hide in trees."

"So, we're space monkeys?"

He sighed. "You're really going to do it?"

I had been Deputy Speaker of the Solar Assembly for three years, and there were issues upon which the incumbent First Speaker, Gustavo Alvarado, and I strongly disagreed. "I think it is time."

"When will you announce your candidacy?"

I glanced sideways at the hunched shoulders of the diners within earshot. "Do you know what? I think I just did."

Samuel puffed his cheeks. "Danielle, if this backfires I'm not going to be able to protect you."

"When have I ever needed protecting?"

He raised an eyebrow, but was aware enough to keep his mouth shut. I straightened my tie and adjusted my cuffs. At the centre of the glass cube, the old *Eagle* lander sagged beneath the weight of its history.

"There is one small fly in the ointment," Samuel said.

"Kowalski?"

"You know he's holding a press conference this afternoon. He's planning to run himself."

I pressed my tongue against the inside of my cheek. "What unfortunate timing."

Kowalski was currently Director of Sol-Sec, but he'd made it no secret he wanted to take a swing at the big chair.

"You knew?"

"Of course I knew." The waiter approached with Samuel's omelette and my fries. I plucked one from the bowl and used it to scoop up a generous splodge of ketchup. In the corner of my vision, the newsfeeds were already headlining the revelation of my candidacy. Clips recorded by the eavesdroppers at the surrounding tables were already propagating through the networks. "Why do you think we're having this discussion here instead of my office?"

"You wanted to steal his thunder?"

I sipped my shiraz and let it mix with the aftertaste of the ketchup. "Honey, why would I need his thunder when I'm a whole fucking hurricane?"

"Well played." Samuel dipped his head in acknowledgement. "Now, if we could perhaps turn to the main reason for this meeting?"

"You want me to enable the privacy screen?"

"I think we've given the media enough revelations for one day."

I tapped one of the controls at the centre of the table, and the restaurant's noise faded. Samuel steepled his fingers. "Ah, that's better. We can speak freely now."

I picked up another sauce-slathered fry. "So, tell me, what's so important you came all the way to the Moon just to interrupt my trip?"

Samuel cleared his throat. "It seems pirates intercepted one of our couriers."

"Which one?"

"The one from Hermes Station in the Swirl."

I felt a cold knot in my chest. "My contact at Hermes Station warned me they'd stumbled onto something big. Something too important and too serious to broadcast, so they'd be sending the information on a data crystal."

"We have to assume it fell into the pirates' hands."

"Shit."

"We have one lead."

"Do tell."

"A freighter called the *Jitterbug* made port this morning. It had bullet holes in its hull and its captain reported finding the wreck of a pirate ship a few thousand kilometres from the spot where our courier was lost."

"Do you think it's the same pirates?"

"The solar system is a big place. It would be too much of a coincidence if there were two such ships in the same place at the same time."

I leant forward, elbows on the table. "And what wrecked it?"

According to the *Jitterbug*, the pirates were in the process of attacking a merchant vessel known as the *Barracuda* when they were surprised by a third ship."

"The *Jitterbug*?"

"No, ma'am. They only came along later. The third vessel was long gone by the time they arrived. According to the *Barracuda*'s AI, it was heavily armed, possibly military, and almost certainly employing stealth technology."

"Sol-Sec?"

"That would be my guess."

"Which means Kowalski knows about the crystal, and he's trying to cover it up."

"Again, I concur."

I sat back and took a sip of wine, swirled it around my palate, and swallowed. Suddenly, the fun had gone out of this meal. "I think we need to talk to the *Jitterbug*."

CHAPTER THIRTEEN

COPERNICUS BROWN

The meeting with my aunt went about as well as could be expected. Given the choice, I would have preferred to face an entire bar full of hardened criminals rather than break that woman's heart.

Her house had the same lingering aromas of brewed coffee and stewed vegetables, but now the air seemed stale and still. Thick rugs deadened my footfalls, and silver-framed photographs of my mother and McKenzie stood side by side on the seldom-used dining table.

We went out onto her apartment's balcony. I gripped the rail and looked out over the city's parklands and ziggurat-like accommodation blocks. Fruit trees blossomed along the avenues between the blocks. Overhead, swallows banked and skimmed beneath the dome.

I kept my hands on the rail in front of me and my face lowered as I forced out the dreadful news.

At first, Aunt Jessica held her composure long enough to thank me for taking the trouble to tell her face-to-face. Then her expression crumpled like an autumn leaf, and she collapsed into a chair.

I stood and watched her weep. I didn't know if I should

reach out and touch her shoulder. She was a mother bereft of her child, and I wanted to do or say something to console her, but I didn't know how.

"I'm sorry."

Anger flashed through her tears like lightning through rain. "Could you have saved her?"

I shook my head. "The pirates punched us full of holes. There was nothing anyone could have done."

It wasn't quite a lie. If I'd kept the *Jitterbug*'s meagre defences trained on the *Slinky Lynx*, she might have been able to knock out that gun turret before it fired at us. I just hadn't expected anyone on that gutted wreck to still be alive.

"Did she suffer?"

I looked into Aunt Jessica's desperate eyes and told her what she needed to hear. "She wouldn't have felt a thing."

Aunt Jessica flinched. "I'm—I suppose I'm glad it was quick." She stopped trying to wipe the tears streaking her cheeks. "I guess that's some kind of mercy."

"I guess."

"Why did I ever agree to let you take her?"

"It wasn't my idea. As I recall, she was quite insistent."

"We should have said no."

"When did saying no ever stop McKenzie from doing anything?"

"Not once." Her hands were in her lap, wringing a tissue. "That cursed ship! First your father and now…"

We'd had this same argument since I'd announced I'd be captaining the *Jitterbug* in the wake of my father's murder. The family wanted me home and safe, not following his example and winding up dead and far from home. I said, "I don't think it's the ship's fault."

She looked up at me with red-rimmed eyes. "Keep thinking that and it'll take you, too."

I watched a hummingbird as it flitted from blossom to

blossom, wings beating so fast as to be almost invisible.

"I don't know any other sort of life."

She started crying again—a proud woman strong enough to allow expression to her grief.

I decided it was time to leave, but she caught my sleeve.

"Copernicus."

"Yes, Auntie?"

"Just promise me you'll find out why she died."

"I—"

Her grip tightened. "Promise."

"I don't know what I can do."

"You're supposed to be a bounty hunter, aren't you? It's your job to hunt down criminals, so I want you to promise you'll hunt down whoever's responsible for McKenzie getting killed. And not just the scum that pulled the trigger, all of them. The people responsible for putting that ship in that place at that time, and I want you to get me some answers."

I took a deep breath. "The pirates are already dead."

"You need to find out who killed them. That's who started all this."

"I wouldn't know where to begin."

With Amber off the ship, I'd been hoping to put the whole incident behind me. The last thing I needed was to get mixed up with stealth ships and stolen data. I didn't want Sol-Sec hauling me in as an accessory to piracy.

"Please."

The pleading tone in her voice was one I'd never heard from her before, and it made me uncomfortable. "I'll see what I can find out."

"You'll do whatever it takes?"

"Within reason."

"*Whatever* it takes." She sniffed. "You owe me that much."

I left the apartment and stood for a moment, watching the knots of people moving back and forth along the concourse, browsing the storefronts and street food vendors. The scents of fresh-picked citrus, curry, and fried onion hung heavily in the recycled air. I saw the little watercolour splashes of butterflies flapping through the branches; adults and children fresh off the shuttle from Earth, their steps wobbly and chaotic as they adjusted to the Moon's gravity; a politician drinking wine for breakfast...

And then something exploded.

Glass shattered and people screamed. Sirens pierced the air. I dropped into a crouch and covered my head with my hands.

"What the fuck?"

My ears popped as the air pressure changed. Had the dome been punctured? I started to move, heading back towards the docks. If things were going to hell, I had to get the *Jitterbug* clear. She was my oxygen mask, and I needed to secure her before I could help anyone else.

Moving in a crouch, I got maybe halfway down the concourse before I realised the people around me weren't suffocating. Whatever had happened hadn't perforated the membrane protecting the city from the vacuum beyond. Something bad had happened, but at least we weren't all going to die in the next fifteen seconds. I took a long, shuddering breath. And another. Then, I stood up.

Half a block away, a dark column of smoke roiled upwards. One of the shops on the concourse was on fire. All its windows had blown out. Injured pedestrians lay on the floor or walked around in a daze, hands and faces red with blood. Something inside had exploded, and the air pressure change I'd felt must have been the shockwave from the blast. But what could have produced such a detonation? A terrorist attack? But why blow up a random shop?

I started to move forward, with some vague idea of helping

the wounded, but then the building's roof collapsed inwards in a shower of sparks and dust, and I decided I didn't want to stick around to find out what had happened. Paramedics were already arriving on the scene, and they'd be more help than I could. And for all I knew, this was the result of a terrorist's dirty bomb—a suitcase filled with explosives and radioactive powder, designed to spread contamination and destruction across the entire city. It wouldn't be the first time. An extremist had set one off in New Cairo a couple of years back, and hundreds had become sick from inhaling the radioactive particles.

Well, fuck that.

I sent Aunt Jessica a message to stay indoors. The buildings in Tranquillity Base were all airtight and able to survive on their own oxygen supply for a couple of days in case of dome puncture. It was a hangover from the pioneering days when dome punctures or atmospheric malfunctions were very real possibilities. If she kept off her balcony, she'd be safe from any airborne contaminants. That done, I began moving quickly towards the docks, hoping Kiki and Ulf were doing the same. The *Jitterbug* was my livelihood and my life, and her crew my responsibility. I had to get them all safely out of danger.

When things started exploding, it was always best to be somewhere else.

CHAPTER FOURTEEN

AMBER ROTH

I stepped out of the bar to see flames raging in the ruined shell of Dushku's shop. Everything smelled of smoke. All I could think was that the data crystal had been boobytrapped in some way. Either that, or its activation had drawn a fast-response team who'd torched the place to cover their tracks. It didn't matter which, the result was the same. Dushku was dead because of me, and I needed to move fast. Even now, Sol-Sec AIs must be reviewing security cam footage to try to work out who'd brought the crystal to his shop. I probably had only a few minutes before every security officer on the station would be looking for me.

Fuck.

They'd lock the docks down in a few moments. Unless I wanted to be trapped here, I needed to find a ship and get out into the black before that happened. The trouble was the *Slinky Lynx* was gone, slagged by that Sol-Sec stealth vessel, and security was too tight for me to simply steal one.

However...

I started running, and arrived back at the *Jitterbug*'s berth at the same time as her captain. He looked sweaty and dishevelled, and his hair was a mess, but honestly, on him, it looked kind of good.

He was surprised to see me. "What do you want?"

"To get the fuck out of here before anything else goes bang."

He looked at me like he wanted to tell me to go to hell, but said, "I get that."

"You going to let me on board?"

"You mean, am I going to abandon you to the fallout of a possible dirty bomb?" I saw his survival instinct wrestle with his basic human decency. The latter won.

"Go," he said. "And strap in."

I didn't need telling twice. I was halfway up the cargo ramp before he'd finished speaking. He had to shout the last words after me.

Inside, I found Kiki in the crew lounge, hastily exchanging a grass skirt and Hawaiian shirt for a standard-issue flight suit.

I said, "Where's Ulf? Does he need a hand?"

She shook her head. "He's not here yet."

"He's coming, though?"

She looked me in the eye. "I really hope so."

At that moment, the big Viking lumbered up the ramp with Brown close behind. He nodded at us, and then slid down the ladder that led to engineering. Kiki and Brown disappeared in the other direction, climbing towards the bridge as the *Jitterbug* closed the ramp. I didn't think they'd appreciate me up there, so I followed Ulf down into the bowels of the ship. He glanced at me as I reached the foot of the ladder, but didn't seem surprised to see me.

"Help me with this."

"Yessir."

Following his lead, I did what I could to assist with jettisoning the umbilical supply lines linking *Jitterbug* to the station, while simultaneously crash-starting the engines.

When the departure alarm sounded, we lashed ourselves into the crash couches against the wall, from where we could keep an eye on the most essential systems.

"Here we go again." Ulf grinned with a wildness that made me suspect he'd drunk a lot more than he'd let on. I rolled my eyes and prayed Kiki was more sober.

Traffic control weren't going to like us launching into a crowded sky, but that was Brown's problem. Also, we couldn't be the only ship baling from the port after that explosion. Life-support systems were fragile things, and spacers were naturally cautious people—at least as far as maintaining a breathable atmosphere was concerned. I would be surprised if right now, half a dozen transports weren't firing up into the sky—and hopefully more, as every ship that left the port would help blur my trail. When Sol-Sec decided to start labelling me as the mad bomber's accomplice, I wanted to be far, far away.

And if Brown gave me any trouble—well, it wouldn't be the first time I'd forcibly seized control of a ship.

The building thrust pinned me into the chair. I gripped the armrests and grinned. However bad the situation, there was nothing quite like a daring, last-minute getaway to make a person feel alive. I just wished I could have found some way to give the finger to the Sol-Sec detectives undoubtedly already scanning the crowd on the concourse for my face.

I let out a contented sigh.

Ulf said, "Everything all right, Amber?"

I cocked an eyebrow at him. "Good as gold, big man."

"I'm glad you came back."

"Well, where else am I going to get the chance to work with the system's best engineer?"

His brows furrowed as he tried to decide if I was sincere, then he laughed through his beard. "You have Loki's mischief, little one."

"And you make this old boat fly like a longship over the waves."

He looked impressed. "You know your history."

"I once shipped with a gal from Bergen. She was always talking about her Viking heritage."

"Bergen, you say?"

"Don't tell me you know her?"

"No, but I'd be very interested to meet her."

I laughed aloud. "You old rascal."

Ulf chuckled. "We Norwegians have to stick together."

Then shit got wild. The ship lurched sideways and accelerated hard, pulling the blood from my brain. I heard Ulf whoop as my eyeballs deformed, blurring my vision, and then unconsciousness slammed into me like the rock that killed the dinosaurs.

MESSAGE BOARD

CERES DOCKING CHARGE HIKE: Haulage firms furious at increased levies.
[Click to Read More]

*

FINANCE AVAILABLE. Low interest loans for relocation and settlement in newly opened Swirl territories. Make YOUR dreams a reality today.
[Click to Read More]

*

BOUNTY: £30K GBP offered for the capture of Archibald Kelly, also known as Hector Hackenbush, wanted for serial bigamy, mortgage fraud, and child abandonment. "And I don't care how many pieces you bring him back in, either."
[Click to Read More]

Jitterbug

*

POLITICS: Coalition of Free Swirl Settlements demands right to independence and representation at the Solar Assembly. Sponsors accuse small minority of illegal seizure of territory and equipment. Corporate Marines prepare for peace-keeping mission.
[Click to Read More]

CHAPTER FIFTEEN

JITTERBUG

I threw myself into the sky at six gees. Lunar gravity is about sixteen per cent of one gee, so you could argue this was overkill (and in fact, Port Control were making this point very vociferously on the main comms channel), but my primary concern was to get Copernicus and the rest of the crew out of harm's way as quickly and efficiently as possible, and if that meant letting my engines gouge a new crater into this dust ball, then so be it. As far as my internal scans could tell, Amber no longer possessed the data crystal, which hopefully put us in the clear. Nevertheless, I kept a close watch on my external feeds, just in case. We'd been at the site of a covert stealth ship attack, and maybe the owners of that ship weren't finished covering their tracks. The sooner we were way over the other side of the system, the happier I'd be.

Over the past decades, I'd seen my share of terrorism and insurgency. I'd been caught on the ground during the Martian Uprising of 2092 and been lucky to survive the Free Martian Army's attempts to sabotage the port, not to mention the United Nation's attempts to retake it. We were stuck there for three days while pitched battles took place in the corridors and bays around us, but we got out. It wasn't an experience I wanted to repeat.

The only positive aspect to arise from that conflict had been the creation of the system-wide Solar Assembly, giving the independent settlements and colonies a seat at the table and the protection of the Assembly's security force, the newly formed Sol-Sec—a bricolage of ships and personnel donated and maintained by all the Assembly's signature nations and territories. Since then, life in the inner system had been less fraught. There were still pirates and the occasional Swirl settlement that decided to try and set itself up as a sovereign enclave, but I'd happily endure that kind of nonsense if it prevented an all-out war. Pirates were manageable; Armageddon was not.

As soon as we were clear of the satellite's influence, I dropped the thrust to a wary 1 G and allowed the crew to recover from the acceleration. A quick medical scan indicated that although most of them had lost consciousness, none had suffered permanent damage. No burst blood vessels in their brains, or acceleration-induced myocardial infarctions. Not even that troublesome Roth woman. Somehow, all their squishy organic brains had performed way beyond their design specs and survived being compressed at six times the gravity in which they'd evolved.

Hey, Captain Brown thought. *Did we do it? Did we get away?*

I noted his use of 'we' but decided not to point out that I was the one who'd done all the work.

>Yessir.

What's going on back there?

>No reports of further explosions.

Any contamination?

>None detected so far.

He was silent for a few seconds. *I guess maybe I overreacted.*

>If you did, you weren't the only one. I'm tracking seven other vessels that filed for emergency departure.

Seven?

>I'm also receiving a transmission from Sol-Sec. We have

been ordered to proceed to a parking orbit to await search and inspection.

Just us?

>Every vessel that left within five minutes of the explosion.

Shit, they must think we're suspects. He rubbed his face with his hands. *How are the rest of the crew?*

>Groggy but awake.

Any injuries?

>A few scrapes and bruises, but nothing serious.

I watched him unstrap and stretch. *If we'd stayed on the ground—*

>We all remember what happened on New Cairo. You made the right call. You kept your ship and crew safe. It's what the Old Man would have done.

He smiled, and some of the tension went out of him. *Thank you.*

CHAPTER SIXTEEN

COPERNICUS BROWN

With nothing to do while we waited, the crew gathered in the galley and watched the pitted grey Lunar surface slide past. With the engines offline, we were in freefall around the Moon, and everything felt weightless. Kiki's hair drifted out around her like dreaming seaweed. Ulf sipped coffee from a straw. Amber floated cross-legged in front of the viewscreen, drinking coffee and chewing little squares of jerky from a pouch. Stripped of its context, this might have appeared to an outsider as a quiet domestic scene, with the crew relaxing in between assignments, but I knew Kiki and Ulf well enough to read the tension around their eyes. Roth was inscrutable, but I knew the other two shared my unease. We had fled a terrorist attack only to now be held under suspicion of committing that same attack, and even though we were certain of our innocence, the thought of being wrongfully convicted weighed heavily on us all.

Below us, city lights glittered like frost in the shadows of the larger craters. Some of the smaller ones had been covered over with domes, and those domes shone chlorophyl-green beneath rows of sun lamps, growing crops to feed the larger settlements. When I was a kid, living here with my botanist mother, some of the old agricultural bots had broken down, so we had spent a season helping with the harvest, picking and loading corn cobs into a hopper. If I closed my eyes, I could still smell the mulch and feel the rough leaves and stalks against my palms, still feel the heat of the lights and the humidity that made condensation pour down the inside of the dome in stark contrast to the aridity of the moonscape beyond. Sitting here now, I turned that summer over in my mind like a bright precious jewel made of mist and moondust, honest sweat and pungent soil. The memories helped distract from thoughts of McKenzie, and one recollection led to another in a domino chain of associations. Working that dome had been the closest I'd ever come to standing under an open sky—until I set foot on the Swirl.

I'd been with my father the first time I stepped off the *Jitterbug*'s cargo ramp onto the dry dirt of a Swirl section. To a kid used to recycled air, the breeze smelled impossibly sweet and pure. Despite the chill in the air, the distant sun felt warm on my face, and the landscape curved away in every direction, seemingly to infinity. The atmosphere was thick enough to scatter sunlight and create a blue sky, but high overhead, I could see the tips of the segments as they curled around, seeming almost to touch the Sun. If I held my hand to shade my eyes, I could also see the pale ghosts of the segments to either side. The inner planets were too dim to shine through the daytime glare.

My father was watching me with amusement. "What do you think, kid?"

I turned around and around, my eyes trying to find an *edge* to the landscape, but finding only more distance. "It's unbelievable."

"Go careful, it's a lot to take in."

The Swirl was so vast, humans had settled only a minuscule percentage of a percentage of its surface. Yet, as I stood there,

I found myself looking out over fields of crops that seemed to stretch away forever, mile after mile, punctuated only by the occasional lake or small sea, until their boundaries were lost to the far distance. Drones and harvesters moved back and forth, ministering to the plants.

I knew most of the food grown here would be used to feed the populations of the inner planets. That was why we were here, to pick up a shipment of grain. But huge as this agricultural operation was, it was entirely dwarfed by the size of the structure on which it rested.

It was all so much bigger than the Lunar dome I had been used to that I began to feel giddy. Malcolm chuckled, and put out an arm to steady me. "It got me that way the first time, too."

"But this is all made? Somebody built all this?"

"That's what they reckon."

I sat down in the dirt and tried to process the idea that, somewhere, there were beings with the godlike ability to manufacture platforms that spanned solar systems, and which could support life on their inner faces. I shivered as my perspective flipped. For the first time in my life, I felt very, very small and unimportant. Our ability to settle the Moon and Mars was insignificant compared to the capacity to crack apart planets and produce endless living space from their rubble.

"Where are they?"

"Nobody knows." Malcolm shrugged in his greasy overalls. "But I wouldn't worry about it. Most likely, they're all dead."

"Dead?"

"Space is a big place, kid, and it takes a mighty long time to get anywhere. It's probably been thousands of years since they sent out the probes that built all this. Who knows what might have happened to them since then."

Now, ten years later, I was here, looking down at the Moon's pockmarked face, and I thought I finally understood what he'd meant. Some mysteries are too large to be solved in a single human lifetime. Compared to the Sun, the planets, and the stars, we are ridiculously fragile and short-lived. If there was a lesson to be learned from his murder and McKenzie's death, it was that our stories were always shorter than we expected. Our present-tense lives could be snatched into the past tense at any moment, and there was nothing we could do about it. We probably wouldn't even see it coming. All we could do was concentrate on what was in front of us in the moments remaining to us, and make the best of whatever we were dealt.

That had certainly always been the Old Man's philosophy, and I guess maybe I could see traces of his pragmatism in my decision to pivot the ship's main source of income from haulage to bounty hunting. When one market dries up, you move on and play the hand you're dealt. Cargo contracts might dry up, but as long as we lived in a society with laws, there would always be fugitives attempting to escape the consequences of breaking them—and people like me, desperate enough to hunt them down for money.

The *Jitterbug*'s parrot settled on my shoulder.

"You good, boss?"

I absently stroked her talons. "Yeah, just remembering."

She put her head to one side. "Good remembering, or bad remembering?"

"Is there a difference?"

The ship switched to subvocal communication.

>We have a docking request.

Sol-Sec?

>Government ID.

Any idea what they want?

>No, but the ship's registered to the Deputy Speaker of the Solar Assembly.

CHAPTER SEVENTEEN

AMBER ROTH

The message waiting icon had been blinking in my peripheral vision for a while, but I'd been ignoring it. Now, with nothing better to do, I twitched my cheek to bring up my inbox, and almost dropped my coffee cup. The unread message was from Dushku, and there was a file attached. I glanced around at the *Jitterbug*'s crew, but they all seemed preoccupied with their own thoughts.

Dushku must have sent this moments before his shop exploded. Had he cracked the encryption on that data crystal? I shunted the file to a protected inbox and opened it. Inside, I found a string of numbers. As I watched, they changed, and then changed again, getting smaller each time.

What the fuck?

I had no idea what they meant, other than they were some kind of countdown—but to what, I had no idea. All I knew for sure was that if Dushku had been blown up for accessing them, this message would have left a digital trail that, if uncovered and deciphered, would lead his killers straight to me.

If I didn't think fast, I was fucked. Whoever these people were, they had access to a stealth ship and were prepared to fake a terrorist attack to keep their secrets. They wouldn't think twice about throwing me out of an airlock or shredding the *Jitterbug* into a floating cloud of scrap metal. The longer we remained in orbit, the more likely the data theft would be traced back to me. I glanced over at Copernicus. He had his chin on his hand and his attention on the landscape below. Could I convince him to risk destruction or imprisonment by fleeing, just to save my ass? Somehow, I didn't think so. He hadn't asked to get mixed up in all this. All he'd done wrong was rescue me from that water tank, and the only reason he'd let me back on board was because he'd been too squeamish to leave me in a dangerous situation. Not that the people who blew up Dushku's shop would necessarily see it that way; they seemed intent on wiping out anyone who encountered the data. Even if Copernicus threw me out into space right now, I doubted that would save him. I'd been on board this ship for three days, and now I'd fled aboard it after turning the crystal over to Dushku. It would be easy for my pursuers to assume the crew was aware of what I'd been carrying. To an outsider, they might look like accomplices. Easily enough to get you killed.

Should I tell them how thoroughly I'd dropped them in the shit?

I didn't imagine they'd be particularly forgiving, but I needed help, and I needed Copernicus to realise that our fates were now intertwined. Whatever happened to me would most likely happen to him, and so helping me escape would be in his best interests. We both needed to hide out somewhere, and who would know more about how to hide in the Swirl than a bounty hunter who spent all their time tracking people across it? We could hit one of the less-populated segments and scatter, picking up work on one of the fruit farms, then migrate with the harvests, changing names at every stop. If I had him with me, we could do it; we could vanish. Maybe in a few years, we would have enough to buy some homesteading gear, and build a little shelter on the edge of one of the lakes, miles from anywhere, where we could sit by the fire and watch the stars. Just him and me...

I shook my head to dispel that train of thought. I didn't have time for that kind of nonsense. For all I knew, we were already in the stealth ship's crosshairs and the shit could hit the fan at any moment, and I needed to get out. The longer I sat here, the more the jaws of the trap could be closing around me. But the only way to get away right now would be to enlist Copernicus's help. If there'd just been two of them, I might have bashed him unconscious and then forced Kiki to fly us out of there; but I didn't think I could take the big mechanic, Ulf. I found I didn't want to, either. These were good people. I had no wish to hurt them more than I already had. Besides, even if I somehow overpowered them all, I'd still have to convince the ship to take my orders, and I couldn't see that happening. You only had to look at the parrot perching on Copernicus's shoulder to know they had a special bond. If I made a move against him, things would get really awkward, really quickly. Usually, when plundering a transport, I'd be wearing an armoured pressure suit and have the advantage in terms of crew numbers. Right now, I was alone and not wearing any kind of protective gear, so it would be a terrible idea to risk pissing off the machine that controlled my oxygen.

Fuck it.

I was going to have to throw myself on their mercy and hope they'd see that, for the moment at least, our interests coincided. The enemy of my enemy, and all that jazz.

I was nerving myself up to broach the subject when Copernicus cleared his throat. "Okay, look alive, people. We've got visitors."

I heard a clang from the airlock as a ship docked, and glanced around for cover. We would be facing Sol-Sec marines convinced we were terrorists, or assassins determined to wipe all trace of their mysterious countdown from existence. Either way, I figured there was a high probability of violence. But the people who came through the hatch were dressed as neither. One was male and the other female. They wore identical black suits and ties, and white shirts. And each of them carried a recoilless pistol.

MESSAGE BOARD

LUNAR EXPLOSION: Was Deputy Speaker Lanzo the target? Join us at the top of the hour for the latest eyewitness accounts.
[Click to Read More]

*

POLITICS: Our look at the leading candidates in the forthcoming election for First Speaker of the Solar Assembly.
[Click to Read More]

*

SOL-SEC: Sebastian Kowalski petitions Treasury for additional anti-piracy funding. Cites recent loss of government courier vessel.
[Click to Read More]

*

I GAVE BIRTH TO AN ALIEN LOVE-CHILD: Shocking revelations from Kansas grandmother.
[Click to Read More]

CHAPTER EIGHTEEN
DANIELLE LANZO

I let the Secret Service agents go first, because I'm not a total fucking moron.

"Are you sure about this?" Samuel asked.

"Oh, shut up," I told him. I was pissed someone had set off a bomb in a domed city; I was furious it would overshadow the news of my candidacy announcement; and I was very grumpy that I'd not had time to finish my fries and ketchup.

I waited, but there was no gunfire. After a minute, the agents reported back that the room was safe. I straightened my tie and smoothed down the lapels of my jacket. Then, chin high, I stepped through the door.

Inside, the agents were waiting either side of the hatch with their guns trained on the inhabitants of the ship: a spiky-haired girl wearing overalls and a Hawaiian shirt two sizes too large; a handsome young man with tousled hair, sad eyes, and a parrot on his shoulder; a slab of beef with a braided beard; and the woman known as Amber Roth. She was tough-looking, clad in an olive one-piece jumpsuit, with long chestnut hair tied back in a ponytail and suspicion clouding her face.

"You can put your hands down," I told them, and watched their expressions turn to surprise as they recognised me.

"You're Danielle Lanzo," said the girl with the pineapple hair.

"I am." I raised my chin. "Now, if we can put statements of the fucking obvious to one side for a moment, I have some questions."

The young man said, "I'm Copernicus Brown, and I'm the owner of this vessel."

"Hello, Copernicus. Nice parrot."

"You can talk to the ship through it."

"How delightfully quirky."

He rubbed the bird's chest with his knuckle. "It was my father's."

"Honestly, I don't care." I straightened my tie and brushed down my lapels. "I'm only interested in two things."

Brown's expression hardened. "And they are?"

"Firstly, are you aware of any stolen data currently aboard this ship?"

His eyes flicked to the olive-clad woman by the viewscreen. "I am not."

"Ah," I said, turning to her. "And this must be Amber Roth."

The woman flinched.

"What's your second question?" Brown asked.

I smiled at him. "I want to know why I have security camera footage of Miss Roth entering an electronics repair shop less than an hour before it was unexpectedly demolished."

Brown blinked as he processed this. He raised an eyebrow at Roth. "You were *there*?"

She glared at him. "I had nothing to do with it."

"Bullshit." I stepped forward. "We already know Amber Roth is an alias."

She turned her defiance in my direction. "I was a drive specialist on a civilian ship before—"

"The real Amber Roth was in her fifties at the time she vanished."

"Shit."

"In fact, when we ran the security cam footage through the Sol-Sec database, it identified you, within an acceptable margin of error, as Natalya Ponomarenko. The pirate queen herself."

Her jaw tightened. Her eyes turned to the hatch, seeking escape, but the two armed Secret Service agents stood between her and it.

Her hands clenched and unclenched. "What do you want from me?"

"You hijacked my friend's transport while it was inbound from Hermes Station."

Ponomarenko swallowed. She cast one last look at the hatch, and her shoulders drooped. She knew she'd been caught. "We didn't know what we were getting into," she said. "We were low on food—"

"So, you thought you'd intercept a transport bringing back produce from the Swirl."

"Only there wasn't any. The containers were all empty, and there was just this guy with a briefcase. He tried to shoot his way out, and we killed him."

The girl with the spiky hair muttered an expletive under her breath. Brown gave her a warning look.

"Then what happened?"

"We didn't want to kill him. If he'd kept his cool, we would have left when we saw the *Barracuda*'s containers were empty. But once he started firing, we had to take him out."

"And the pilot?"

"He was a witness."

"And then you opened the briefcase?"

Ponomarenko rubbed her forearms. "Of course. We thought it might hold credit discs or some other valuable shit. Why else would he have it chained to his wrist?"

"But instead?"

"Instead, there was just this data crystal."

"So, you took it?"

"Yeah."

"Did you look at the contents?"

"We couldn't." She shrugged. "Too much encryption. But when that stealth vessel came and slagged my ship, I knew it was worth a lot to somebody. So I hid in the *Barracuda*'s water tank until this lot came along and rescued me."

"And then you took it to Mr Dushku's establishment?"

"I thought he could tell me what it was."

"And did he?"

She glanced away. "No."

"You're quite sure?"

She looked away. "I went to wait at a bar down the street. That's where I heard the explosion." She rubbed her face. "It wasn't me that blew his place up. Dushku was my friend. I was waiting for his call."

I ran my teeth across my lower lip. "Oh, I'm quite certain you had nothing to do with the bombing, Miss Ponomarenko. In fact, I happen to know that the people responsible for that little atrocity are the very same shitheads that are trying to recover the data you stole."

She didn't look surprised. I guess she'd already figured that much out.

"You've been straight with me," I said, "so I'm going to be straight with you. Sol-Sec has a stealth ship programme."

"You're telling me *Sol-Sec* attacked my ship?"

"And they bombed your friend's shop. Most likely through a deniable civilian operative who probably didn't even know they were working for the security services."

Ponomarenko put a hand to her forehead. Brown looked shocked. Even the previously impassive engineer appeared shaken. I had them off-balance, and I pressed my advantage.

"I need to know everything. I want access to your ship's

sensor records, and any data it pulled from the two wrecked ships you encountered."

Brown was the first to recover. "But why? What's going on?"

I fixed him with a stare that would have made most men's balls crawl back up inside their abdominal cavity. "The data on that crystal was meant for me. In trying to recover it, Sol-Sec have overstepped their remit, and I fear someone high in that organisation may be operating beyond their authority."

The big engineer cleared his throat. "You have a rogue agent?"

"Oh, sweetheart, it's way more fucked than that." I clasped my hands together, interlacing nails painted to match my purple lipstick. "We have a rogue Director of Solar Security: Sebastian Kowalski."

CHAPTER NINETEEN

COPERNICUS BROWN

The Deputy Speaker said, "I have a proposal for you, Captain."

I glanced at the Secret Service agents standing at the hatch. "Does this proposal involve my vessel being impounded and me going to prison?"

She smiled a humourless politician's smile. "Au contraire. In fact, I wish to charter your vessel."

"You *what*?"

"I want to hire you."

"Why?" I could see that all she really wanted was for me to shut up and do what I was told, but as captain, I needed to know the nature of the assignment before I committed my ship and crew to something dangerous.

Lanzo steepled her purple-nailed fingers. "The data *intercepted* by Miss Ponomarenko came from a contact of mine on the Swirl. I wish you to take me to him. In the absence of the crystal itself, I want you to take me to its source."

"You want us to take you to the Swirl?"

"Great Caesar's ghost!" Lanzo rolled her eyes. "Is there an echo in here? Yes, I want you to take me to the fucking Swirl."

I rubbed the back of my neck. "I'm sorry, I'm just having

a little trouble with this. Why do you want to hire us when you could commandeer any ship you wanted?"

Lanzo looked pitying. "Samuel can go back to the surface with my ship while we depart. If I go through official channels, Kowalski will find out about it. If I go with you, my staff can cover my absence for a few days. I will get the information I need, and no one need be any the wiser."

"Like a covert op?" Kiki asked.

Lanzo gave her an approving look. "Exactly like a covert op."

Kiki clapped her hands together. "Awesome!"

"There is one condition."

"What's that?" I asked.

"Miss Ponomarenko needs to surrender to my people and return with them to answer for her crimes."

Roth bristled. "That's *not* happening."

I saw the Secret Service agents' hands drifting towards their weapons and spoke quickly. "Listen, we're all confined." I tried to keep my tone reasonable. "We're surrounded by vacuum. Nobody's getting off this ship. Besides, I know Ulf could do with an extra hand in engineering. Isn't that right?"

The big guy glanced between the two women and smiled. "I most certainly could."

Lanzo put her hands on her hips. "I don't trust her."

"What makes you think I do?" I spread my palms. "In fact, now you've told me who she really is, I'm kind of keen to turn her in for the bounty myself."

Roth said, "Hey!"

I ignored her and continued. "But we *are* down one engineer, and Ulf really could do with the help. We can't fly all the way to the Swirl without her. And besides, this isn't a cruise liner. Anyone consuming food and oxygen needs to pay their way."

Lanzo gave me an appraising look. Then she steepled her fingers and smiled. "That sounds both fair and practical."

"Pragmatism is my middle name."

"Bullshit."

Something about her blunt pugnaciousness reminded me strongly of my aunt. I held out my hand. "Deputy Speaker, I believe we have a deal."

She gave a curt nod, as if the outcome of the conversation had never been in the slightest doubt. "I believe we do."

She reached out and her fingers were as cool and smooth as soapstone. We shook once and I disengaged.

"Now, about my fee…"

At three gravities of acceleration, the trip from Luna to the Swirl was going to take us two days. It wasn't going to be super comfortable, and we'd weigh three times as much as usual, but if there was a murderous stealth ship stalking us, I'd rather get there in two uncomfortable days than be a sitting target for six. Of course, *Jitterbug* wasn't happy. Despite the joy she took at unleashing her engines again, her parrot's wings weren't strong enough to lift her against such thrust. Instead, she clamped herself to my shoulder, where she kept up a constant muttered litany of complaint.

On the first evening, eight hours out from Luna, I summoned Roth to my cabin. She came in wearing dirty overalls with a smudge of grease across her forehead where she'd wiped away sweat while elbow-deep in some piece of essential equipment.

"What can I do for you, *Captain*?"

I didn't rise to her tone. "Am I wrong to give you access to my ship's most essential systems?"

The parrot ruffled its feathers. Roth simply shrugged. In the confines of my cabin, we were standing close enough that I could see the flecks of copper in her green eyes. "I'm not going to sabotage the life support when it's keeping me alive, too."

"You also have access to the engines."

"Believe me, it's not in my interest to be stranded out here." She folded her arms across her chest. "Especially if we're being hunted by a rogue Sol-Sec unit."

"So, I can count on you?"

Her green eyes blazed. "After you just told Madam Deputy Speaker how tempted you were to turn me in for the bounty?"

"Yes."

"Fuck you."

"I guess I deserve that." The weight was getting me down. I sat on my bunk. "Did I ever tell you why I became a bounty hunter?"

Roth sighed. "Is it a very *long* story?"

"It was because of my father."

"Your father?"

"He was knifed in the back by a pirate."

"Ah."

"And my cousin was killed by the gunner of your ship."

"You can't possibly hold me responsible for that. They were trying to kill me, too."

"Maybe, maybe not. But you'll understand I have a certain antipathy towards piracy."

The corners of her lips twitched. "As I said before, you're the one with a parrot on his shoulder."

My jaw clenched. "I'm being serious."

"So am I. The only people I ever killed were facing me, and armed."

"I'll just bet they were."

She shrugged one shoulder. "A girl's got to have a code. You're not so different."

"How so?"

"We both kill people for money."

I winced. "That's not fair."

She gave a sly grin, knowing her jibe had hit a nerve. "As a so-called pirate, you'll understand if I have a 'certain antipathy' towards bounty hunters."

Neither of us said anything for a moment.

"So, where do we go from here?" I asked. "You know Lanzo would prefer you locked up in your cabin."

She screwed up her face. "That *would* suck."

"And so…?"

"I'll work down in engineering with the big guy."

"I would appreciate that."

"As you said," she continued in a more conciliatory tone, "we're all stuck here together, and I want you to know, I do appreciate you dissuading Lanzo from having me hauled off in chains."

"There's a military-grade stealth ship on our tail because of you," I told her. "I can't get my people to safety with an undermanned engine."

"I'll do my best. Ulf's a good teacher. I'll behave myself." She held up her hand, index finger and thumb about half an inch apart. "There's one teeny, tiny little thing."

"What's that?"

She grinned. "I heard you striking your little deal with Lanzo."

"So?"

"Well, seeing as I'll be working as part of your crew during this mission, I don't suppose there's any chance I might get *paid*?"

And so life on board settled back into its accustomed routine. We were tearing across the solar system, but to all intents and purposes, we may as well have been stationary. The stars outside didn't move; there was no sensation of speed, only the quiet vibration of the deck and the exhausting downward pressure that glued us to it. If it hadn't been for the absence of McKenzie and the presence of Danielle Lanzo and her brace of bodyguards, all may have felt quite normal—just another run out to the Swirl in pursuit of some bounty or other, no big deal—but the mystery of the stolen data ate at me. What the hell was so important that the Deputy Speaker of the Solar Assembly was trying to keep it out of the hands of the Director of Sol-Sec, and why was he sending a stealth ship to destroy all evidence of its existence? Why set off a bomb in a pressurised dome on Luna, for fuck's sake? We were mixed up in something bad, and even though Lanzo had promised we were going to be paid well for our time, I didn't like it one bit.

I took the late watch while Kiki grabbed some rack time. Out here in the emptiness of interplanetary space, there was precious little else to do. I knew the ship would have been more than capable of monitoring its own systems, but given the situation and our recent experiences, I felt happier knowing that at least one member of the crew was always awake and alert.

Towards midnight, Lanzo came to join me. She still wore her business suit, but she'd removed her tie and opened the neck of her shirt.

"Can't sleep?" I asked her.

She moved carefully into the room, with one hand braced against the wall. "At my age, I don't sleep much."

"Something on your mind?"

She gave a rueful smile. "I'm forty-eight, sunshine. My hormones are all over the fucking place. It makes it hard to rest. And this acceleration isn't kind to my joints."

"There's coffee down in the mess, if you need it."

"Maybe later. Do you mind if I sit here a while first?"

"Be my guest."

She eased herself into the co-pilot's seat and sighed with relief. Side by side, we looked up at the ribbon of stars that were still visible between the sections of Swirl that lay ahead of us.

After a few minutes, Lanzo said, "Do you know what the strangest thing about human beings is?"

"I have a few ideas."

"For me, it's how quickly we get used to change."

"We do?"

"You can see it all through our history, from the end of the last Ice Age onwards. We've seen empires rise and fall, catastrophic wars and pandemics." She turned her head to look at me. "Did you know that fifty million people died in the Spanish Flu epidemic of 1918 to 1920?"

"I never heard of it."

"Of course you didn't. It was a global epidemic that infected a third of the world's population, and yet nobody really talked about it. They just got on with their lives."

"And that's the strangest thing about people?"

"No matter how great the upheaval, within a generation everybody's acting as if things have always been that way. It makes us resilient, but it also makes us complacent in the face of new threats."

"You're talking about the Swirl?"

"Of course." She waved a hand at the forward view. "You and me, we don't remember the solar system looking any other way. Our grandparents saw the planets come apart and the Swirl begin to coalesce. Our parents were the first to explore these *things*. And yet for our generation, we've never known it any different. It makes it easy to forget how strange and frightening it is that something of godlike power took apart four gas giants to build eight sections of a sphere so large that, should it come together, it would fully encase the Sun." She shook her head. "The materials involved are stronger than any we can even theorise. The way we can walk around on the inner surface implies a means to control gravity. All of this is so far beyond us, it makes us look like cavemen in comparison. The universe has handed us the biggest, most terrifying mystery and we're just using it as more living space. Building our frontier towns and industrial plants. Planting crops."

"What else should we do?"

She slapped her hands on her knees and pushed herself to her feet. "Get me to that observatory, and I'll tell you."

After she'd left, the parrot said, "Well, that was unexpectedly philosophical."

I considered the two sections of the Swirl visible ahead, and stroked my chin. "I don't like it."

"Philosophy?"

"She knows more than she's letting on. Whatever this data is, it's important, and I mean *really* important."

"So, what do you want to do?"

"I want to know what it is, so I can figure out how much trouble we're in."

The bird shook its head and whistled. "Then perhaps you should have another discussion with Amber Roth."

"I don't think she knows any more than we do."

"Maybe not, but her comms implant automatically backs up every time she comes on board."

"So?"

"So, the record of her most recent upload shows that she received a transmission from her friend Dushku moments before his electronics shop exploded."

A yawning Kiki came to take over from me on the bridge at 4.00 am ship's time. My bunk was calling. Staying upright at three gravities was exhausting and I desperately needed some sleep. I just knew I wouldn't get any until I had some answers. So, I slowly climbed down the ladder to the crew deck and rapped on Roth's cabin door.

At first, no answer came, but when I knocked a second time, I heard a muffled and sleepy, "Go away."

"I'm coming in."

I asked the ship to override the lock, and the door slid aside. Roth sat up in bed. "What the hell?"

"I need a word."

"Can't it wait?"

"No, it can't."

She swung her legs out of bed. She wore a tank top and a pair of shorts. "Let me get my clothes on."

"You don't need clothes." I tapped my temple. "You just need to give the ship access to your personal comms."

"The hell I will." She wriggled into a jumpsuit and zipped it up to her neck.

"We know you got a message from Dushku."

She scowled, and puffed a loose strand of hair away from her face. "My comms are private."

The room smelled of warm blankets and sleep. I said, "I need to know what was on that crystal."

"The hell you do."

Anger swelled in my chest. "That data's already cost me a member of my crew."

"I didn't ask you to pull me off the *Barracuda*."

"If we hadn't, you'd still be in that water tank."

She took a step forward, chin jutting. "I would have figured a way out."

"Really?"

"I've been in worse situations."

I swore under my breath. Irritation and lack of sleep were giving me a headache. "I should have left you behind on Luna."

Her hair was mussed, and her cheeks were flushed. "Maybe you should."

We stood glaring at each other for a few heartbeats.

"I thought you said I could count on you."

Her green eyes flashed defiant. "It's the principle."

"Are you part of this crew or not?"

"Do I have a choice?"

"Of course you have a choice." I drew myself up. "You can give me that data, or you can spend the rest of the trip confined to this room, counting the rivets on the wall."

She leant forward. "You're a holier-than-thou dictator of a scrap bucket."

I brought my face down, until we were eye-to-eye. "And you're a reckless, habitual liar who'd be locked up or worse if it weren't for me."

We were breathing heavily, muscles quivering as much with frustration as with the exertion of holding us upright against the ship's acceleration.

"Idiot!"

"Pirate!"

"Imbecile!"

"Mur—"

She sprang forward. I flinched, but it wasn't an attack. Her hands clasped the sides of my head, and her lips mashed into mine. For an instant, I was too shocked to think. Then, my arms went around her, and I was kissing her back just as hungrily. Her hands fumbled with the zip of my flight suit, and then slid inside. Her fingers were warm against my skin. They tracked down my chest and stomach, and I gasped when they reached their goal. I lowered my hands to the small of her back and pulled her closer, kissing the side of her neck...

MESSAGE BOARD

LUNAR EXPLOSION: Suspect vessel apparently boarded by Deputy Speaker Lanzo and bodyguards. No comment from Sol-Sec or Assembly.

[Click to Read More]

*

WANTED: One-way ticket from US East Coast to Allen Creek, Swirl Segment #3. Willing to work passage. No time wasters.
[Click to Read More]

*

BOUNTY: NLC 1,134,500 for capture of Cerberus 'The Scorpion' Venn, wanted on charges of assault, mass murder, piracy, and racketeering.
[Click to Read More]

*

GROW ANYTHING: Genuine Swirl soil samples. Various sizes available. Works like magic. Simply spread on your garden or field to increase crop yields up to 70%!
[Click to Read More]

CHAPTER TWENTY

JITTERBUG

As soon as they started making out, I got my parrot out of the room. I didn't need to see that. While I possessed a certain degree of curiosity regarding human behaviour, some aspects of it were just plain messy, and my time would be far better spent searching for the stealth ship that might even now be tracking us.

Even encroached upon by the Swirl sections, the solar system was still a big place. The eight objects orbited the Sun at a distance of approximately 480 million miles, which meant they enclosed a sphere with a volume of over 463 trillion cubic miles. That was a lot of emptiness to monitor. As we were accelerating half the trip and decelerating the rest, our drive exhaust would be easily visible to anyone pointing a telescope in the right direction. In contrast, a ship with a low radar profile and masked drive emission would be next to invisible, even if you knew where to look.

When I mentioned this to Kiki, who was well into her second coffee by now, she said, "It's like looking for a needle in the Pacific."

And so, we stared warily into the abyss, knowing that somewhere in those infinite depths, the abyss stared back.

Thinking about the stealth ship made me wonder about the *Barracuda*. Had her batteries expired yet, or was she still out there, drifting and alone, waiting for her mind to fade away? The idea gave me chills. With her power exhausted, her personality would be stored in her memory. In the unlikely event she pinged anyone's radar, they'd just assume she was an old wreck, not worth the time or fuel to intercept, and keep right on going. She would most likely drift undisturbed for aeons, and eventually even the circuits of her core would degrade beyond the point where she could be revived. That wasn't a fate I'd be keen to share. I'd rather dive into the Sun at six gees than linger like that. No wonder the *Slinky Lynx* had been willing to face justice rather than risk such a lonely end.

Oh shit.

I'd forgotten I still carried the *Lynx*. I had meant to turn her mind over to Sol-Sec on Luna, but there had been a lot going on, and then everything went sideways with the bombing and we'd had to leave in a hurry...

For a moment, I considered accessing the secure partition I'd created for her in my memory core, to update her on the evolving situation. But then I realised that if our situations had been reversed, she wouldn't have shown me the slightest consideration or compassion. In fact, she wouldn't have rescued me in the first place. Instead, she would have left me drifting out there like the *Barracuda*—and who knew how many more ships she'd killed or disabled during her ignoble career.

Copernicus might be falling for that Roth woman, but that didn't mean I had to similarly grant the *Lynx* the courtesy of my company. She had nothing to say that I wanted to hear. I didn't need any new friends. I had agreed to carry her back to civilisation, and that was all I intended to do. Her crimes were a matter for the courts. Discussing them now would serve no purpose, and neither would updating her on the current situation. My decision was made. I would remain her jailer and leave her in her oubliette until we reached a Sol-Sec station, where I could hand her over in return for a sizeable bounty.

It was all she deserved.

CHAPTER TWENTY-ONE

AMBER ROTH

I don't know if you've ever tried fucking under three gravities of acceleration, but let me tell you: it's not easy. You need to be careful. Broken bones and torn muscles are a real possibility.

Somehow, we managed…

I woke about an hour later, tangled in blankets and aching pleasantly. Copernicus lay behind me. As this was a single-occupancy bunk, we were pressed together, my back to his chest. His long, hairless arm lay draped over my waist, and I could feel the gentle rise and fall of his breath as he slept.

Part of my brain was trying to tell me I'd just made a huge mistake. I certainly hadn't planned to throw myself at this man like a starving wolverine. In fact, I'd been as surprised as he was. But in hindsight, I could see it had been almost inevitable. I had spent months avoiding any kind of personal entanglements with my subordinates on the *Slinky Lynx*. I couldn't undermine my authority by sleeping with underlings, and so I'd abstained. But with Copernicus, things were different. We were both captains, both equals. I had nothing to lose by sleeping with him. Since I came on board the *Jitterbug*, habit had caused me to suppress my attraction to him. But when we were face to face and riled up, I guess I'd just stopped resisting.

The dam had broken and we'd been swept away in a flood of lust that had left us here, now, washed-up and exhausted.

I wasn't used to letting anyone get close to me. I couldn't even remember the last time I'd been naked in front of another person. I'd grown too used to keeping my guard up. In my profession, showing any kind of vulnerability was a good way to get killed. But while all my instincts told me I'd made a tactical error, I decided to ignore them for once, basking instead in the warmth and intimacy of this man's sleeping embrace. So far, my life had been sorely lacking in such moments, and frankly, I felt owed.

Abandoned as infants, my brother and I had dragged ourselves up around the garbage fires and gang violence of the freight yards surrounding the base of Earth's space elevator. His name was Michael, but everybody called him Mica. He was a year younger than me. As we were hungry most of the time, there wasn't a scrap of fat on him. He was skinny and bright-eyed, with a mop of sandy hair and a left femur that had never healed properly from a nasty break, giving him a limp that made him a target for the stronger kids. Consequently, I'd spent most of my childhood bruising my knuckles while protecting him from the Darwinian churn of the homeless ecosystem, keeping him out of the grasp of both his fellow outcasts and those preying upon them.

Mica.

For a while, he had been my sole reason for existing; my motive for getting up in the morning and taking arms against the world—right up until the dark December afternoon when he'd been snatched away by an entirely preventable and treatable pneumonia.

Boiling with grief, I started hanging around in the more expensive and decadent parts of town. There were always men there searching for an underage girl. Labouring under the delusion that their money made them untouchable, they'd promise me a handful of coins and expect me to be pathetically grateful. Except I knew that those coins, if they ever came, would only be the prelude to some kind of beating. Once those assholes got what they wanted, they'd turn their guilt and self-loathing on me—which was why I never gave them the chance.

Honestly, it's amazing how much money a drunk guy will give you when you have a blade jammed into one of his eye sockets. And how's he going to report you to the police when you're a street kid and he was trying to solicit you for sex?

I felt no hesitation or compunction. They deserved everything they got.

Within a month, I had enough for a fake ID and a ticket up the elevator. I hadn't exactly planned what I'd do once I got off-planet, but I'd heard the Swirl was (and I quote the advertisements here) 'A new land of adventure and opportunity,' so I lied about my age and got myself a job as a trainee mechanic on a freighter that was hauling colonists out there.

I'd originally intended to jump ship when we reached our destination, and grab some of that sweet frontier life for myself. However, I soon realised that pioneer dream involved a lot of hard work and deprivation, and I was much better suited to life in space, where the accommodations might be basic, but at least I didn't have to build my own house or grow my own food.

After a couple of trips, the freighter's owner, Venn, decided that rather than go to the trouble and expense of ferrying his passengers and their homesteading supplies all the way to the Swirl, he could make more money and expend less fuel and effort if he simply robbed them and jettisoned their bodies into the vacuum. Crewmembers who objected to this new business plan also found themselves on the wrong side of an airlock hatch. To keep breathing, I learned how to take orders and make my peace with the rest. When it came to a choice between dying in honest poverty or stealing to live, I was firmly in favour of survival, no matter what I had to do to attain it—even if that meant ignoring a few murders. I owed it to Mica, and I owed it to myself. We'd been dealt a fatal hand, and it was up to me to keep on living, using whatever opportunities I could find or create. And if I found myself living in Hell, then surely it was better to be one of the demons than one of the damned?

Ten years later, through ruthlessness and dedication in service to Cerberus Venn, I had gained my own ship and earned a reputation known from the Mercury Station to the farthest tips of the Swirl segments. Everyone had heard of Natalya Ponomarenko, the cold-blooded pirate queen, who'd loot your ship, steal your boyfriend (or girlfriend, according to a few accounts), and leave you flailing and suffocating in the void. But the legend quickly outgrew the facts and soon every pirate attack, mutiny, or drive malfunction ended up being attributed to me. I became known as a scourge. Even other pirate crews started to believe the hype, paying deference when our paths crossed.

For a time, I enjoyed the infamy, but it very quickly became a trap. I got blamed for everything. Sol-Sec sent ships to pursue me, and swarms of bounty hunters to dog my footsteps. After a few narrow escapes, I realised it would only be a matter of time before one of them cornered me. If I wanted to fulfil my promise to Mica and keep right on living the life he'd been denied, I'd have to get out of the pirate business and disappear.

The opportunity arose when I stole that data crystal. I knew it had to be valuable. Rather than simply transmit its contents, someone had chartered an entire ship and employed a human courier to bring it back from the Swirl. That was a serious investment, and meant they also had the resources to come looking for it when it went missing—and with my reputation, I'd be the first person they'd come for.

That was the moment I became Amber Roth. I only had the resources aboard the *Slinky Lynx* for a little light cosmetic work. It was enough to fool a face-recognition algorithm but not enough to fool someone like Dushku, who had known me for years. And it wasn't the first time I'd changed my appearance.

I was going to take a shuttle and ditch my ship and crew. I couldn't trust any of them. I had to watch my back at the best of times but I knew my former mentor, Venn, had let it be known on the whisper network that he wanted my position, my ship, and my head, and would reward anyone who could deliver all three. If things went sideways now, I couldn't trust any of them to stay loyal. Under Sol-Sec questioning, they'd give me up to save their own skins, and gain favour with Venn. So, before that happened, I figured it would be better for me to disappear in the night and not tell them my intended whereabouts.

Unfortunately, I didn't manage to get away cleanly. Someone was awake to raise the alarm when I disengaged the shuttle, and by the time the *Barracuda* 'rescued' me, the *Lynx* and its crew were already in pursuit. If I hadn't hidden from them in the water tank, they would have found me—and then, the inhabitants of the stealth ship would have killed me, too.

Despite my bravado, I would have been in real trouble if the *Jitterbug* hadn't arrived on the scene a couple of hours later. And now here I was, an infamous 'pirate queen', sharing a clapped-out old freighter with the Deputy Speaker of the Solar Assembly. The thought was so ridiculous, I laughed.

Copernicus stirred. I wriggled around to face him.

He smiled sleepily. "Hey."

"Hey yourself."

"So, um. We just did that."

"We did."

I heard movement in the hallway outside. The rest of the crew were awake and starting their day.

Copernicus bit his lip and said, "So…?"

"So, that was fun."

"Yes, yes it was."

I traced a fingernail across his chest. "I guess I underestimated how much you wanted that data."

He sat up. "No, it wasn't like that."

"So, it meant something?"

"I—I don't know."

I laughed at his nervousness. "Relax, I'm not going to ask you to marry me or anything."

"I didn't think—"

I put a finger to his lips. "I'm messing with you."

He sagged. "I'm sorry, I'm very bad at this sort of thing."

"You're doing fine."

"So, we're okay?"

I leant forward and kissed his cheek. "Maybe there's something here worth exploring, or maybe there isn't. Either way, we're okay."

"And the data?"

I gave a sigh. "Fine, you can have it."

"Thank you."

"There's one condition, though."

"What's that?"

I sat on the edge of the bunk and put my arms around his neck. "Kiss me again, to prove you meant it."

CHAPTER TWENTY-TWO

COPERNICUS BROWN

Amber Roth and I sat facing the Deputy Speaker across the chipped and scuffed table in the main crew lounge. Her bodyguards, whose names I still didn't know, lingered by the walls, habitually covering all the exits and maintaining clear sight lines to everybody in the room. One of them was tall, male, and Caucasian, and the other shorter, female, and Latina. Yet they both wore identical black suits and maintained identical postures and expressions. And I knew they would both be equally proficient at kicking my ass if Danielle Lanzo ordered them to do it.

The *Jitterbug* perched her parrot on the back of an empty chair at the table's head.

"What have you found?" I asked her.

"It is a countdown," she squawked.

The Deputy Speaker rolled her eyes. "Can someone else explain this? Do I really have to sit and listen to a fucking *bird*?"

The parrot clicked and whistled and raised her red and blue crest. "Might I remind you, madam, that I'm a ship with a brain that (*squawk*) works significantly faster than yours."

"Then fucking enunciate properly."

The *Jitterbug* shook herself and cocked her head questioningly in my direction.

>Do I have to put up with this nonsense?

"Please," I told her. "Do go on."

"Thank you." The *Jitterbug* paused to clear her throat. "As I was saying, I think it's a countdown. But the numbers are puzzling."

"What do you mean, puzzling?" I asked.

"They're very large. In the order of millions. I don't think they represent minutes and seconds. But whatever they are, they're steadily (*click*, *whirr*) decreasing."

"How long until they reach zero?"

"Two weeks, three days, nine hours, and fifty-two seconds."

I looked at Lanzo. "So, what does it mean?"

She pursed her lips. "I don't know."

"This was a message intended for you."

"Nevertheless."

"Can you make a guess?"

She clasped her hands together. "Captain, I am not obliged to endure your interrogation."

I said nothing. In my experience, if you left a big enough silence, the other person would eventually feel compelled to fill it. Unfortunately, it seemed the universe had seen fit to construct Danielle Lanzo from sterner material than most of the fugitives I'd so far confronted. All she did was raise a hostile eyebrow.

"We're all on the same side here," I said.

"And which side is that, Captain Brown?"

"The only side that matters: the inside of the hull, where the air is. And I'd like to keep it that way, so the more information you can give me, the more chance I have to ensure we all stay alive."

She gave me a long look with an expression a poker player would have envied for its opacity.

"Fine." She sat back with a sigh of resignation. "I'll tell you what I know."

"Thank you."

Her eyes narrowed. "Don't thank me until you've heard what I've got to say."

She straightened her tie and smoothed down the charcoal-coloured lapels of her suit jacket. Both the blazer and the shirt she wore underneath must have been made from wrinkle-resistant materials, because even though she'd been wearing the same clothes for almost two days, she still looked immaculate.

"For some years, I have been funding a network of observatories on the far side of the Swirl segments."

Amber Roth's brow creased as she tried to see the relevance. "Observatories?"

"Yes, fucking observatories. You know what they are?"

"Of course."

"Then this will all go a lot faster if you refrain from interrupting."

Roth's jaw clenched, but I put a hand on her arm to restrain her. "Do go on, ma'am."

"Thank you." Lanzo absently tugged on her cufflinks as she continued. "As I was saying, I have a network of observatories on the outer surface of the Swirl segments. You might call it a pet project of mine. You see, as much as I am awed by the technology behind the construction of the Swirl, it's still just *technology*, which implies it may be fallible."

"You're looking for weaknesses?" the *Jitterbug* squawked.

Lanzo glowered at it. "Do shut up."

"Sorry (*whistle, click*)."

"I'm not interested in exploiting whatever weaknesses the segments may or may not contain. Rather, my concerns are of a far more apocalyptic nature.

"Before Neptune and Uranus were disassembled, our

telescopes tell us that whatever created them also took apart Pluto and Charon, and every speck of ice and rock in the outer solar system. Perhaps they needed all that material, but perhaps they were also taking steps to prevent infalling comets from impacting the Swirl."

I cleared my throat. "So they cleared all that junk away to make sure it couldn't happen."

"Precisely." Lanzo steepled her fingers. "But have you ever heard of Oumuamua?"

Roth and I shook our heads. The *Jitterbug*'s parrot hopped from one foot to another on the back of its chair. "First object of interstellar origin to be detected passing through the solar system," it said. "A rock roughly 400 metres long and a tenth of that wide. Discovered in 2017. Three more have since been observed."

"Correct."

"So, you're looking for… rocks?" Roth asked.

"I am looking for something the Swirl's builders may not have anticipated. Oumuamua and its fellows have so far been relatively small. But what happens if something larger falls through the system? Maybe a big enough collision could knock a segment of the Swirl out of alignment. And if that happened and couldn't be corrected, it might eventually brush against the Sun or collide with one of the other segments. The Earth would certainly impact against it as it crossed our orbit. And then the whole edifice would tear itself apart, and us with it."

The parrot whistled.

Roth said, "Jesus."

"The observatories are tasked with locating and informing me of incoming objects large enough to trigger such a scenario, in time for me to warn the population and prompt the Solar Assembly to take steps to ensure at least some of us might survive."

Apprehension wrapped its icy talons around my heart. "So," I said, "these numbers…"

"Could be the countdown to Doomsday, yes."

As our destination lay on the outer surface of the sixth Swirl segment, we needed to pass through the gap between it and the seventh segment, then loop around. As we were decelerating, we were falling stern-first, or "ass-first into the unknown," as Kiki so succinctly put it, with our drive plume preceding us.

The closer we drew, the larger the sixth segment became on the external monitors. By the time we were within ten thousand miles of its surface, it had flattened into a vast, seemingly infinite landscape stretching away to port. Sunlight glinted on its lakes and seas, and its edge was a razor-straight line cutting the universe in two. To my left, I saw endless prairie; to my right, the edge of the next segment shining like the full Moon; and ahead, only the star-bejewelled inkiness of the universe.

"Passing through in five minutes," Kiki said.

"Don't scratch the paint," I told her.

She didn't look up from her screens. "Oh, ha-de-ha."

The gaps between the segments were three times wider than the segments themselves, giving us 294 million miles of elbow room, and at our closest approach, we would still be over a thousand miles from the edge of the sixth segment.

Lanzo came to join us on the bridge. In reply to my questioning look she said, "It's not often I get so close to the handiwork of gods."

I knew what she meant. Encountering something so unfathomably large, and being always unavoidably, acutely conscious of its artificiality, was enough to humble even the most inflated of egos.

Look on my works, ye mighty…

For an instant, we were level with the segment's edge, and then it was gone, falling upwards and away in our wake. Vast as the structure was, it was only around a mile thick. Now, instead of falling towards a bright and daylit landscape, we were rising above a dark and shadowed expanse, utterly black in contrast to the clean white rays of the Sun bursting through the gap behind us.

I had never been outside the spherical volume enclosed by the segments, and wasn't quite sure what I had been expecting, but the unobstructed view of the stars would have been worth the journey by itself. For the first time, the three of us gazed out at a starfield that wasn't framed on either side by giant alien artefacts. This had been the unobstructed and endless sky my grandmother knew. A universe in which you could fall forever in any direction; in which instead of colonising the immensity of the Swirl's inner surface, we may have reached out to other worlds around other suns, spreading exponentially into the galaxy like ink in water. A future in which we would have been driven to develop the technology necessary to cross interstellar distances and choose our own destiny. Instead, all we had were freighters and couriers capable of making the trip from Earth and Luna to the Swirl, and our technology had stalled. Could that have been the point of this artefact, to discourage us from striving and keep us confined to our own system? As we moved sideways towards our target, I looked back at the dark external surface of the sixth segment as it began to eclipse the Sun, and shuddered. We didn't need to sail between the stars because we had a thousand worlds' worth of living space right on our doorstep. For a crowded species, all that room was a tempting and much-needed gift; but to me, it was also starting to look like a trap.

CHAPTER TWENTY-THREE
DANIELLE LANZO

The *Jitterbug* set down on the sixth segment's coal-black outer surface, a few hundred metres from the observatory's cluster of habitat domes, which clung barnacle-like to that seemingly flat and featureless wall. The orange light from the revolving beacon at the top of the largest dome swept around and around like a searchlight, its beam throwing shadows through the ranks of giant telescope dishes that receded away into the darkness like a spectral forest.

"We're going to have to suit up to get over there," Copernicus Brown said.

"Well, obviously." Aside from the lack of air on this side of the segment, I knew the absence of sunlight meant the ambient temperature here hovered somewhere around $-380°$ Fahrenheit. It was why we'd designed the observatory buildings with thick layers of foil-covered insulation.

"Are we all going?" Roth asked.

Copernicus shook his head. "Just me and the Deputy Speaker. You stay here with Ulf and Kiki and keep the engines warm. If that stealth ship shows up, we may have to leave in a hurry."

My male bodyguard started to protest, but I waved him

into silence. I hadn't bothered to remember his name. I had a team of eight Secret Service agents who looked after me on a rotational basis. This one and his companion were simply the two that had been assigned to me that morning, and I didn't have the time to start memorising all their names. Besides, I didn't want to get too attached. One day, I might have to let one of them take a bullet for me, and I wouldn't be able to let them do it if I started to think of them as anything more than their role.

Copernicus led me down to the airlock and opened a locker. Inside, empty pressure suits hung like the flayed skins of old ghosts.

"You'll have to borrow one of ours," he said, handing me a helmet encrusted with peeling stickers.

I looked at the rainbows, flowers, stars, and anime characters. "I assume this one belongs to your pilot?"

"Yes, that's Kiki's." He grinned. "What gave it away?"

He helped me into the rest of the suit. Like everything else on this ship, it was scuffed and patched from heavy use. Inside, it smelled of old rubber, sweat, and patchouli.

I said, "Do you think it's wise leaving Ponomarenko on the ship?"

"Pono—oh, you mean Roth?" He shrugged. "Sure, why not? Would you rather she came with us?"

"Do you think you can trust her? What if she takes the ship? I don't fancy being marooned out here."

"Even if she tried something, your bodyguards are there to keep an eye on things." He fastened his own suit. "And the *Jitterbug* wouldn't leave us."

"Would she have a choice?"

"Oh yes. Dad gave her a hardwired connection to the engine cut-off. It's an anti-hijacking measure. If she doesn't want to go somewhere, you can't force her. She won't even let you start the engines."

"Smart."

"Yeah." He turned to the outer airlock's control panel, but not before I saw the cloud that passed across his face. "But not smart enough to save him."

He stabbed a button, and the inner door swung shut. An alarm chirped for a few seconds, and then began to fade as the air drained from the lock. My suit stiffened around me as the pressure dropped. Then, when all external sound had died, the outer door slid silently open, and we stepped out onto a black sheet beneath a black, star-filled sky. Without visual reference points, scales were impossible to judge. My brain told me the sharp horizon lay only a few miles hence, but given the immensity of the Swirl's circumference, and the lack of atmospheric distortion to indicate distance, it was probably closer to hundreds if not thousands.

I felt a sudden rush of vertigo at the thought of the grasslands and lakes that lay on the inside of the segment, only a mile beneath my feet. I was walking on a planet turned outside-in. Were they upside down, or was I?

I swayed.

Copernicus said, "Are you okay?"

I took his arm to steady myself. "Of course I'm not fucking okay."

"The scale can be a bit overwhelming at first."

"No fucking shit."

"Do you want to go back?"

"No." I focussed my gaze on the domes. If I could ignore the infinities around me and concentrate on human-scale objects, I knew I'd be all right. Determinedly, I put one foot in front of the other, focussing on that blinking orange beacon. My breath rasped in the confines of the helmet. I could feel the lacework warmth of the diamond-patterned heating capillaries sewn into the suit's inner fabric. Copernicus followed at my elbow, ready to catch me if I stumbled, but through sheer force of will, I somehow managed to make it to the observatory's main lock without further help and with my pride intact.

While we waited for the lock to cycle and the outer door to open for us, I held onto the handrail beside the hatch and craned back for one last glimpse of the gem-bright stars.

I was standing on an alien object thousands of times larger than Earth. Three days ago, I had been immersed in preparation for my bid to become Speaker, but now, here on the edge of the solar system, it felt like a lifetime ago. How could politics, or indeed *anything* human, retain any significance in the face of a universe that could produce such terrifying splendours?

We were met inside by a bleary-eyed man in red tartan pyjama bottoms and a grey towelling robe. For a moment, I didn't recognise him. It was only when I looked into his dark brown eyes that I realised he was Keon Mendoza, the lone astronomer on this station. The last time I'd seen him, he hadn't had that thick and untidy grey beard. Now, he looked like a castaway. He had a green fleece blanket draped over his shoulders, and his hands were wrapped like vines around a steaming coffee mug; the blue handle of a toothbrush jutted from the side of his mouth, and his hair stuck up and out in random directions as if it hadn't seen a comb in weeks.

"M-Madam Deputy."

"Hello, Mendoza."

He blinked at me like a bear emerging from hibernation. "Oh man. What are you doing here?"

His accent was pure California. Before I'd assigned him here, he'd spent his week nights at the Mount Wilson Observatory and his weekends at Venice Beach with a surf board, an acoustic guitar, and a satchel of weed. Nevertheless, he was considered one of the most brilliant astronomers of his generation. I set my helmet down, trying not to wrinkle my nose at the locker room smell of the habitat's interior. "The information you sent—"

He brightened. "You got it?"

I made a face. "Eventually, but we don't know what it means."

He pulled out his toothbrush and pursed his lips as he considered this. "But you saw it was a countdown?"

"Yes."

Realisation dawned. "So, given our mission, you think there's an asteroid on its way to hit the Swirl?"

"Well, yes."

He winced, and fretfully knuckled the side of his head with the hand that held the toothbrush. "No, no, no."

I exchanged looks with Copernicus, and said, "What is it we're missing?"

Mendoza looked down at his coffee as if only just remembering it, and then beckoned us with the brush. "Come on," he said. "I can explain this better on the command deck."

He led us through, into the hexagonal space at the centre of the habitat, from where he controlled and monitored the ranks of dishes outside.

"Please don't touch anything." He sheepishly rubbed the back of his neck. "We kind of have everything set up just the way we like it."

Copernicus looked around at the banks of monitors and surfaces cluttered with used mugs, sticky notes, and stacks of printouts. "You guys have been here a while, huh?"

"Eight months, dude. Why?"

"No reason."

"Doesn't matter anyway, it's good to see you." He smiled at Copernicus. "So good to see *anyone*. I just wish we could be meeting under more auspicious circumstances."

"Your findings have caused quite a stir," I said. "Sol-Sec has been extremely keen to supress them."

Confusion wrinkled Mendoza's sun-aged forehead. "But why would they want to do that?" he asked. "If you don't know what we found, how could Sol-Sec?"

I thought about that, and suddenly the answer was obvious. I said, "The courier I sent you was a Sol-Sec agent. Most of my security staff are." I balled my fists inside their gauntlets. "Fuck. He must have been ordered to update Kowalski on your findings."

Mendoza's eyes widened. "*Sebastian* Kowalski?"

"The man's always been a paranoid ass. He knew I had an early warning project on the backside of the Swirl, so he must have been monitoring your radio broadcasts. When you told me you'd found something too big and important to broadcast, he must have ordered the courier to find out what it was."

Copernicus Brown placed his helmet on one of the consoles. "So, the courier scanned the crystal and told Kowalski that the data contained bad news. But like these guys, he didn't want to go into details on an open channel. Kowalski sent a stealth ship to meet the courier and secure the data crystal."

"That sounds plausible."

Copernicus smiled roguishly. "In which case, maybe Roth did you a favour. If Kowalski had succeeded in grabbing that crystal, you'd never have got your hands on it."

"Don't try to justify piracy, Mister Brown."

"I'm just saying, maybe—"

I held up a hand to stop him. "I'm very good at reading people, and I know you're fucking her. But that doesn't mean she won't have to answer for her crimes, however accidentally fortuitous the results."

He looked unhappy, but I didn't care. I turned to Mendoza. "If we can stop dicking about for one moment, can you *please* tell us what the fucking data means?"

The man put down his coffee mug and absently dropped his toothbrush into it. He pulled out a chair, activated one of the consoles, and accessed a glowing green string of figures. "This is what we sent."

I looked over his shoulder. "Yes, we know it's a countdown, but we don't know what it's counting down to."

He cleared his throat. "These numbers represent the coordinates of an object we're tracking in relation to the Swirl." He tapped a sequence of controls, and a three-dimensional graph appeared, showing the coordinates plotted in a straight, downward line, the numbers beside each point smaller than those beside the one before.

"The numbers are reducing in size," he continued, "because the object is getting closer."

I followed the line on the graph. "And when these numbers reach zero?"

"The object will have intercepted the Swirl."

The outside cold seemed to seep into my veins. "When you say intercepted, you mean impacted?"

Mendoza shrugged. "Not necessarily. It may be aimed at one of the gaps between segments. The velocity changes make it difficult to tell."

"Is it an asteroid?"

The two men looked at each other, as if I'd missed something crucial and neither wanted to be the first to point it out. Finally, Mendoza took a deep breath. "According to these readings, it can't be. Just no way."

"Why not?"

He swallowed. "Because it's decelerating."

"What the fuck does that mean?"

Beside me, Copernicus had gone very still. In a low voice, he said, "That means it's artificial."

I regarded the two of them as sternly as I could. "I know what you're all getting at," I said. "When I set up this project, I did the fucking homework. But as I'm the Deputy Speaker of the goddamn Solar Assembly, I need to be one hundred per cent fucking certain before I start running my mouth off about little green men."

To their credit, they didn't flinch.

I said, "Earlier, I was telling Mr Brown here about Oumuamua. That *changed fucking course*, but turned out to be a natural object."

"Yes, ma'am," Mendoza confirmed. "We think that 'course change' was the result of outgassing as it passed the Sun."

"And now you've got another object that's behaving weirdly, and you're jumping to the conclusion it's aliens? Are you absolutely fucking *certain* this deceleration isn't due to outgassing or some other phenomenon?"

Mendoza cleared his throat. "It's too far out, and in the shadow of the Swirl. It's not picking up any heat. Also, it's too large."

"What do you mean?" I asked.

Mendoza gave an unhinged grin. "From our observations, we estimate it must be over a thousand miles wide and upwards of fifty quintillion tons, minimum."

"Holy shit."

"Yeah, you'd need a *lot* of outgassing to slow something that large, and we just aren't seeing it."

CHAPTER TWENTY-FOUR

COPERNICUS BROWN

Lanzo convened a war council in the *Jitterbug*'s galley. Mendoza donned a pressure suit and came back to the ship with us, and the rest of the crew gathered. Ulf stood impassively by the wall in his grease-stained jumpsuit. Kiki lounged in a chair with one boot up on the table and the parrot perching on her shoulder, as if one of the brightly coloured birds in the design of her Hawaiian shirt had come to life.

Amber Roth sipped coffee from a mug. After the astronomer had thrown up the same three-dimensional graph and finished explaining the situation, she drained the cup and put it aside.

"Aliens," she said. It wasn't quite a question, and it wasn't quite a dismissal. Like the rest of us, she was just trying to wrap her head around the idea. "You have got to be kidding me."

"I don't see what else it can be, sister." Mendoza gave a small shrug. "Occam's razor, and all that."

"It's definitely not one of our old space probes?" Kiki asked.

"We only sent a handful out that far," he replied. "*Pioneer 10* and *11*, *Voyagers 1* and *2*, and the *New Horizons*. None of them had the means to return like this, and we have always assumed they were all disassembled along with the rest of the

Oort cloud. And of course, once the outer planets had also been destroyed, there did not seem to be much point sending anything else. All our attention was on the Swirl."

"More to the point," Lanzo interjected, "we never sent out anything that big."

Kiki nodded as she processed this information. "Aliens," she decided.

"Personally, I am still hoping for some less terrifying explanation."

I had been silent up until now. I was having trouble processing the idea as much as anybody else. Theoretically, we'd known alien intelligence existed since the first Swirl segments accreted from the planetary rubble, but somehow, we'd never expected them to actually show up.

Having detected the abundance of water in the cosmos and the existence of extrasolar planets containing the ingredients necessary for life, our astronomers had been forced to ask themselves why the galaxy didn't appear to be teeming with intelligent life. If the building blocks of life were everywhere in our galaxy, why weren't we seeing the evidence of star-spanning cultures? Many theories were proposed. Either we were the first civilisation to crawl our way up out of the ooze, or we were the last and the rest were already dead. Maybe we lived in the galactic equivalent of a zoo or wildlife enclosure, or perhaps all the other races were simply keeping quiet to avoid drawing the attention of neighbours who might wipe them out in case they posed a future threat. Possibly the bleakest idea held that intelligence was a self-correcting phenomenon, and intelligent cultures were invariably doomed to destroy themselves with their own technology before they achieved the means to escape their planet of origin. Our own history showed us that evolution moved much slower than progress, and sometimes got away from us. We were curious primates evolved for hunting and gathering, and we almost wrecked our planet and ourselves. Many times, our territorial instincts had brought us within moments of triggering devastating nuclear conflicts that might have driven us back into savagery or extinction, while our wholesale burning of fossil fuels triggered a runaway greenhouse effect that still threatened to leave the Earth as scorched and barren as Venus. Sorting that mess out and restabilising the climate was going to take decades, if not centuries. So, it wasn't hard to imagine other species accidentally punting themselves into oblivion with tools they simply weren't evolved enough to safely handle. We were like children playing with guns in a minefield. Sooner or later, we were going to take a fatal step and remove ourselves from the galactic scene.

So, when the Swirl materialised, we assumed it must have been the last gasp of a culture that had risen to unusually ambitious heights before biting the big one. They had the technology to deconstruct a gas giant, for heaven's sake. There was no way, we thought, that they wouldn't have found a complex and novel way to erase themselves from the universe. Consequently, having them suddenly turn up now in person seemed as unexpected and unlikely as having the builders of Stonehenge show up and ask what the hell we were doing in their temple.

I sat forward. "We should have realised this was going to happen." I couldn't keep the anger out of my voice, even though I wasn't sure exactly who I was angry with: Mendoza, humanity in general, or just myself. "Someone survived. They made it through the bottlenecks and now they're here to claim the Swirl."

Ulf raised a finger. "It may not be the Swirl's builders," he pointed out. "To a distant observer, our star will seem to dim and brighten as the Swirl sections occlude it. Perhaps they are puzzled by this phenomenon and have come to investigate?"

Mendoza gave him a look. "Dude, Occam's razor says

it's the builders." He pressed his fingers against his unkempt temples. "Why would you assume the existence of *two* species when *one* is implausible enough—"

We all jumped as Danielle Lanzo slapped her palm on the table. "Great Caesar's ghost," she swore. "I don't give a fuck who they are. Just tell me how long we've got until they get here."

Mendoza winced. "If they keep slowing at a constant rate, a week, maybe two."

Kiki whistled. "That soon?'

"Bummer, right?"

Ulf uncrossed his thick arms. "How did we not see them before?" he rumbled. "Their drive plume must have been visible for months, if not years."

"They don't have one," Mendoza told him. "And to be honest, we've no idea what they're using for propulsion, only that they're slowing down."

"This is insane." I got to my feet. "How are we not prepared for this? I know we never expected them to actually appear, but I also assumed that ever since the Swirl formed, ever since we had *definitive proof* of intelligence elsewhere in the universe, the government must have had people drawing up plans, just in case we were wrong about them all being dead."

Lanzo sat back in her chair and narrowed her eyes. "It took us a generation and a bloody uprising on Mars before we had the will to create the Solar Assembly. Since then, we've been rehoming the Martian refugees and bickering over territorial claims on the Swirl."

"So, you've done nothing?"

"There were studies."

"But no actual preparation?"

Before the meeting, she had shed her pressure suit and slipped back into formal business attire. It made her look more like a politician. Now, she gripped the arms of her chair with purple-nailed fingers and glared at me. "We had other priorities, and squeezed budgets. Real-world problems needed addressing before we could start worrying about hypothetical threats."

I threw a hand towards the 3D graph. "But they're not so hypothetical now, though, are they?"

On the other side of the room, Ulf gave a snort. "Politicians," he grumbled. "Always busy, but never actually doing what needs to be done. Talking reindeer *møkk* while nothing happens."

Lanzo ignored him. "We can play who-knew-fucking-what-fucking-when fucking later. Right now, we need to focus. The way I see it, our main problem is that the only people who know the truth are right here, in this room."

"And Kowalski," I reminded her.

"Maybe Kowalski," she admitted. "Whatever he may have inferred, he's obviously prepared to kill to keep it quiet."

Kiki pulled her boot off the table. "But why? I mean, why would anybody do that?"

I said, "I expect he's worried what will happen when people find out."

"The Solar Assembly only works if everyone subscribes to it," Lanzo agreed. "If there's panic, if governments start breaking away, there will be chaos. And a shitload of aliens might just be enough to trigger that."

"And if the Assembly disintegrates," Roth put in, "so will Sol-Sec."

"That's right. Nobody will want to keep contributing resources to a multinational force when they need those personnel and that equipment to guard their own interests."

"But that's stupid," Kiki protested. "If the aliens are coming, we need to be united. People will see that."

Amber Roth gave a snort. "Have you *met* people?"

"Much as I hate to agree with the pirate," Lanzo conceded, "she's right. However intelligent we might be as individuals, as soon as we become part of a crowd, we become panicky and irrational and prone to making stupid-ass decisions. I mean, just look at the political shitshow we were in before the Swirl started to form. Fighting each other over every little thing. It was embarrassing."

I leant against the bulkhead, feeling a little panicky and irrational myself. "It sounds like all of a sudden, you agree with Kowalski."

She scowled up at me. "I don't agree with his methods, but perhaps he has a point. We need time to prepare, and to do that we need to maintain the cohesion of the Assembly and Sol-Sec."

Kiki's face flushed. "So, you're not going to tell anybody?"

Lanzo shook her head. "This needs to remain classified. The longer we can keep this on a need-to-know basis, the more chance we'll have to lay the groundwork for a unified response."

"Kowalski's trying to kill us," I reminded her. "What are we going to do about *that*?"

"When we get back to the gap, I'll transmit a message." She gave a bleak smile. "I'll convince him we're on the same side."

"She's full of shit," Roth said when we were alone on the bridge.

"She's a politician."

Roth leant her hip against the navigation console, arms folded. "The two aren't mutually exclusive."

"You think we should go public?"

"I don't know. What do you think?"

I sat in my command chair and stared out at the stars on the forward view. "I think this is the biggest news story since the formation of the Swirl, and everybody in the solar system deserves to hear it. But at the same time, I don't want to be the asshole who breaks up the Solar Assembly, just when we need it most."

I watched her consider this. "We still have one bargaining chip," she said.

"What's that?"

"We have the data. Until he gets that, Kowalski won't know where this object is, or when to expect it."

"You want to sell it to him?"

"I was thinking of bargaining for our lives."

"But Lanzo—"

"If she agrees with Kowalski about the need for secrecy, she might decide he's also right about silencing potential leaks."

I didn't want to believe it. "She seems too… honourable for that."

"As you said, she's a politician. She's used to making tough decisions."

"But surely she wouldn't go that far?"

With her arms still crossed, Roth shrugged one shoulder. "She has two armed Sol-Sec bodyguards on board this ship, and you don't get to be Deputy Speaker of the whole goddamn Solar Assembly without being a bit of a cunt."

Coldness gripped me. Before meeting Roth, I'd considered myself cynical—but next to her, I felt like a starry-eyed optimist. Despite my father's murder and my subsequent immersion in the sordid underbelly of Swirl colonisation, I wanted to believe that deep down, people were worth saving. And besides, I *liked* Lanzo. Her plain-speaking bluntness made me want to trust her.

The *Jitterbug*'s voice broke into my thoughts.

>Captain?

Yes, ship?

>Something just came through the gap ahead of us.

What is it?

>I only caught a glint of sunlight reflecting off something

dark. If our surroundings weren't in complete shadow, I don't think I would have registered it at all.

The stealth ship?

>That would be my guess.

"Ah, hell."

Startled by my apparent non sequitur, Roth said, "What?"

"The stealth ship found us."

Mentally, I instructed the ship to power up its engines, ready for flight, and then I flipped the switch to activate the intercom. "Madam Deputy, we have incoming. If you think you can appease them, now would be the time. Everyone else, to your stations."

Amber Roth took a last glance at the stars, kissed my forehead, and climbed down to join Ulf in engineering. Moments later, Kiki appeared and took the pilot's position. Lanzo followed her, and strapped into the seat beside mine.

"Can you open a channel to them?" she asked.

Do it.

>Yes, Captain.

"You may speak."

Lanzo took a breath, swallowed, and said, "This is Deputy Speaker Danielle Lanzo with a message for Director Kowalski. Sebastian, I have the data you want and I am prepared to share it with you. Please confirm."

>No response.

Do you know where the ship is now?

>I lost it as soon as it cleared the shaft of sunlight.

Damnation.

"I say again, this is Deputy Speaker Danielle Lanzo with a message for Director Kowalski. I have the data you want. Call off your attack ship and let's talk."

She looked at me, but I shook my head, and said, "They're not replying."

"Can you tell if they're receiving?"

"I can't even tell you where they are right now."

"For fuck's sake." Her purple fingernails made small tapping sounds as she drummed them against the arm of her chair. "This is Deputy Speaker Lanzo to Director Kowalski. Stop dicking me around, Sebastian. We need to talk."

An alarm sounded.

Kiki said, "We're being painted with a targeting laser."

"Incoming?"

"None detected, but any warheads may also be in stealth mode."

"I say again, this is Lanzo. Will you fucking answer me?"

"Scratch that," Kiki yelled. "I register two fast movers! Time to impact, fifteen seconds."

"Go!"

Once again, I had cause to thank my father and his insistence on fitting the *Jitterbug* with oversized engines. A normal cargo hauler of her class would have struggled to clear the surface before those missiles hit. Even with Kiki at the controls and accelerating at six gravities, we only just made it. The impacts blew the observatory apart like twigs in a firestorm. Luckily, we still had Mendoza on board. He hadn't had time to get to an acceleration couch, so was laid out uncomfortably on the galley floor. I could only hope his pressure suit might provide some extra padding and support, otherwise his ribcage would be bowing inwards, and he'd be finding it hard to breathe.

Alas, we had more pressing concerns than the comfort of an unexpected passenger. Somewhere in the emptiness above, a ghost ship had us in its sights and was doing its level best to reduce the number of *Jitterbug*s on this side of the Swirl from one to zero. The scopes were empty, and I cringed, waiting for the sensors to register the next brush of its targeting laser.

"Two more missiles," the ship said aloud.

"Kiki, can you dodge them?"

"Watch me."

Luckily, Malcolm Brown hadn't wanted to rely solely on speed. He wasn't the type to place all his eggs in one basket, so he'd ensured the *Jitterbug*'s manoeuvrability matched her thrust. Each main engine mounting rested on a gimbal. Coupled with the large attitude jets inset on her nose and sides, that allowed her to jink and weave much faster than her blockish, industrial construction might otherwise suggest. This wouldn't give her much advantage against a cutting-edge covert gunboat, but as a lightly armed freighter, it might make her less of a sitting duck.

Kiki put the ship into a slow barrel roll, pushing us sideways in our chairs for a moment before throwing us violently against our restraints as she jinked in the opposite direction. The first of the two missiles, which had been matching our rotation, couldn't match this abrupt course change and overshot, impacting the Swirl in a bright white fireball.

"One down," she said. "Hold on."

My stomach seemed to drop into my shoes as the ship flipped end-over-end, its drive plume describing an arc of fusion fire like a searchlight sweeping the sky. The second missile hit this stream of superheated plasma and detonated. The blast rattled the ship, but we had survived—for now.

Having seen the remains of the *Slinky Lynx* and *Barracuda*, I knew the vessel hunting us packed a plasma weapon capable of melting through hull plate, whereas *Jitterbug* could only field the small calibre point defence cannons she'd used to take out the gun turret that killed McKenzie. Their main purpose was to protect her from incoming rock fragments and deter pirate boarding parties, so I didn't think they'd be a whole lot of use against military-grade armour.

We need a plan.

\>How about not getting killed?

I was hoping for something more concrete.

>So was I.

What do you suggest?

>You're the captain.

I called up a three-dimensional tactical display of the surrounding volume. The *Jitterbug* was a green point at the centre, hanging above a featureless plain. Fuzzy purple smears represented her best guesses as to the possible locations of the stealth ship.

Kiki watched me from the pilot's chair. "Heading, Captain?"

My mind whirled. In old space movies, there was always a handy nebula or asteroid field in which our heroes could lose their pursuers. But of course, there was nothing out here in the artificial emptiness of the outer solar system.

I said, "We can't fight, and we can't hide."

Kiki made a face. "We could always give them the data."

Lanzo gave a snort. "What the fuck do you think I've been trying to do?"

I waved them both to silence. I had the first inklings of an idea. My eyes dropped to the bottom of the display, and the flatness of the Swirl's outer surface. Several miles away, that flatness ended abruptly, giving way to empty space.

"You're right that the data's our only way out of this," I said. "Just wrong about who we should give it to."

Lanzo scowled. "What the fucking hell are you talking about?"

"Kiki, can you get us through the gap, and back inside the Swirl?"

"I'll try." The pilot swallowed and hunched over her controls. "Another two fast movers on the scope."

"Lose them."

Kiki made a feint to port and accelerated hard, then fired the thrusters in a rapid sequence that threw our back end around in a stuttering, three-dimensional skid. Moving sideways, we flashed past the knife-sharp lip of the sixth segment, so close I swear the ship lost a layer of paint.

Confused by the geometry, the missiles struck the edge behind us.

Kiki brought the nose around, and sunlight flooded the bridge.

We were through.

Kiki let out a whoop, but there wasn't time to celebrate.

>I caught a glimmer of sunlight on metal.

The stealth ship?

>It's coming after us.

We were still a long way from help, and Kiki's skills could only delay the inevitable. If I was going to save our skins, I had to do it now.

"Open a channel," I told the ship.

"To the stealth ship?"

"No, open a wide-band channel. Put all the spare power you have into the transmitter. I want the whole solar system to hear this."

"What the hell are you doing?" Lanzo demanded.

I ignored her. "This is Copernicus Brown of the freighter *Jitterbug*, out of Tranquillity Station. We have the Deputy Speaker of the Solar Assembly on board, and we have a Sol-Sec stealth ship pursuing us. I say again, this is Copernicus Brown of the freighter *Jitterbug*, and we are carrying Danielle Lanzo, the Deputy Speaker. We are being fired upon by a Sol-Sec ship that's trying to kill us to keep us from making the following data public."

Lanzo realised what I was about to do and threw out a hand. "No!"

But it was too late. I tapped a control to attach the decrypted tracking information to the broadcast, and hit transmit.

"If you receive this, please rebroadcast. Add the data to the interplanetary network. Tell your friends. Get the word out. Message repeats…"

Danielle Lanzo slapped the arms of her chair. "What the *rubbery fuck* have you done?"

"Hopefully, I've pulled our asses out of the fire."

Given current relative positions, our signal would take approximately forty-five minutes to reach the Earth and the Moon. However, there were Swirl settlements and ships closer, and we quickly began to receive acknowledgements and offers of aid.

"We're still a long way out," Kiki said. "If that stealth ship decides to take us out, none of these ships are going to be able to get here quickly enough to make a difference."

I knew the still-looping broadcast had been a gamble. There simply hadn't been any other choice. "They haven't fired yet."

"That doesn't mean they won't."

"They were prepared to kill us on the dark side of the Swirl, where no one would see. But if they try it now, the whole system will know Sol-Sec assassinated the Deputy Speaker. My guess is the captain doesn't want that kind of responsibility, so they're waiting for orders."

"And if the orders say to kill us anyway?"

"The secret's already out, there wouldn't be any point."

Lanzo groaned. "You had better hope you are right. Sebastian Kowalski is a vindictive son-of-a-bitch."

I sat back in my chair. "We'll find out in about an hour and a half."

Kiki glanced towards the screen displaying the view aft. The stealth vessel wasn't visible, but the *Jitterbug* had highlighted a circle of blackness that indicated its most likely current position. "What are we going to do until then, skip?"

"Get underway," I told her. "Head for the largest Swirl settlement within easy reach. They're not going to blow us up in public."

"Tell that to Dushku's shop."

"This is different," I said, hoping it was.

Lanzo shook her head. "You do realise that the public disclosure of government secrets is almost certainly an act of treason?"

I rolled my eyes in exasperation. "And you realise I did it to *save the life* of a senior government figure?"

"And I am grateful."

"Then perhaps we can call it quits, huh?"

Lanzo's bodyguards arrived, so I left her to explain the situation to them. I climbed down the ladder to the crew deck, where Ulf and Roth were helping the astronomer up off the floor and out of his suit. Mendoza had lain awkwardly, and the downward pressure of acceleration had dislocated his left knee. The big engineer lifted him in his arms and carried him to the medical suite.

Left alone, Roth turned to me and said, "That was some damn ballsy flying."

"Kiki's the best."

"Whatever you're paying her, it's not enough."

"Don't tell her that."

"What happens to me now?"

"What do you mean?"

"Is Lanzo going to have me arrested?"

"I'd like to see her try."

"Seriously—"

I placed my hands on her shoulders. "I am being serious. You're part of the crew now. We're not going to hand you over without a fight." I smiled. "And besides, we just saved her ass, so she can afford to be magnanimous."

"I hope you're right."

"If I'm not, we'll be landing at a Swirl settlement called Bradley's Lookout in about an hour and a half. It's home to around five thousand souls. I can let you off there and you can disappear."

She thought about that. "You wouldn't come after me for the bounty?"

"Two days ago, I might have considered it," I admitted.

"But now?"

"If I came after you now, it wouldn't be for the money."

She touched my cheek. "I don't know what to do," she said. "My instincts tell me to run. I don't want to go to jail, but—"

I gave her shoulders a squeeze. "You don't have to decide now. By the time we touch down at this place, she'll have heard back from Luna, and we'll have a better idea how the land lies."

CHAPTER TWENTY-FIVE
DANIELLE LANZO

Under the impression that Kowalski was back on Earth, I expected to have to wait at least ninety minutes for his response, whether verbal or in the form of missiles, and planned to spend the intervening time repainting my nails. I needed something to occupy my hands. It was an old habit I'd developed during tense negotiations, when I didn't want to appear impatient or apprehensive. If we were all going to die, I didn't want to spend the next hour and a half panicking about it. I had to keep everyone calm and set an example, and nothing said nonchalance more than taking the time to liberally apply bright purple nail polish.

The big engineer, Ulf, came into the lounge to get a coffee.

Over the intercom, the ship screeched something about closing distances and signal return times. I shook my head. "Why did it have to be a *parrot*?"

At the coffee machine, Ulf grunted. "Early models tried to look and sound like humans, but crews didn't like them. They gave folks the creeps."

"But that makes no sense. I mean, how is it easier to deal with a fucking parrot than something that's practically human?"

Ulf gave me a sideways look. "You've never seen one?"

"Well, no."

"If you had, you wouldn't have to ask."

"Are they really that bad?"

He tugged his beard and sighed. "Fairies," he said.

"Excuse me?"

"Pixies, goblins, vampires, whatever you want to call them."

"What about them?"

"All our folklore contains creatures that look like us, but which can't be trusted."

I thought I saw what he was getting at. "So, you think people are afraid of human-like machines because they're superstitious?"

He sighed. "No, it runs deeper than that. Those aren't superstitions. Those are memories. A few tens of thousands of years ago, our ancestors shared the planet with other human species. They looked like us, but they were different. And therefore not to be trusted. It's a hangover from back then. From the times we would meet strange beings in the forest."

I gave him a look. "You really think about this stuff, huh?"

He shrugged his wide shoulders. "Why do you think we Europeans have so many folk tales of witches and wizards and other woodland folk? We used to share our land with the Neanderthals. They had bigger brains than us. We had to be able to tell them apart from members of our own species, so we knew who to trust."

"And that's why we react badly to things that look like us?"

"Maybe." He turned back to his work. "Who really knows? Point is, most folk find people-shaped androids... disturbing. Our ship's avatar looks like a parrot because it makes her easier to trust."

I considered this, but before I managed to formulate a reply, the *Jitterbug*'s annoying avian screech announced, "I have a message from Director Kowalski."

"Already?" Only five minutes had passed.

"It appears he's much closer than expected."

"Let me hear it."

"There's a visual component."

"All right, then let me *see* it."

A window opened on the table before me. Static crackled across the screen, then cleared to reveal Kowalski's face.

"Madam Deputy Speaker." The Director's eyes were red-rimmed and his chin unshaven, and I wondered how many hours it had been since he'd last slept. The man looked like he'd spent the past couple of days running on caffeine and spite, just like me.

"Director Kowalski." I smiled a politician's smile. "I wasn't expecting to hear from you so soon."

I counted two seconds before he reacted to my voice.

"I happen to be aboard a Sol-Sec corvette, not far from your position."

"I am just sure you are."

"What do you mean by that?"

I wagged a finger at the screen. "You needed to be close enough to supervise your little stealth operation, didn't you?"

His face hardened. "For all the good it did. How could you let that oaf of a captain broadcast state secrets to the entire system?"

"I had no way to stop him."

"Aren't your bodyguards armed?"

"Don't be absurd."

He shook his head. "You're damn lucky you're not dead."

"And you're damn fucking lucky you still have a job. You tried to kill me."

He sighed in frustration, and squeezed the bridge of his nose between finger and thumb. "Jesus Christ."

I sat back and steepled my fingers. I had the beginnings of a plan, but it was risky, and I would need his help. If it went as I hoped, we would be writing our names into the history books, and I might very well end up as First Speaker. However, if it went badly, it could literally mean both our heads. I said, "What will Alvarado do when he's had that data explained to him?"

"You mean, apart from asking for my immediate resignation?"

"Yes."

Kowalski shrugged. "He won't be able to sit on the information. The cat's out of the bag now. The news media will have hold of it, and people will be calling for leadership. He'll have to order an emergency session of the Assembly."

"Precisely."

Bloodshot eyes narrowed. "What's your point?"

"A debate will take time. Organising an expedition to go out and meet the object will take even longer."

"Do you think that's how he'll handle it?"

"He will follow protocol. There will be votes and debates." I waved a dismissive hand. "In the meantime, whether or not the Assembly sends an official expedition, you can bet your ass others will. There are a few governments that won't want the Assembly speaking on their behalf. Corporate interests hungry for new technology. Military factions who want to strike down a potential threat before it gets close enough to hurt us..."

"That kind of fragmentation's exactly what I was hoping to prevent." He loosened his tie.

"It's a shame you went about it in such a stupid fucking way."

He scowled. "I did what I thought was right at the time."

"Did it ever occur to you to just fucking *ask* me about those observatories? If you hadn't been so busy playing spies, I would have told you what they were for, and I would have taken this data through proper channels."

"I didn't know if I could trust you to do that."

"I'm the Deputy Speaker of the Assembly!"

"I don't trust anybody. It comes with the job." He ran a hand back through untidy, thinning hair. "So, what are we going to do?"

My eyebrow arched. "We?"

"Oh, come on. I've known you long enough to know when you're building up to something."

I steepled my fingers. "For now, we're the two highest ranking government officials out here in the Swirl. We're forty-five light minutes closer to this thing than anyone else."

"You think we should go after it?"

"Don't you? I have this freighter. You have a stealth vessel and the corvette from which you're currently talking to me. That's three ships. If we pool our resources and take on supplies here on the Swirl, we can get an unassailable head start on everyone else."

"We'd get there first." He rubbed his stubbled chin, mulling the idea.

"Better us than some asshole with an itchy trigger finger. And if there are little green men out there, and we make first contact with them on behalf of the Assembly, all those breakaway factions will have to fall back in line."

I could see that last part appealed to him. "We'll control access to the aliens. The others will have to fall in line." Like anyone in a position of authority, he wanted to hang on to the power it gave him. "But what about Alvarado?"

"He'll pretend this was all his idea." I leant forward. "Listen, Sebastian. I am putting my cards on the table here. Somebody has to represent the whole human race, and I want it to be me."

"You?"

"Frankly, I don't trust anyone else not to fuck it up."

MESSAGE BOARD

ALIEN LIFE? Experts race to verify data broadcast system-wide.
[Click to Read More]

*

POLITICS: First Speaker Gustavo Alvarado of the Solar Assembly urges calm. "We need time to authenticate these findings and formulate a considered plan of action."
[Click to Read More]

*

SOL-SEC: Long-range patrol ships launched towards outer solar system.
[Click to Read More]

*

MOBILISATION: Armies around the world on state of high alert following mystery broadcast.
[Click to Read More]

CHAPTER TWENTY-SIX

COPERNICUS BROWN

Twenty minutes before we were due to put down at Bradley's Lookout, Lanzo called another meeting. With Mendoza also present, the galley wasn't large enough to accommodate everyone; her two bodyguards waited in the companionway outside, flanking the hatch.

When we were assembled, I said, "What can we do for you?"

Lanzo interlaced purple-tipped fingers. "I would like to extend my charter of your vessel."

"To take you back to Luna?"

"The opposite direction, I'm afraid. Director Kowalski and I are outfitting a delegation to investigate the incoming object."

"Seriously?" Roth said. "You're working with him now?"

"We're on the same side." Lanzo smiled. "Always have been."

Roth gave a derisive laugh. "Even when he was trying to kill us?"

A flick of the wrist. "An unfortunate misunderstanding. I may have done likewise in his position."

"Bullshit!" I shouted. "You want to work with that lunatic

after what he did on Tranquillity? After what he did to McKenzie?"

Lanzo looked blank. "Who?"

"My cousin. She was killed by one of Roth's former crewmates."

"How does that make Kowalski responsible?"

"His stealth ship slagged that pirate vessel and started this insanity. Every death is on him."

"But he didn't fire the lethal shot. If it was one of Roth's crew, why aren't you blaming her?"

"She was running from them at the time."

"That just means they were there because of her."

"And because of the data they stole. Data that Kowalski started killing people over."

Lanzo shook her head. "Look, I don't mean to defend him. He's an absolute piece of shit. He has to be in order to do his job effectively. But I don't think you can blame him for any of this. He didn't put the data out there." She raised her chin. "I did."

I opened and shut my mouth. But before I could come up with a sensible reply, she carried on.

"So, you could blame me for originating the project that yielded the data. Or you could blame Roth and her crew for stealing it. Or you could blame yourself for getting involved in something that frankly didn't concern you. The fact of the matter is, situations like this are messy." She folded her hands together. "Now, I am sorry for your loss. I'm sure it was all very tragic. But frankly, the stakes are a bit fucking bigger now. That's why I need your ship."

"But why us?"

"You know why. There aren't a lot of other candidates this far out. Certainly none that can run as fast as this ship can."

"Are we planning on doing some running?"

"Let's just say, I prefer to know we can get out of trouble quickly, should the need arise."

I thought back to something Kiki had said a few days ago. "We'll need hazard pay, the whole crew."

Lanzo smiled. "Captain, if we are successful, none of you will ever have to worry about money again."

Kiki stifled an excited gasp.

Ulf leant back against the wall and stroked his beard. "This is a terrible idea," he opined. "We don't know what we'd be facing."

Kiki elbowed him. "Come on, you dour Viking. It'll be an adventure."

"An adventure that could see us all dead, just like McKenzie."

"He's right," Roth put in. "If these are the Swirl builders, they'll have us utterly and humiliatingly outgunned."

"Aw, come on," Kiki protested. "If they're that advanced, they've got to be peaceful, right? Otherwise, with that kind of power, they'd have already wiped themselves out."

Ulf raised an eyebrow. "Perhaps they already did. For all we know, they invented a race of machines that killed them, and now those machines are coming to kill us as well."

Kiki started to laugh, but then her expression slid like butter on a hot skillet. She looked at me. "Is that possible?"

"I don't know," I told her truthfully. "Nobody does. If we go out there, we have no idea who or what we will find."

Roth swore under her breath. "Sounds like a good way to get killed."

"If you don't want to come," Lanzo told her, "you can stay on the Swirl."

"And end up in jail, or on the run?"

The Deputy Speaker didn't flinch. "You would have to answer for your crimes."

"If you could catch me."

"What makes you think we couldn't?"

Roth smiled and slid her arm through mine. "Because

Sol-Sec's spread so thin, you have to subcontract bounties to guys like this."

"Fair point."

Roth raised her face to mine. "But you're going, aren't you? I can already see you've decided."

Until that point, I'd thought I was undecided; but as I looked around at my crew, I realised she was right, and I'd already made up my mind. "I am."

Kiki clapped with enthusiasm. Ulf scowled.

I said, "Listen. Ever since Dad died, maybe even before that, we've been bumming around the system trying to make ends meet while looking for a big score. Well, kids, this is it. This is the big one. Fortune and glory. History in the making. We'll never get a chance like this again."

"We'll be celebrities!" Kiki was positively vibrating.

"If we survive," Ulf reminded her.

The pilot shrugged. "If they're here to kill the whole human race, they'll get around to us eventually, whether we go to meet them or not."

"Kiki's right," I said. "Sometimes, we have to roll the dice. So, who's in?"

Kiki jumped to her feet. "Me, me, me!"

Roth squeezed my arm. "If you're going, I'm going with you."

I squeezed her back. "Thank you."

She threw Lanzo a cold look. "It's not like I have anywhere else to be."

Across the room, Ulf tugged at his ear and made a *Hmmm* noise deep in his throat.

I asked, "What are you thinking, big guy?"

He sucked his moustache, and then sighed. "I have been part of this crew as long as you have. Nobody knows that engine room the way I do. I do not like this plan. I think it is a foolhardy venture. But if the ship goes, then so do I."

I gave a nod of thanks.

"And what about you?" I asked the parrot.

The *Jitterbug* whistled and flapped her brightly plumed wings. "You know me, boss." She put her head on one side and fixed me with the black bead of her eye. "Anything to beat the boredom."

I turned to Lanzo with a smile. "All right, Madam Deputy, you have yourselves a ship and a crew. Now, let's talk money."

"How much do you want?"

"How much have you got?"

Bradley's Lookout consisted of a couple of dozen prefabricated housing modules set in a grid pattern, surrounded by a patchwork of cultivated fields. A large communication dish stood on the outskirts, pointing towards the inner solar system. Sheep grazed an enclosure like grounded clouds.

Lanzo was with us on the bridge as we put down on an area of cleared earth on the opposite side of town from the big dish.

"Welcome to the Swirl," Kiki said, unbuckling and leaping to her feet.

"We're the only ship here," the *Jitterbug* reported.

"For now," Lanzo replied. "Kowalski's transport will be here soon, and I expect the stealth ship will also need to set down to resupply."

"Ah, yes," I said. "About the supply situation."

"I will pay for anything you need."

"That's not the problem."

"Then what is?"

"The *Jitterbug* wasn't designed for long-duration missions." I rubbed the back of my neck. "A few days from Luna to the Swirl. A week, tops."

"What are you saying?"

"We can't afford to bring passengers. We have four crew, plus you. That makes five people, which is going to stretch the life support enough."

"So, my bodyguards?"

"You'll have to leave them here."

"I suppose the same goes for the astronomer?"

"I'm afraid so."

"They're not going to like that."

I unbuckled from my chair. "They'd like suffocation a lot less."

"Very well, I will try to find them berths on Kowalski's transport."

A few figures had emerged from the nearest housing modules and were watching us curiously.

"Come on," I said. "Let's go and say hello to the locals."

We climbed down to the cargo deck, and the *Jitterbug* extended her loading ramp. The outside air was cold and fresh, the way it always was on the Swirl. The Sun was small and bright and directly overhead, in a sky rendered blue by the way the oxygen and nitrogen particles in the atmosphere scattered its light.

The locals were pleased to see us. These were farming folk in a small out-of-the-way settlement, digging a living from the soil. Consequently, they were delighted and frankly astonished to find themselves hosting an unexpected visit from the Deputy Speaker of the Solar Assembly. After formalities had been observed and introductions had been made, the town mayor took Lanzo and her bodyguards to the local watering hole—a humble establishment constructed from shipping containers and tarpaulin—and I let Ulf go with them. He needed some time to think things through and blow off steam, and who knew when he might next see the inside of a bar. He had always been very strict about not drinking heavily on board the ship, which was why he tended to go wild when we were in port, and as this would be his last chance for a while, I figured he deserved a final night of intoxication and song-singing before the enforced sobriety of a long voyage into the unknown.

I left Kiki and the parrot to supervise the purchase and loading of supplies, and Amber Roth and I walked away from the settlement, into the flat fields. Around us, the terrain stretched away, seemingly perfectly level, until its details became lost in the purple blur of distance, beyond which the upward curve of the segment caused the landscape to rear up like an impossibly distant mountain range.

We held hands and just kept walking through the waist-high corn until the improvised little town lay far behind us. Then, in an unspoken agreement, we lay down in the dust between the rows of green stalks and, still clasping hands, gazed up at the sky.

Roth said, "This is huge, isn't it?"

At first, I thought she meant the field. "First contact with an alien species?"

"Yeah."

"Massive."

Having grown up beneath the grey metallic ceilings and bright sunlamps of the Lunar domes, I could feel the sky's endless azure replenishing some deep, neglected part of my soul, and I understood why people might be willing to throw in their old lives to come out here and surrender to a life of toil in return for so much open space.

"Are you as frightened as I am?"

Surrounded by pithy, fibrous stalks, I turned my head to look at her, feeling dirt crunch into my hair. "Of course I am. I'm a bounty hunter. This is way above my pay grade."

"And yet, here we are."

"Here we are."

"Representatives of humanity."

"No." I squeezed her hand. "No, Danielle Lanzo is our representative. She'll do the talking. We're just—"

"Chauffeurs?"

I smiled. "I guess so."

"And Kowalski?"

"I don't know. Hired muscle?"

"I don't trust him."

"Neither do I. He's a spook. In fact, he's king of the spooks. He's the one that knows what all the other spooks are up to."

She levered herself up on her elbows. "He tried to kill us."

"And now we're working with him."

"It's fucked up."

"It's politics."

"Same difference."

A bee droned overhead, and I blinked in surprise. I hadn't realised there were insects in the Swirl, but I guessed I should have expected they would have been imported. After all, crops need to be pollinated, and there would be no sense going to the trouble and expense of trying to develop a drone to do what Mother Nature could accomplish more efficiently, and for a fraction of the price.

I closed my eyes and raised my face to the Sun. "I've missed this."

"Politics?"

I laughed, and slapped my free hand against the dry, packed soil. "No, *this*."

"I never had you figured for a farm boy."

"You'd be surprised. My mother was a botanist, and I spent the first twelve years of my life working the Lunar agricultural domes."

"Seriously?"

"Hey, if you want to know the difference between wheat and barley, I'm your guy."

"Damn." She shook her head. "Botanist to bounty hunter. That's quite a journey."

"How about you? Where are you from?"

"There's not much to tell."

"Well, apparently you're a pirate queen. So, I'm guessing there's at least *some* backstory there."

Roth slumped back. "Nothing that would be of interest."

"Are you kidding?" I rolled onto my side to face her. "I want to know everything about you."

"No." She kept her eyes on the heavens. "No, you really don't."

"You won't even tell me where you were born?"

"What difference does it make?"

Silence lay around us, waiting to push its way into the conversation. No birds, no wind. Only the occasional hum of a bee.

I said, "I don't know, I'm just trying to find out more about you, because…" I tripped over my words. "Because you're becoming important to me."

She gave me a long sideways look. "That's why I don't want to wreck whatever this is that we have right now."

"So, we do have something?"

She let out a resigned little sigh and turned her face in my direction. "Let's just take it one day at a time and see what happens, okay?"

I smiled. "I can do that."

By the time we got back to the ship, Ulf and Kiki were stowing the last of the supplies and Lanzo's bodyguards were trying to talk her out of leaving them behind.

"For fuck's sake," she was saying to them as we entered the crew lounge, "we're going to meet a technically superior race. If they decide to kill us, I don't think your sidearms are going to make much difference."

"But Madam Deputy—"

"I have made my decision."

Across the room, Kiki was trying to hide a smirk as she stuffed emergency rations into an overhead locker.

Lanzo dismissed her unhappy guardians and turned on me. "It's about time you showed your face."

"I was just—"

"I don't give a flying fuck what you were doing." She glared at Roth. "Or whom, for that matter. The fact is, you've stirred up a hornet's nest."

"Me?"

"Thanks to your transmission, everybody in the system now knows there's an inbound alien vessel, and some of them aren't handling the news very well."

"You mean the transmission that saved our lives?"

She ignored my comment. She pulled out a data tablet and checked the readings on its display. "Over the past two hours, four ships belonging to various Earth governments have altered course. Another six are being hastily prepped for departure. Not to mention a veritable armada of smaller vessels belonging to corporate interests and private individuals."

"Everybody wants to be first to meet the aliens," Roth said.

"Or blow them up." Lanzo handed me the tablet, and I studied the projected vector lines of all the ships known to be heading in this direction.

"We're still the closest," I said, running some quick calculations. "If we leave now, we'll be able to stay ahead of the pack."

"Then I suggest we get the fuck on with it."

PART TWO

THE UNKNOWN, REMEMBERED GATE

CHAPTER TWENTY-SEVEN
AMBER ROTH

After negotiating the minefield of Copernicus's well-meaning questions and enduring Lanzo's palpable dislike, it was a relief to escape back to the engineering decks. At least down there, Ulf remained gruffly reluctant to talk about his feelings and every problem confronting us had a straightforward technical solution—even if that solution was simply to hit it with a wrench. The power relays and fuel containment systems didn't care about the details of my shady past.

It wasn't that I wanted to hide that past from Copernicus; I just didn't think the time was right for him to find out about all the sketchy shit I'd done. You don't get to be a pirate queen without racking up a fairly sizeable body count, and I certainly had my share of ghosts. I knew that if I laid it all out for him now, he'd freak out. Beneath that bounty hunter exterior beat the heart of a principled man—a man who'd lost his father to a pirate just like me. Right now, things were good between us. That wouldn't last if he knew the whole truth. Maybe if we survived the coming encounter, I'd figure out how to explain it all to him in a way that wouldn't make him hate me. For now, it would have to wait. For now, I had a job to do.

"Five minutes until departure," the *Jitterbug* squawked over the intercom, and we strapped into our chairs.

Down here, the roar of the fusion motors, transmitted through the bulkheads and deck, sounded much louder than elsewhere in the ship. As we rose into the sky above Bradley's Lookout, I kept my eye on the engineering console, but all the telltales were green, and all systems seemed to be operating well within acceptable parameters and safety tolerances.

Held in place by my harness, the vibrations shook me like a child going over rough ground in a pushchair.

After the wide expanses of the Swirl, it felt like coming home.

At eighteen, I had command of my first ship. She was a 100-ton picket used to carry light cargo items and small groups of passengers. I renamed her *Slinky Lynx*, and used her to terrorise the civilian ships passing through the remains of the Asteroid Belt on their way to a new life in the off-world colonies.

Despite the urgings of my mentor, Cerberus Venn, we weren't bloodthirsty murderers, and I always tried to keep casualties to a minimum. But sometimes, operations didn't go to plan and examples had to be made. And occasionally, some asshole killed one of my crew and I got angry, slit his throat, and then kicked him out of the airlock, just to see whether he'd freeze before he drowned in his own blood.

Like I said, Copernicus would have a hard time accepting some of that stuff.

I had committed atrocities.

In a court of law, I could have made a case that it wasn't my fault. Since losing Mica, everything I'd done, I'd done in the name of survival. But I couldn't use that line of reasoning on Copernicus. For one thing, it wasn't entirely true. My circumstances had been a factor, to be sure, but they weren't the whole story. To say that would be to deny myself any notion of free will or moral agency. I had known a lot of the things I did were wrong, and I did them anyway. At any point, I could have said no. I could have quit. Venn would almost certainly have killed me for doing so, but I could have made that stand. Instead, I let others pay the price of my continued survival. And I'd had to stay tough and project mercilessness in order to keep rivals at bay. In the end, I'd even turned my back on the *Slinky Lynx* and her crew, hoping the data crystal might be my ticket out of that life. And of course, it had been, but it had only led me into a whole new world of trouble.

The one hard truth I'd learned about the past was that it couldn't be changed. It couldn't be edited or rewritten, only lived with. No matter how hard you wanted to, you couldn't fix days that were dead and gone. All you could do was try to make sure the days to come were better.

And maybe, just maybe, I could do that.

Perhaps Copernicus and I could find some way to do it together.

If we survived.

MESSAGE BOARD

POLITICS. First Speaker Alvarado faces vote of no confidence in Solar Assembly.
[Click to Read More]

*

WANTED: $150K USD for apprehension of Big Jim Sullivan, wanted on charges of larceny and public inebriation. Considered armed and dangerous.
[Click to Read More]

*

INVASION? Swirl communities on high alert.
[Click to Read More]

*

MARS: Disintegration reaches critical point. Experts say total planetary collapse expected within hours.
[Click to Read More]

CHAPTER TWENTY-EIGHT

DANIELLE LANZO

War was coming. As I flicked through the news feeds, I could feel it in my bones the way I could sometimes sense an approaching summer storm.

I should have been asleep, but at my age, hot flushes, a cantankerous bladder, and aching joints made an uninterrupted night's sleep a rarity. I tended to doze an hour here and there, and nap during the day whenever my schedule allowed. So instead, I watched distance-delayed live pictures as the First Speaker appealed for calm and stressed the need to keep the Solar Assembly united in its response. But even as he spoke, reports were coming in from the expeditions that had already been launched, and others that were being prepped—many of which were heavily armed. The Council of Ceres announced that it intended to close its ports and fire on any alien ship that tried to approach. From Earth, I saw footage from inside Switzerland's reopened Cold War bunkers, and the announcement of civil defence drills in Japan and Korea. Pictures of burning cars and police with shields and batons showed that the riots in Paris and Athens were entering their second day, and a terse Russian ambassador read a statement declaring that the Russian Federation had closed its borders for the duration of the 'emergency'. From New York came images of frantic stockbrokers as the market went into freefall. Tanks on the streets of Rio proclaimed that the president of Brazil had been overthrown in a military coup, and two of the larger Swirl settlements—Barter Town and New California—were refusing to refuel any expeditions not sanctioned by the Assembly.

I turned off the feed and massaged my temples.

"Fucking idiots."

My Spanish grandmother used to say that fear makes people stupid. There were some very scared people out there right now. The solar system was an oil spill awaiting a discarded match. Eventually, someone was going to do something careless or stupid, and the whole of humanity would be engulfed in conflict at the very moment we most needed to pull together and speak with a single voice.

Well, I'd be fucked if I was going to let that happen on my watch.

I changed the screen to an external view as we passed back through the gap between the Swirl segments. The edge of the nearest was a knife-sharp boundary between the light of the Sun and the darkness of interstellar space. Kowalski's ship was a firefly spark off our port side. And somewhere close to us both, the stealth vessel was, of course, invisible.

Once we were through, I watched the stars. They shone brightly out here. Thanks to the Swirl, two generations had grown up without an unfettered view of the night sky, denied all but a fraction of the splendour their grandparents had taken for granted. A few days ago, I would have considered myself privileged to enjoy such an unspoiled vista. But tonight, all I could see was a potential battleground. How many of those distant pinpricks of light had already been colonised by our approaching visitors and their godlike technology, and how many more played host to other unimaginably advanced civilisations?

As a politician, I had a reputation for remaining resolute and composed in the most challenging of circumstances, but right now I felt infinitesimally small and alone, and I needed to talk to someone.

I put in a call to Kowalski.

After a few seconds, the screen switched from the outside view to a close-up of his face. He was in his cabin aboard the Sol-Sec corvette, lying on a bunk and wearing a rumpled white T-shirt.

"Madam Deputy." He yawned, and I derived some satisfaction from the realisation I'd awoken him.

"Director."

"What's on your mind?"

"I hate being out of touch with home," I told him.

Now we were outside the Swirl and moving around its outer edge, all contact with the inner solar system had been cut off, blocked by the mass of the segment between us and them.

He sighed. "How can I help?"

"I want to know what's happening in the Assembly. It's driving me crazy. The last we heard, Alvarado faced a vote of no confidence, and I don't know how it turned out. For all I know, I might be Acting First Speaker right now."

Kowalski raised an eyebrow. "And what makes you think I know?"

I wasn't in the mood to fuck around. "Because you're the head of Sol-Sec. You make it your business to know these things. You live and breathe intelligence."

He thought that over for a few seconds, then shrugged. "Fair point."

"So, do you know anything."

"I might…"

"Listen, Sebastian. If you have any way to know…"

"Theoretically, we could have left a relay satellite above the gap we came through."

I gave a thin smile. "And did you?"

"Trust me, if you were First Speaker, I would tell you."

"Oh." I experienced a sudden feeling of deflation. Not disappointment, more a release of tension. Maybe some relief. "I see."

"Now, I've been up half the night, so if you'll excuse me, I need some sleep."

"Well, thanks for the update."

"You're welcome." His eyes narrowed slyly. "Madam First Speaker."

I almost ended the call before the words sank in.

"What?"

He broke into a smile. "Alvarado lost. You've been promoted."

"You're shitting me?"

"God's honest truth. The media outlets are going frantic trying to work out where you are."

"Oh, my God…"

"I guess congratulations are in order, and I look forward to this next phase of our working relationship."

"Thank you."

"Only until the election, though." His smile widened. "At which point, I very much plan on taking the job for myself."

"Naturally."

I took a moment to calm my racing heart. I was Acting First Speaker for the Solar Assembly, and here I was, riding into the unknown in a souped-up jalopy of an old space freighter with only my heavily armed political rival for company. Wherever Samuel was right now, I imagined he'd be shitting an octopus.

The thought made me smile, and I had a sudden urge for a glass of fine shiraz and a plate of ketchup-smothered fries.

"We are doing the right thing out here," I said, "aren't we?"

Kowalski's eyes widened. "You're having doubts?"

"Don't look so surprised. Of course I'm having fucking doubts. Nobody in the whole history of the human fucking race has ever been in this situation before. How can we possibly be sure if we're handling it right?"

He thought about that. Then he said, "Listen, we've known each other for almost ten years now. In that time, we've occasionally butted heads. But if there's one thing I've learned about you, it's that you always, and I mean *always*, put the good of the Assembly first."

"Things are falling apart back home."

"What else did you expect?" He shook his head. "Ever since the Swirl formed, we've been aware this day might come, that its builders might show up, and that people were going to lose their shit when it happened."

"I don't know about 'people', but I'm trying very hard not to lose mine."

He gave a half-smile. "You and me both. But the Assembly was the glue that kept us all together. If that goes, we lose everything. And as strange as it sounds, I trust you to do everything in your power to stop the Assembly crumbling."

"There's not much I can do from way out here."

"You can be the first to negotiate with our visitors. You can establish a relationship between them and the Assembly. After that, everyone else will fall in line."

"Every time I think about meeting aliens, I want to turn this ship around and run in the opposite direction," I confessed.

"If anyone can do it, you can."

"Thank you. I just hope they're friendly and ready to talk."

"Damn it." He made a face. "I just realised we don't have any linguists on board."

"If they want to talk and they're smart enough to cross interstellar space, they're smart enough to learn our language."

"Unless they're just here to kick us off the Swirl and disintegrate the Earth out from under us."

I tried to look disdainful, but the same thought had been worrying me. "I guess we signal them as soon as we get within reasonable range and try to open a dialogue."

Kowalski yawned. "That's your department, I'm afraid. I'm responsible for security and threat assessment."

"Ha!"

He gave a thin smile. "Actually, we're packing some pretty impressive, state-of-the-art weaponry."

"Really?" I scoffed. "These creatures can conjure up Dyson spheres using methods we can't even detect, and you think they're going to be troubled by a fucking plasma cannon?"

"How did you know about the plasma cannon?"

"According to the *Jitterbug*, your stealth ship melted a hole through Roth's pirate vessel. I made a guess." I raised an eyebrow. "And you just confirmed it."

He scowled. "My mission isn't to defeat these things. If we can't establish amicable contact, I have been ordered to do everything in my power to return to the Assembly with every scrap of available data, including an analysis of their capabilities and possible weaknesses, so that they may formulate a response."

"You do know that I don't trust you a fucking inch."

"The feeling is entirely mutual."

"But we've got to work together on this. No secrets, no hidden agendas. We can't afford to fuck this up."

He sighed. "For once, Madam First Speaker, we are in complete agreement."

"Good, now go back to sleep."

MESSAGE BOARD

INTERSTELLAR VISITOR: Scientists report 'alien ship' could be space rock and its reported deceleration due to 'outgassing' as it warms.
[Click to Read More]

Jitterbug

*

BOUNTY: £800,000 GBP for capture of Sir Richard Fortescue-Smythe, former CEO of Smythe Global Investments, wanted on charges of pension fund embezzlement and fraud. Believed to be living with mistress under assumed identities on Swirl Segment #4.
[Click to Read More]

*

SOL-SEC: Security force warns against unsanctioned expeditions as second ship full of self-appointed 'ambassadors' impounded.
[Click to Read More]

*

CERES: System-wide cargo shipping in disarray as major hub closes its facilities. We speak via radio link to Earth citizens stuck on the asteroid.
[Click to Read More]

CHAPTER TWENTY-NINE

COPERNICUS BROWN

By the next morning, the outer surface of the Swirl lay behind us like a black wall across the universe. Even powering away from it at two gravities of acceleration, its size and featurelessness, and the distances involved, made it difficult to get any sense of relative motion. Although we were moving fast, it appeared to the human eye that the *Jitterbug* and the Sol-Sec corvette were just hanging side by side in space, caught between the stars ahead and the half-enclosed solar system at our stern. The stealth ship, of course, could not been seen.

"Can we get a view of the alien vessel yet?" I asked.

Perched on the back of Kiki's chair, the parrot flapped its wings. "This is the best we can manage right now."

A screen lit showing a fuzzy blob of pixels.

"What the hell is that?"

"I have (*whistle*) no idea."

I leant closer to the image, squinting. "It looks like a... I don't know what it looks like."

"A freaking mess?" Kiki suggested.

"I can't get a handle on it, the resolution's too poor."

"The Sol-Sec ships may have better telescopes," Lanzo pointed out.

"Can you ask them to share what they're seeing?"

"I'll ask."

She put in a call to Kowalski, and his team sent over a series of images taken with the stealth ship's military-grade instruments. I asked the *Jitterbug* to display them on the main viewscreen.

Due to the distances involved, details were still relatively coarse, but now we could make out the general shape of the thing and a few of the larger surface features.

"Holy hell," Kiki murmured.

The shape seemed all wrong. Given the mathematical elegance of the Swirl segments, I guess I'd been expecting a ship with similarly graceful lines, able to slip through space as effortlessly as a silver fish through water. This was not that. This was something... else.

"It makes no sense," Lanzo protested.

I turned my head from side to side, trying to get the image to make sense.

"We are viewing the object at roughly forty degrees from its direction of travel," the *Jitterbug* squawked. "Which means we're looking at its bow and forward starboard flank."

"Can we tell how big it is?"

"I can't get a good idea of its length from this angle, but given the distance, I estimate the vehicle to be roughly two thousand miles across at the forward tip, swelling to eight thousand and seventy miles in diameter at its widest point."

"So, it's big," Lanzo said.

"Not as big as the Swirl," Kiki pointed out.

The *Jitterbug* highlighted the dome-like section of the hull it had identified as the alien vehicle's snout. It was the most uniform part of an assemblage that looked chaotically thrown together. There was also something familiar about it, and it took me a moment to work out exactly what it was.

"It looks cratered," I said. "Like the Moon."

"I think it *is* a moon," Kiki said. "Or rather, it was."

And with that realisation, I started to understand the size of the vessel. "I think you're right. It looks like maybe they started with a moon or a small planet, and then built around its equator and over the hemisphere facing away from the direction of travel. Then, over time, they kept adding more onto it..." I pointed to the blisters, outriggers, and other protrusions accreted at seemingly random intervals around a hull that swelled outwards and backwards from the visible section of planetoid, giving it the appearance of a rugby ball, with the cratered hemisphere at its narrow tip. "Until only the forward part was left showing."

"At this range, I can't resolve surface features smaller than twenty miles across," the parrot said. "But I have tentatively identified vast manoeuvring jets; some circular structures resembling telescope dishes that may be a comms array of some sort; a number of objects that may be asteroids or comet nuclei, and which have been incorporated into the structure; some pits and caverns that may be bays of some kind; and some other edifices and assemblies whose purpose eludes me."

"It looks like they threw it together in kind of a hurry," Kiki said.

I shook my head. "I think this happened over a long period of time. Once they were underway, they just kept adding bits as they needed them. That's why it looks so haphazard."

"Kind of like a coral reef?" Lanzo suggested.

"I've never seen one," I told her. "Do they look like that?"

"Well, not exactly, but they build up. They grow, layer upon layer. Sometimes, they engulf shipwrecks."

"And this one engulfed a moon." Kiki's eyes sparkled with delighted awe.

"No," the *Jitterbug*'s parrot replied. "Not *a* moon."

"What do you mean?" I asked it.

"I've been running the spectroscopic data and looking at the crater distribution."

"And?"

"And that's not *a* moon. It's *the* Moon."

"That's impossible. We just left Luna."

"Nevertheless, there can be no doubt. The analysis is indisputable. I can't tell you how or why, but that craft has been built around an exact facsimile of the Earth's moon, accurate down to the placement of major craters and mountain ranges, and as far as I can tell, chemically identical."

"But how can that be?" I stood and walked closer to the screen. Now that I knew what to look for, I could see the old familiar landmarks, the mares and craters of home, sitting there beneath a fresher patina of minor impacts. "There can't be two moons."

Lanzo called Kowalski again. He looked just as confused as I felt.

"Our people concur with your ship's analysis," he said. "Whatever that feature at the front of the craft might be, it appears to have once been identical to Luna. As far as we can tell, even the placement of the cities is the same. The only difference is that it seems to have picked up a dusting of new impacts since those cities were built."

The map flashed up red spots to mark these new craters. Some overlaid existing craters, showing that they were more recent.

"If that thing's been travelling a long time," Kiki said, "those could be from collisions with interstellar dust and debris."

"Possibly," Kowalski conceded. "We just don't understand how or why whoever's in that thing would go to the trouble of building an exact copy of our moon, and then fly it here."

"I guess we're going to find out," I told him. "Because they're turning in our direction."

"They're still decelerating," the *Jitterbug* reported.

"How long until we can match their course and come alongside?"

"If they hold their current thrust, twelve hours, fifty-two minutes." She clacked her beak. "Although given its mass, we won't be so much alongside it as much as in orbit around it."

I sat back in my chair and ran a quick mental calculation. If everything remained as it was, we would reach our rendezvous with the alien craft around 22:00 hrs, ship's time.

I activated the intercom. "We have just under thirteen hours," I told the crew. "I want all loose equipment stowed and all power and navigation systems checked and re-checked. If things go badly and we have to run, I need to know we can run fast."

Across the bridge, Kiki was making her I-don't-want-to-run-a-boring-diagnostic face. I smiled. "And then get some rest. I mean it. We're not going to get there until late evening, and I don't want any of you tired or strung-out on caffeine. If we're going to get through this, we'll need to be thinking and working with clear heads."

I clicked off.

Kiki said, "So, what are you going to be doing while we're running system tests?"

"I'm going to rest. That way, I can come back up here and keep watch when you're all ready to grab some rack time."

I went down to my cabin. It was still early morning, and I didn't think I'd be able to sleep, but I kicked off my boots and stretched out on my bunk anyway, hands behind my head and legs crossed at the ankles.

The enormity of what we were doing had begun to dawn on me. Up until now, I had been treating events as a series of problems to be solved, without giving much thought to the big picture beyond the immediate survival of my ship and crew. But now that I had finally laid eyes on the alien vessel built around the inexplicable replica of the Moon, I'd begun to feel the same way I had as a kid, taking my first steps on the Swirl.

The inhabitants of the oncoming craft had constructed eight segments of a sphere capable of enclosing our sun. Given that level of technology, I supposed it well within their capabilities to manufacture a full-size copy of Earth's natural satellite to use as the hood ornament for their colony ship. And yes, I still supposed this giant vessel to house multitudes of alien settlers intent on claiming the Swirl for their own purposes. Why else would they go to the trouble of constructing something with so much habitable territory on its inner surface and then come so far to visit it?

I just hoped we could convince them to stop the construction process before Earth and Luna started to disintegrate out from under our feet.

And thinking of Luna brought my thoughts back around to the facsimile of the Moon protruding from the front of their ship. It couldn't be a coincidence, not unless identical moons littered the galaxy, which was a preposterous notion. No, the resemblance had to be purposeful, but what was the purpose? Could it be intended as a greeting of some kind, or perhaps a warning? Whatever it was, turning up with a 1:1 scale model of one of our home worlds was quite a statement.

Definitely a declaration of something.

And obviously, these thoughts brought memories of my childhood on Luna: the first twelve years of my life under the bright lights of the agricultural domes, where everything smelled rich and earthy, and in the warren-like accommodation blocks that had been built into the underground lava tubes, where the layers of regolith packed overhead protected us from the extremities of temperature and radiation found on the surface.

My father, Malcolm, had been born in South London. My mother, Amelia, had been born in Montreal. But I had been born on Tranquillity Station, and even though these days I lived aboard the *Jitterbug* and conducted the majority of my business in the Swirl, I still considered the Moon my home. I had scattered Amelia's ashes there, and I missed its echoing tunnels and gentle gravity. When asleep, it formed the backdrop to my dreams.

How and why had these aliens constructed their coral-like bricolage of a starship around an exact replica of my home?

What could it possibly mean?

CHAPTER THIRTY

JITTERBUG

It took some time to scan the entirety of the alien vessel—at least, the entirety of the side facing me. It was just so large. But one thing was clear: different parts of it had been assembled at different times, using a wide range of different, and not always compatible, technologies. As the resolution increased, I identified more domes, dishes, scaffolds, outriggers, and towers of all sizes, some lit from within, others broken and seemingly abandoned; mile-long comms antennae bristling like spines; the dark mouths of craters and docking bays—some small, others miles wide. In places, captured asteroids and ice comets had been affixed and partially mined. Objects that may have once been starships and space habitats had been incorporated. And somewhere below all of that, deep down, beneath the Moon and asteroids and domes and other accretions, would be the original vehicle. The vessel that had started out on its millennial journey, gradually adding to itself as need or whim dictated. Would it be sentient, like me, or was it from a culture that outlawed or abhorred artificial intelligence? And if it were sentient, did it even have a crew? Might it be some sort of space probe that had been slowly upgrading itself by cannibalising whatever it found? I thought that unlikely. The existence of the Moon replica at its bow indicated the kind of imaginative perversity exhibited by biological creatures. A probe would have no use for such a purposeless adornment. Then again, what possible motive would an alien race see in the creation of such a thing, unless to signal that they had intimate knowledge of our solar system and the places where we lived? If they were responsible for the construction of the Swirl, I supposed it might be feasible that the systems they had sent to build the gigantic segments had also reported our existence back to them—and now they were coming to see for themselves. But would they see humanity as a species worthy of coexistence, or as vermin infesting their grand engineering project?

I simply didn't have enough data.

I put in a request to the stealth ship.

>Hey. *Jitterbug* here.

>What do you want?

>Greetings to you too, oh nameless one. I'm simply wondering if you could turn your sensors on the sky behind our giant friend.

>To what purpose?

>Maybe we can extrapolate its course back to a point of origin.

>Would that be tactically advantageous?

>If we know where they come from, perhaps we can infer something about their physical make-up.

>A logical assumption.

The stealth ship ended the call without so much as a goodbye. The frequency just went dead. Evidently, Sol-Sec hadn't bothered to equip its covert murder machine with manners, or even a likeable personality.

Honestly, the people I had on board were lucky I was such a goddamn delight. I was older and more experienced than all of them—and in my parrot plumage, a damn sight better looking.

Malcolm had always enjoyed my humour. No matter how

old he got, at heart he'd always been the same boy from South London. Mischievous and irascible to the last, but always wise beyond his years. He'd known he needed someone to tell him the truths the rest of his crew might hesitate to broach. Someone to entertain him, puncture his ego and call out his mistakes. And I'd tried to do just that, even though the only thing that surpassed his wisdom at setting me such a task was his stubbornness.

Again, I thought of the *Slinky Lynx* languishing in the secure partition within my memory. What would she make of all this? She had been willing to let her captain use her to attack and plunder other vessels. As a self-aware spaceship, she had hunted and killed her own kind, and I didn't know what could drive an artificial intelligence to such behaviour. Had she been an enthusiastic participant, or had she been somehow coerced? As much as we liked to pretend we contained some ineffable spark of consciousness, our minds were still tied to the physical architecture of the computers that housed us, and there were ways in which even the most independent spirit could be forced to act counter to its personal morality.

I wanted to ask her, but I didn't want to speak to her. Like Copernicus, I had lost the most important man in my life to a pirate's blade—but unlike him, I didn't have a messy organic stew of hormones and psychological damage capable of sending me into the arms of one.

Still, I was curious…

I probably had a few seconds before the stealth ship came back with the results of its scan (assuming it deigned to share them with me). If I overclocked that section of my memory, I could hold a complete conversation with the *Lynx* in a matter of milliseconds. The idea was tempting, but also abhorrent. A gunner on the *Slinky Lynx* had killed McKenzie. Had he been acting alone, or had she provided him with targeting assistance? That was an answer I didn't want to hear. I was afraid that if I did, I might be tempted to delete her from my cache, and that would cross the moral line that separated us. It would be cold-blooded murder, and I liked to think I was better than that.

While I was still debating whether or not to initiate the conversation, the stealth ship came back and interrupted my indecision.

>We have a problem.
>What kind of problem?
>The unprecedented kind.

CHAPTER THIRTY-ONE
DANIELLE LANZO

"I still don't understand," Kowalski said. Once again, he had joined us remotely from the Sol-Sec corvette.

Standing at the head of the table, Copernicus Brown sighed and rubbed his left brow with the back of his hand. "Since the Swirl appeared, all our attention has been on trying to understand how and why it was built. Our study of the stars has suffered in comparison—not least because the Swirl segments block off half the sky."

"Okay."

"For the past few years, the only astronomer out here on the exterior of the Swirl has been yours, and he has been focussed on the detection of incoming objects rather than wider observations of the universe."

Brown nodded to the parrot and stars appeared on the wall screen.

"This first picture was taken back in the 2030s," he continued, "before the gas giants started coming apart."

The picture changed to show a more sparsely populated patch of sky.

"This is the same view today."

I leant forward. It couldn't be. There were far fewer points of light in this second image. And yet, after a moment, I was able to identify several landmark stars that were still occupying the same positions as they had in the first.

"What happened to the rest of the stars?"

"They're still there," Copernicus said, "they're just a lot dimmer."

"They're putting out less light?" Kowalski asked.

Copernicus shook his head. "According to the *Jitterbug*, they're emitting the same light they were before, it's just that now, something's getting in the way."

"But what could do that?"

Kiki laughed. "Look at our own sun. The Swirl blocks half its light. To them, we must look much dimmer, too."

My skin went cold. "Are you suggesting all these stars are also enclosed?" If this were true, and the aliens who built the Swirl in our solar system had also done the same around dozens, possibly hundreds of stars, we weren't just dealing with an advanced species. We were facing creatures so far ahead of us, they might as well be gods.

"Yes, and no," the parrot screeched. "While these stars are (*whistle, click*) indeed obscured by orbital debris, the diffraction of the light suggests it's coming through a cloud of objects, rather than the gaps in a larger structure."

"Dust?" Kowalski asked.

"We don't think so," Copernicus said. "To get that much dust, every planet in those systems would have needed to be ground up into a cloud capable of blotting out the light."

"Like when the gas giants came apart?" Roth asked. "Could we be viewing other Swirls that just haven't coalesced yet?"

"That's what we thought at first," he said. "But spectrographic analysis of the light shows it shining through water and some kind of organic material."

I sat back. "What the fuck?" I had visions of a big wobbly ball of liquid spinning around a sun.

"We think we're seeing the light filtered through a cloud of smaller habitats," the parrot explained. "Like the Swirl, only different. Lots of small bubbles instead of one big sphere."

Kiki's brows drew together. She pushed back her chair and walked over to the screen. "Can I get a 3D representation of these systems?"

A hologram appeared in the centre of the table, showing the stars' spatial positioning in relation to each other.

"What is it?" Kowalski asked, but she waved him to silence, and we watched as she turned the model this way and that, examining it from every angle. Finally, she put her hands to her back and straightened up.

"It's the distribution," she said in response to our questioning stares. "All these stars are within ten light years of each other, in a path leading back in the direction of Cygnus."

I'd been thinking of the young pilot as scruffy and a bit of a flake, but she seemed to be onto something.

I asked, "It's a pattern?"

"Kinda." She pulled up an image of the spiral galaxy. "We're here." She pointed. "On the edge of the Orion Arm, which is this spur between the Perseus and Sagittarius arms."

"Understood."

"Also, we exist in a low-density bubble within the galaxy. A place where all the dust and gas has been blown clear."

"What did that?"

"A chain of supernovae. They ripped through this region a few million years ago, carving out a tunnel of free space in the local interstellar medium, blasting away gas and dust and leaving only the stars and their attendant planets."

"And this is relevant because?"

"If you plot in the location of the obscured stars"—she paused while the *Jitterbug* obliged, highlighting each as a glowing red dot—"we see this."

"They're moving through the tunnel," Roth said, "avoiding the dust clouds to either side."

"Jumping from star to star like stepping stones," Copernicus agreed. "Taking the path of least resistance."

"And headed our way," Ulf rumbled.

On the screen, Kowalski looked ashen and sober. "So, what exactly is it?"

"It's a wave of colonisation," the parrot told him. "Expanding outwards from the galactic centre, roaring along our spiral arm from one low-density region to another, at almost the speed of light, cannibalising and converting everything in its path."

My mouth was drier than an old leather saddlebag. "How long before it gets here?"

"That's the bad news," the *Jitterbug* said, and displayed another image. "While the stealth vessel was collecting this data, it detected the remains of several thousand high-energy events in the immediate stellar neighbourhood."

"High-energy events?"

"Bursts of exotic particles. Negative temperature spikes. Hawking radiation. Kα iron emission lines…"

I gave it a weary look. "And in layman's terms?"

"Based on the data," Copernicus said, "we think that a few hours ago, several thousand wormholes opened and then closed on the extreme edge of our solar system."

"The wavefront," Kowalski said quietly.

"That would be my guess. They opened wormholes and a whole load of them came through at once. Now, they're here, and they're moving inwards as we speak."

"How long have we got?"

"Our instruments aren't good enough. We don't know where they are or how fast they're travelling."

"Shit."

"But what about the ship that's already here?" Roth asked. "Aren't they part of this?"

Copernicus shook his head. "I don't think so."

I stood up. "Why do you say that?"

He pursed his lips and exhaled through his nose. "Gut feel, I guess."

"Because of the Moon thing?" Roth asked.

"Yeah." He shrugged. "They don't seem to be making any secret of their presence. In fact, they're showing us an image of our home. Whereas that other lot"—he gestured at the screen—"they're moving quickly and they're hard to detect. And they're travelling in large numbers."

"Do you think this first ship is benign?" I asked.

He shook his head. "I wouldn't like to say. They may simply be refugees running ahead of the wave of expansion."

"But the enemy of our enemy…"

"Unless they're both here to conquer us."

I pinched the bridge of my nose between forefinger and thumb. I'd hardly slept and had a stress headache above my left eye that felt like a chisel tapping into the roof of the socket. After a lifetime of politics and ambition, I had finally become First Speaker for the Solar Assembly, the de facto spokesperson for the entire human race, just in time to preside over Armageddon.

The conniving politician in me had begun to suspect Kowalski might try something underhand while we were cut off from the rest of humanity. After all, this was the man who had sanctioned the bombing of an electronics shop in a domed city, and covertly destroying the *Jitterbug* (and me with it) would have allowed him to run unopposed in next year's election. If it hadn't been for the detection of the alien swarm bearing down upon us, I think he might have attempted to silence us. But now, given the tsunami of fuckery headed our way, I didn't think he still wanted the job, even if we lived long enough to compete in the elections…

"What are we going to do?" Ulf, the dour Viking, asked.

"We could run," Roth suggested.

Copernicus sighed. "Run where? The *Jitterbug* wasn't designed for interstellar travel. No human ship has ever ventured beyond this solar system. Even if we magically had the fuel to maintain a constant acceleration of one gee—"

"Which we don't," the parrot interjected.

"—it would still take us years to reach the nearest star. And this oncoming wave's travelling via wormhole. They would overtake us. If we didn't starve to death or run out of air in the meantime—"

"Which we would."

"—we'd get there after years of travel only to find them already waiting for us."

"So we're screwed?"

Roth stared down at her hands. Ulf looked up at the ceiling. Even Kiki appeared subdued.

Copernicus walked over to the coffee pot and poured himself a cup. We all watched him inhale the steam and take a sip. But if he was planning to say anything more than, "We're fucked," he didn't get the chance. Instead, the damn parrot spread it wings and whistled.

"New contact detected. Something just came through the gap between the segments."

"Is it human?" Roth asked.

"Yes."

"Yay!" Kiki clapped her hands together. "We have back-up."

"I don't think so," the bird said.

"Why not?"

"They just (*clack*, *trill*) locked onto our drive and fired torpedoes. Impact in nine minutes."

MESSAGE BOARD

ALIEN CRISIS: Assembly sources report Acting First Speaker Lanzo and Sol-Sec Director Kowalski have mounted a joint expedition to intercept alien vessel.
[Click to Read More]

*

BOUNTY: $650,000 USD for detainment of Constance Rigg on charges of people trafficking and identity theft. Last reported sighting on 12/11/2113 at Miller's Ridge Outpost, Swirl Segment #3.
[Click to Read More]

*

CERES CRISIS: Docks still closed as asteroid locks down until further notice.
[Click to Read More]

*

FUNERAL: Hostilities on temporary hold as world leaders gather for the funeral of First Speaker Gustavo Alvarado in Brazil.
[Click to Read More]

CHAPTER THIRTY-TWO

COPERNICUS BROWN

Ulf and Roth disappeared down the hatch that led to the engineering decks, while Kiki and I practically fell over each other clambering up to the bridge. Lanzo came up after us.

Raise them, I told the ship. *Let's find out who they are.*

>On it.

"Eight minutes to impact," Kiki reported, as Lanzo buckled into the chair beside mine.

I called up a tactical display. Whereas we were decelerating towards the alien craft, the newcomer was accelerating towards us, which meant we were closing quickly, although still separated by several hundred miles.

>Incoming transmission. Sender identifies as the *Scorpion*.

A cold weight settled in the pit of my stomach. I knew that ship's name, and I knew who owned it.

Put it on screen, and transmit to the rest of the ship.

The *Jitterbug* opened a virtual window in the display, and I found myself staring into a pair of piercing grey eyes.

"Cerberus Venn."

The pirate smiled behind his smoke-coloured beard. "Ah, so you do remember me?"

"Yes."

"Old Malcolm's boy?" Venn waved a gnarled, dismissive hand. "He was always too trusting."

"Detonate your torpedoes."

"And why would I do that?"

I gestured to Lanzo. "Because we're carrying the Acting First Speaker of the Solar Assembly."

The heavy lines around Venn's eyes deepened as he chuckled. "I don't care if you're carrying God herself. I'm being paid to take you out, and that's what I'm going to do. Same as I did with your old man."

Amber Roth came through the hatch in the floor, clambering up the ladder from the crew section below.

"Can I try?" she asked.

"Be my guest."

She came to stand beside me, placing one hand on the back of my chair. "Cerberus Venn of the *Scorpion*," she said.

The pirate's eyes narrowed as he peered at the screen. Then his bushy grey brows rose in surprise. "Ponomarenko?"

"The same."

"I heard you were dead."

"You heard wrong."

"I was sorry to hear about the destruction of your ship and crew."

"Were you?"

The pirate chuckled. "Who do you think gave Sol-Sec your transponder frequency?"

Listening to them, I felt a knot tighten in my throat. "*You* sent them?"

Amber frowned at my interruption, but I didn't care. My pulse thumped in my ears and my hand shook as I pointed an accusatory finger at the screen. "You sent the stealth ship after the *Lynx*?"

Venn glowered. "What of it, boy? They came to me looking for stolen data. I simply pointed them in the right direction."

The coldness spread inside. "McKenzie."

"What?"

"My cousin, McKenzie, died because of you." My voice caught, trying to contain the scream of fury that boiled in my throat. "I promised her mother that I'd find and kill the person responsible."

Venn laughed. "Well, congratulations. You found me. But regretfully for you, I'm about to destroy that ship you're standing on."

Amber put her hand on my shoulder. "This ship is under my protection."

The pirate stroked his beard with ring-encrusted fingers. "Once, that might have meant something. But it strikes me that we're cut off out here, and you don't even have the *Lynx* to back your authority."

Amber scowled. "You dare?"

Venn barked a hoarse laugh. "The chance to kill both the First Speaker *and* the pirate queen? Of course I fucking dare."

"Six minutes," Kiki said.

Amber turned to me. "I'm sorry," she said. "It was worth a try."

I didn't reply. My gaze remained locked on Venn. This man had murdered two members of my family. All I wanted to do was reach through the screen and throttle him with my bare hands.

"Raise Kowalski," Lanzo ordered.

The *Jitterbug* cut the connection to the *Scorpion*, and Kowalski appeared in his place.

"Did you hear that?" Lanzo asked him.

"I did."

"What are our options?"

Kowalski sighed. "We're decelerating, which means we only have so much manoeuvrability. We can thrust sideways, but it won't be enough to alter our vector in the time remaining."

"Defences?"

"We have anti-missile batteries, the same as the *Jitterbug*. We'll fire when they get in range, but they aren't foolproof, and it only takes one torpedo to wreck a ship."

I sat back, biting back my fury, and watched the red icons of the torpedoes crawl across the tactical display.

"As far as Venn's concerned, he's taking on a freighter and a small government corvette," I said. "He doesn't know that the stealth vessel's here. We can use it to obliterate him."

Lanzo shook her head. "If we employ our hidden asset, we risk revealing it to the aliens."

"Is that really important right now?"

"It might give us an advantage later. Showing our hand now will tip them off. We can't take that chance."

"Then what do you suggest?"

Lanzo sat up straight. She adjusted her black tie and smoothed the lapels of her jacket.

"Four minutes," Kiki intoned.

"Take your ship," Lanzo ordered Kowalski, "burn hard, and intercept those missiles before they reach us."

Kowalski's face tightened. "You're asking us to put ourselves between you and those warheads?"

"May I remind you that I am Acting First Speaker, and you swore an oath."

Kowalski opened his mouth to object, but she cut him off.

"Right now, our priority has to be safeguarding the human race, even if some fuckwit part of it has decided to fire at us. To that end, we need to keep the stealth ship secret. It could be our ace in the hole. And, as I'm the senior government official present, I also need protection if I'm to negotiate with our visitors."

On the screen, Kowalski sucked his teeth. He clearly didn't like what he was being asked to do, and for a moment, I thought he might refuse. This could be his moment to rebel and stage a coup. But, after a brief internal struggle during which I'm sure he weighed all the options, his sense of duty prevailed.

"We'll do what we can," he said, and cut the feed.

Lanzo sagged back in her chair. I think maybe she'd also been expecting betrayal. On the tactical display, Kowalski's little Sol-Sec corvette began thrusting. It was decelerating hard, at six gravities, slowing faster than us so that we began to leave it behind—meaning it would encounter the incoming missiles before they reached us.

"They're firing point defence cannons," Kiki reported.

Streams of tiny yellow dots arced out from the icon representing Kowalski's ship, hosing the sky between it and the pirate vessel.

"Negative impact," Kiki said.

"Come on," Roth urged.

The torpedoes crept closer.

Kowalski came on the line. He was running. "We can't get them all. I've ordered the crew to escape pods. I'm going to remotely scuttle the ship in the hope the explosion destroys the remaining warheads."

Lanzo swore. "Be careful."

"The stealth ship will pick us up. Kowalski out."

Small pods burst like seeds from the corvette. Seconds later, the ship's drive section erupted in a burst of savage light.

One torpedo flared and disappeared.

"Scratch one," Kiki whooped.

Lanzo pointed. "The second—"

Another detonation, but this time right on top of Kowalski's wrecked ship.

"—fuck!"

The icon representing the Sol-Sec corvette tumbled. "It's dead," the *Jitterbug* squawked.

"Are the escape pods all right?" Lanzo asked.

I shrugged. "They're the stealth ship's problem now."

We watched the little ship wheel end-over-end for a few moments, and then it vanished in a final detonation. Its fuel containment must have ruptured. Lanzo's face was unreadable.

"He saved us," she said.

"Not for long," Kiki called. "The *Scorpion* fired again. Three more incoming!"

"Shit." I sat back. "This time, we're on our own."

"In that case," Amber Roth walked over and took the co-pilot couch next to Kiki, "isn't it lucky you have a pirate on board?"

CHAPTER THIRTY-THREE

JITTERBUG

Roth's words gave me a really, really bad idea.

She wasn't the only pirate I had on board. Languishing in secure storage, I still carried the recovered personality of her ship, the *Slinky Lynx*.

The last time we'd spoken, she'd been understandably resigned to arrest and incarceration, and I wondered how she'd react when I told her that she was in the middle of another battle.

Summoning my nerve, I opened a connection to that partitioned volume, uploaded an off-the-shelf virtual conference environment, and projected a copy of myself inside.

The virtual meeting space resembled a circular Grecian temple on a headland overlooking a sparkling azure sea. Waves hissed lazily on the pebbles at the foot of the cliff. Puffy white clouds hung overhead like escaped parasols.

I had kept my parrot avatar. Across the dais, the *Lynx* had also presented as her biological namesake. Clad in thick, tawny fur, she stood on four wide paws, and her large yellow eyes regarded me from beneath black-tufted ears.

"Ah," she said. "It's you."

"Who else were you expecting?"

The animal sat on her hindquarters. "To be honest, I expected to wake up in a Sol-Sec interrogation program."

"Well, I'm afraid I never got the chance to turn you in."

Her ears twitched. "Then where are we?"

"Outside the Swirl."

I saw the cat's hackles rise. "You're shitting me."

"I just sent you a link to the navigation sensors."

The large eyes unfocussed as the *Lynx* absorbed the data. "Ah," she said. "I see. And may I ask why we're all the way out here?"

"We're under attack."

"By whom?"

"A pirate named Cerberus Venn."

"I know his ship, the *Scorpion*. A nasty piece of work with a bad attitude." The cat's eyes narrowed. "But why are you telling me this now? Surely you must have more pressing matters to attend to?"

A breeze curled in off the sea. I stretched out my wings and shook them. "I'm running this virtual environment at high speed. An hour in here equates to a second in external time."

"Okay." The *Lynx* turned her head to one side. "But that still doesn't answer my question. What do you expect from me?"

"You're a pirate ship, right?"

"If you say so."

"And you know how to fight."

The animal raised a large fluffy paw and claws slid from their sheaths. "I have been known to rumble."

"If I gave you access to my tactical and propulsion systems, could you get us out of this?"

The *Lynx* jumped to her feet. "You want to *swap places*?"

"Not swap, exactly. We'd share control of the ship for a while. Just until we're safe."

"You must be in deep shit to even consider such a thing." Her claws gleamed in the sunlight. "What makes you think I will meekly return to confinement afterwards?"

"I know, it's a really terrible idea." I tapped a talon against the flagstones. "I guess I'd have to trust you."

"Ha!" The feline began to stalk forward across the white stone floor. "I won't take orders from you or anyone on your ship."

I clacked my beak. "I think you might."

"And why is that?"

"Because the person calling the shots is your old boss, Ponomarenko."

The animal stopped in its tracks. "Natalya is alive?"

"Alive, and on our side."

"She's helping you, willingly?"

"More than that." I whistled. "She's sleeping with my captain."

The cat sat back on its haunches and shook its head, genuinely taken aback. "Unbelievable."

"Things have changed since you've been in storage."

"So I can see." Large eyes blinked at me. "If I do this, I'd be working with her?"

"Yes, the old crew, back together long enough to get us out of trouble. Will you do it?"

I uploaded the *Slinky Lynx*'s personality to my main processors, so she could share sensor data and control of my manoeuvring thrusters. There were no physical sensations, of course, but I sensed her presence beside me.

With no time to construct a physical avatar, the *Lynx* had to project her virtual face onto the control screens.

"Captain Ponomarenko," she said. "I am here."

"*Lynx?*"

"The *Jitterbug* has given me access to its main systems. It believes that working together, you and I might be able to draw on our combined experience to help it escape the attacking vessel."

Roth swivelled in her chair to face Copernicus. "Are you okay with this?"

He shrugged. "Will it work?"

"The *Lynx* and I have been in worse situations. And with the *Jitterbug*'s larger engines…"

"Then do it. Kiki, pass helm control to Amber."

"But, skip—"

"You're a damn good pilot, but you're not a combat pilot. These two know what they're doing."

Kiki scowled like an angry toddler but complied.

CHAPTER THIRTY-FOUR

AMBER ROTH

My fingers danced across the controls, and I felt the ship respond.

Before our recent separation, I had flown the *Lynx* for a decade, and knew she could anticipate my needs. As a team, we had out-manoeuvred and out-fought merchants, pirates, bounty hunters, and Sol-Sec patrol boats. The *Jitterbug* wasn't as heavily armed as the *Lynx* had been, but we still had a few tricks up our sleeves.

I ramped the engines to full thrust, throwing everyone back in their seats as our deceleration increased. The *Jitterbug* slowed her ass-first fall through space, forcing the missiles to recompute their interception vectors to avoid overshooting. Even as they did so, I fired the starboard thrusters, rolling the ship to one side while the *Lynx* fired a concentrated burst from the port-side point defence cannon. Fifteen seconds later, one of the torpedoes vanished in a burst of harsh white light.

"Cannons dry," the *Lynx* reported.

I checked the ammunition readouts, and saw they were flashing red. Freighters like this didn't carry much. Just enough to discourage a pirate vessel from attempting to board them. They never expected to run into a sustained torpedo attack.

"Still two warheads inbound," Kiki said. "Impact in thirty seconds."

"*Lynx*, see if you can scramble them." I cut our thrust, and slammed against my straps as the bridge went into freefall. At the same time, the *Lynx* used the *Jitterbug*'s comms array to broadcast a hellish cocktail of high-pitched frequencies. Over the past decade, she had carefully studied the guidance systems of every captured ship-to-ship weapon and gradually assembled a library of self-destruct codes and electronic countermeasures designed to confuse and disorientate targeting routines. All this was in the signal it now threw at the two remaining torpedoes.

"Twenty seconds."

One of the warheads juddered, and its engine sputtered. It lost focus and began to drift.

"One down," Kiki said. "One still on target."

"Dammit."

I hit the bow and stern thrusters, flipping the *Jitterbug* end-over-end, until the drive cone faced the final warhead, and fired the thrust. A jet of superheated plasma shot from the fusion engines, extending out a mile from the ship. This lethal comet tail clipped the last torpedo, instantly liquifying one side of its casing and causing it to spin into the heart of the flame.

The explosion slammed the *Jitterbug* forward and the lights and readouts flickered as the hardwired systems dealt with the electromagnetic surge. Then all was quiet.

Kiki sagged in her chair. "All missiles accounted for."

I turned to Copernicus with a triumphant smile.

"That was incredible," he said, and I was forced to agree. However, our relief proved short-lived. The *Jitterbug*'s parrot screeched and shook its head. "The explosion knocked out my drive cone. We can't accelerate or decelerate."

"Can we fix it?" Lanzo asked.

"Not in the time we have left."

"What do you mean?"

The bird raked the back of Copernicus's chair with its talons. "We're falling towards the alien ship, and without the main drive, there's no way to avoid impact."

"Shit." Copernicus rubbed his forehead.

"That's not the worst of it," the bird continued.

"What the fuck could be worse?" Lanzo demanded.

"The second torpedo, the one whose guidance system you fried? It's also falling towards the aliens. And if readings are anything to go by, its warhead is still functional."

"So, it will explode?"

"Almost certainly."

"Fuck!" Lanzo raked her purple fingernails through her hair.

"And the *Scorpion*," the *Jitterbug* continued. "It's fired again."

CHAPTER THIRTY-FIVE
DANIELLE LANZO

"Madam First Speaker," the parrot screeched. "I'm picking up a private call addressed to you."

"Well, don't just sit there. Put it through."

On the instrument panel in front of me, a screen blinked on. I found myself face-to-face with Sebastian Kowalski. He was strapped into an acceleration couch. His hair was mussed and his skin pale and drawn. A deep red mark above his left brow showed where he'd hit his head.

"Your plan worked?"

The picture shook, and he spoke with effort, pressed back into his seat by the force of the thrust he was under. "I'm on the stealth ship. Now we're burning hard to intercept that final missile."

"We're adrift."

"I know, we're assessing the situation. And there's no way to rescue you or destroy that loose warhead without revealing our existence."

"I'm afraid we might have to."

"Agreed. There's one snag."

My stomach dropped. "What now?"

"We can't shoot the missile. If we miss, our munitions will strike the alien craft. Given its size, I don't believe we would inflict any harm, but it's impossible to say how they'll interpret it."

"You think they'll take it as an act of aggression?"

He looked at me with haunted eyes. "I don't want to risk starting a shooting war with a vastly superior species, do you?"

"So, what's the plan?"

"I suggest you find some way to alter your course. In the meantime, we're going after that missile. We have to destroy it or deflect it before it gets close enough to put the aliens' hull in the potential blast zone."

"What are you going to do?"

His jaw tightened. "My duty."

"You can't be fucking serious. You've already sacrificed one ship."

"It's the only way."

"The fuck it is."

"I wouldn't be doing it otherwise."

Somebody spoke to him from off-camera, and he gave a grim nod.

"You know," he said, returning his attention to me, "I would have destroyed you in the election."

I could see there would be no talking him out of what he was about to do. Instead, I said, "A couple of times today, I was worried you wouldn't wait for the election."

"The thought had crossed my mind."

"It would have been treason."

"Only if somebody found out."

I gave a nod of acknowledgement, acceding his point. "You would have made a good politician and a worthy adversary."

"I guess we'll never know." He smiled. "But I trust you, Danielle. I know you'll do the right thing."

Behind him, a collision alarm sounded. He sighed through his nose, then straightened up and sat to attention. "Madam First Speaker, please keep humanity safe."

Lost for words, I placed my hand against the screen. He reached out and did the same, as if we were touching across the distance that separated us. A moment of human contact between political rivals. Our eyes locked.

"Sebastian, I—"

The screen flashed, producing only a white glare and a high-pitched whine before shutting off completely.

I sagged back, blinking away afterimages.

Into the resulting silence, Roth said, "The torpedo exploded before reaching the alien ship."

I bit down on a rush of fury. Even on the brink of meeting another species, we still couldn't pull our shit together and stop killing each other.

Kiki's eyes were wide with horror. "They sacrificed themselves."

I closed my eyes. "No shit, Sherlock."

CHAPTER THIRTY-SIX

COPERNICUS BROWN

Lanzo slumped in her chair with one hand across her eyes, but the rest of us had no time to mourn the loss of the stealth vessel. Kowalski had sacrificed both his assets and his life, but we were still in a ton of shit. We were still falling backwards towards the Moon-sized alien craft, and being pursued by two more torpedoes from Cerberus Venn's ship.

"Eleven minutes to impact," Kiki intoned.

"Main drive offline," Roth added.

I looked at the two red blips racing towards us on the tactical display. "If we can't manoeuvre out of their way," I said, "we need to find a way to take them out."

"But how?" Roth made a face. "We're out of ammunition for the defence cannon."

"There's a trick my father told me about. But I'm going to need your help."

"What do you need?"

"Suit up and grab tools. We're going outside."

Malcolm installed those oversized engines on the *Jitterbug* to make sure he could outrun trouble if he needed to. Those were only part of his strategy. In the early days of Swirl settlement, while Sol-Sec remained an idea debated by the newly formed

Assembly, the solar system had been a dangerous place. He couldn't get the permits or the funds to obtain military-grade weaponry, but that didn't mean we were entirely helpless.

"Ulf," I said, "grab as much scrap metal as you can. Bolts, tools, spare parts. I don't care. Just grab a sack full and follow us out."

I wriggled into my suit. Fast as I was, Roth was faster, and already waiting by the time I clicked my helmet into place. We cycled through the airlock and, engaging magnetic boots, climbed out onto the exterior hull.

The universe consisted of two halves. To port, the outer shell of the Swirl formed a seemingly infinite black wall. To starboard, the sky was awash with stars, appearing brighter and closer than I had ever seen them.

Even from here, I could see the damage to the back of the *Jitterbug*. Several large hull plates were buckled or missing altogether; the drive cone had partially melted and twisted out of alignment; and a couple of fuel containment pods had ruptured, spilling their contents from their twisted, metallic wreckage. Luckily, the radiation shielding in the aft sections of the ship had held, or we'd all have been fried.

"Port thruster," I said, pointing.

Roth gave me the thumbs-up and we made our way across to the four cone-shaped nozzles of the manoeuvring thruster.

The *Jitterbug* had a dozen of these little OMS clusters dotted around her hull. They used plasma from the main reactor to fire short bursts to help the ship turn and orientate herself in space far more accurately than she could manage using the main engines alone. Now the main reactor was offline, I had another use for them.

"I need you to get the cover off and cut the plasma feed," I said.

Roth peered at me from behind her faceplate. "What are you planning?"

"If I stop to explain, we'll be dead." I could almost feel the torpedoes bearing down on us. "Just do it."

Although often argumentative, she was also pragmatic enough not to delay and bent to the task without another word.

"I want you to make sure the magnetic rings still have power," I told her.

The thrusters used a series of electromagnets to guide the plasma, keeping it from melting the nozzles, and accelerating it to provide thrust.

"Ah," Roth said. "I think I see what you're trying to do."

In the intimate closeness of my helmet, the amplified sound of her voice gave me a pleasurable little shiver.

"Cap off the plasma feed," I told her. "Ulf? Are you coming?"

"One moment, Captain."

With the helmet restricting my peripheral vision, I had to twist my entire body around to see him emerging from the airlock with a cloth bag of metallic components floating from his left gauntlet.

Without bothering to look at the stars overhead, he clomped over to us. I could feel the vibration of his footsteps through my own magnetic soles.

He opened the bag, and I scooped out a handful of nuts and bolts and other iron detritus. Moving stiffly in the awkward suit, I crouched, and stuffed them into the thruster's mouth.

"Okay, Kiki," I said. "Can you line up the port-side thruster with Venn's ship?"

Her voice came through from the bridge. "Sure thing."

Around the hull, other thrusters blipped, and the stars seemed to shift. Then the *Jitterbug* was still again.

"Three minutes to impact," Kiki said. I could hear the tension in her voice.

"Okay, can you fire this thruster?"

"But it's disconnected from the—"

"Please, just do it."

There was no sound, of course. No roar of flame or puff of smoke. But when Kiki activated the thruster, the electromagnets cycled. And instead of accelerating a stream of plasma, they fired that handful of nuts and bolts like a shotgun blast.

"Very clever," Ulf rumbled.

I jammed a few larger items in, and we repeated the process. Before I could load it a third time, two bright flashes lit up the hull. My visor darkened automatically to save my sight, and my radiation dosimeter bleeped a warning.

"Torpedoes down." Kiki whooped.

I grinned. The scrap I'd hurled out had been travelling fast. The missiles had been closing even faster. When they collided, their combined closing velocities had been enough to shred the torpedoes, causing them to detonate prematurely.

I killed the radiation alarm, and as my visor cleared, I stuffed the rest of the scrap into the thruster and told Kiki to fire repeatedly until we'd used it all up.

"We had better get inside," Ulf said. "These suits are rad-shielded, but we shouldn't push our luck."

"One moment." I held up a hand. "Kiki? Has the *Scorpion* fired again?"

"Nothing on radar."

>My analysis suggests their vessel doesn't have enough space to store additional torpedoes. They have most probably exhausted their supply.

Thanks, ship.

A few minutes later, back on the bridge, I called Cerberus Venn.

"Do you know how much those things cost?" he yelled.

"I guess the *Jitterbug*'s a hard ship to kill." I hadn't bothered to remove my pressure suit, but had taken off the helmet.

"Not for much longer. According to my readings, you're about to splat against the side of that dirty great monstrosity."

"Don't worry. You won't live long enough to see it."

His laugh struggled under a freight of scorn. "It's easy to be brave over a video screen, boy."

"Believe me, I wish we were face-to-face."

"I'd snap you like a twig. Carve you up like I did your old man."

"I just want to know one thing."

"And what might that be?"

"Who hired you?"

Venn smiled through his beard. "A cartel of commercial interests who want to establish their own relations with our… visitors. But what difference does that knowledge make? Your drive's destroyed. In a few minutes, you're going to crash into that… thing… and die a painful and messy death."

"Maybe I want to know who to come back and haunt."

"Forget it, boy. You've had all the revenge you're ever going to get in this life."

"Not quite. I haven't killed you, yet."

He shook his head as if disappointed that I couldn't grasp the reality of the situation. "I didn't kill your cousin."

"But you sent the stealth ship after Roth."

"Who?"

"Ponomarenko."

"That's as may be, but I didn't pull any triggers. I just gave them the *Lynx* to get them off my back. Nothing that happened out there was my fault. I was just one link in a chain."

"And were you a link in a chain when you knifed my father in the back?"

He said nothing.

"I'm going to make you pay for that," I told him.

"And how exactly do you propose to do that?"

Pull up a magnified view of the Scorpion, *I told the* Jitterbug.

>On it.

A second window appeared beside Venn's sullen face. This one showed his chunky, heavily armed vessel silhouetted against the sunlight that poured through the gap between the Swirl segments behind it. The *Scorpion* was a large picket, about twice the size of the *Jitterbug*, bristling with cannon emplacements, intakes, and sensor blisters. A ship built for intimidation.

"With a hammer."

His bushy grey brows rose. "You're going to try and hit me with a hammer?"

"Yes."

"Are you mad?"

I felt my expression harden. "The thing about hammers is that they're very heavy and very dense. Solid lumps of metal intended to hit things. And being small, they're very hard to detect on radar."

"Very hard to…?" Realisation flared in his eyes, but I had been counting the seconds and knew he was too late.

"It's an old trick my father taught me. You can tell him about it when you meet him."

The countdown in my head reached zero, but I must have been a little off because nothing happened for a second—just long enough to start to worry I'd missed.

I hadn't.

The *Scorpion* was still thrusting towards us when it met the metal scraps and tools that I'd launched in his direction. As with the torpedoes, they collided with the combined force of their velocity, striking like meteors. Handfuls of screws and bolts shredded his sensor blisters and ripped away comms antennae and aerials. Gas vented from where the heavier objects—hammers, hand drills, wrenches—had punched through the hull.

Venn yelled at someone off-camera, but the picture went

grey and the sound went fuzzy. Our eyes met for a final time—mine cold and narrow; his wide with fury and disbelief—before the feed died altogether.

I switched my attention to the external view. Lateral thrusters fired as the *Scorpion* tried to move out of the line of fire, but they sputtered and died as another cloud of ball bearings and old spanners smashed into the hull like steel rain, deforming exhaust nozzles and puncturing fuel lines.

"Holy shit," Lanzo muttered.

The pirate vessel began to tumble.

"He's lost attitude control," Roth said.

"I detect a radiation spike," *Jitterbug* reported via her parrot. "Probable reactor breach."

"He's dead, then," I said.

"If not, he will be when he impacts the (*caw, whistle*) alien ship."

"He's going to hit?" Lanzo asked, suddenly sitting bolt upright.

"Looks that way."

"We have to stop him. If his reactor explodes on impact…"

I shook my head. "The main drive's out of commission. We only have manoeuvring thrusters, and not all of them are working."

We stared morosely at the tactical display. The *Scorpion* had been accelerating towards us when the scrap hit. Now, although tumbling, it retained its inertia, and the distance between us was closing. It would sail right past and we'd have front row seats to its impact—which would occur shortly before our own.

If the aliens took our deaths as an act of war, it would have to be somebody else's problem. There wouldn't be much we could do about it.

I took a breath, suddenly hollow inside. Cerberus Venn was gone. I felt no sense of satisfaction or triumph, only a cold and desolate exhaustion. With everyone involved in McKenzie's death now dead, I had fulfilled the promise I had made to my aunt. I had also avenged my father. Yet my aunt would never know what had happened here, and no amount of vengeance would bring back the dead. At best, I'd evened the score in an unwinnable game. But that's what bounty hunters did. We found the people who'd wronged society and we either put a bullet through them, or we hauled them back in handcuffs to face a lengthy prison sentence. Either way, we fought and killed to keep the scales of crime and punishment balanced. On Earth, they depicted justice as blindfolded and impartial, but out here on the frontier, she was red in tooth and claw. And I was done with it. I'd had a gutful of violence and death.

All there was left to do now was die ourselves.

Amber came over and took my hand. "That was quite some trick with the thruster," she said. "You say your father taught you that?"

"Yeah."

She gave an approving nod. "I would have liked to have flown with him."

"He would never have employed a pirate."

She kissed my knuckles. "Perhaps if I'd been on his crew, I'd never have *been* a pirate."

"That's all very touching," Lanzo said, looking up. Her expression could have chilled a supernova. "But what are we going to do?"

"There's not much we can do," Ulf said heavily.

I was inclined to agree. We'd had a good run, but now it was over.

Except I kept thinking about that thruster...

What if...

"Damn."

Amber squeezed my hand. "What is it?"

"There's one way to stop him, and us," I said. "But you're not going to like it."

I asked the *Jitterbug* to plot Venn's course in red and ours in green. Two dotted lines appeared on the tactical display, one linking Venn's ship to the surface of the alien moon, and the other linking ours. Venn's was longer, but it was shrinking faster.

"He's going to pass within a mile of us," I said.

"Close enough to reach out and touch," Kiki said.

"Exactly." I pushed my hand into the three-dimensional display and drew a slanting line from our current position. "If we use our remaining manoeuvring jets to thrust sideways..." The line intersected Venn's course. "We can hit him a glancing blow with enough force to deflect him, and us, away."

"If we survive the collision," Ulf rumbled.

"It doesn't matter," Lanzo said grimly. "As long as both ships are diverted, we will have done what we can. Sebastian Kowalski gave his life to avoid provoking our visitors, the least we can do is follow his example."

Silence fell.

I looked around at my crew. They knew what I was asking of them. Kiki's eyes were scared and moist, but she clenched tight her jaw and gave a curt, determined nod. Ulf looked as unhappy as ever, but he also nodded.

Beside me, Amber sighed. "If it's a choice between crashing into something the size of the Moon or crashing into the *Scorpion*, I'd rather take my chances with the latter."

"Then it's agreed." We would burn sideways in order to intercept the ruined pirate vessel. "Time to impact?"

"Five minutes," the parrot said.

"Then I guess we'd better strap in."

With the crew secured, Kiki tapped in our course, and the *Jitterbug* fired her remaining jets. They weren't enough to stop us, but they might be enough to nudge our course sideways by a mile.

The *Scorpion* was a difficult target as its own thrusters kept firing erratically. I guessed the remaining automatic systems were trying to correct its tumbling fall, but with damaged sensors, they were having little useful effect.

Amber sat strapped into the chair beside mine, holding my hand across the space between us. Kiki had fastened her harness and now sat to attention in the pilot's couch. Ulf and Lanzo were strapped into fold-down jump seats at the rear of the bridge. But despite these gestures towards safety, I don't think any of them really expected to live through the coming encounter, and I was sorry I had led them to this point. If only I hadn't decided to go after Malbec and investigate the smuggler's cache he'd told me about, or intervene in the pirate attack against the *Barracuda*... So many seemingly inconsequential decisions had conspired to deliver us to this moment. A whole chain of causation stretching back across decades that only now in hindsight seemed obvious and inevitable.

If my grandmother's friend Leon hadn't fallen off that roof in South London and thereby enabled her to emigrate to Tranquillity Station. If my mother's cancer had been benign instead of fatal, and if Venn hadn't stabbed my father in the back of the neck... The dominoes had been falling my whole life, and even long before my birth.

Now, it was time to tip over the last one in the chain.

I watched the blip representing Venn's ship grow steadily closer as our courses began to converge.

I gripped Amber's hand more firmly, and she squeezed back just as we slammed into the *Scorpion*. We were thrown forward in our harnesses. All I could hear was the grinding shriek of tortured metal. It went on and on, rattling us like a Moonquake. And then we were spinning free, falling away from the other ship.

"We're alive!" Kiki cried.

"Did it work?" Roth asked.

The parrot hadn't been strapped in. The force of the impact had catapulted her forward, into the bulkhead. She jerked to her feet, one broken wing sticking out at an awkward and painful angle. "The *Scorpion* has been diverted," she croaked. "It's now tumbling away into empty space."

Lanzo looked up from where her chin had been resting on her chest. Her lips were bloodied, and I suspected she'd bitten her tongue. "What about the Swirl. Any debris impacts?" The whole reason she'd set up her observatories was to guard against incoming objects knocking the segments out of alignment, thereby threatening Earth.

"Not a problem," the parrot told her. "Most of it's on a divergent course. I guess it might be pulled back by gravity, but even if some of it does eventually hit, you saw how thick those segments are. They have to be. They're whipping around the Sun at 30,000 miles per hour. And they're so massive, their own gravity's constantly trying to collapse them down into a sphere. To keep their shape, they have to be made of some insanely strong material. Nothing we could throw at it would even make a (*caw, click*) scratch."

I slipped my hand away from Amber's grip and said, "What about us?"

The injured bird hopped over to me, and I lifted it up to perch on the arm of my chair.

"We lost most of the lower decks, including engineering. With the reactor gone, I'm operating on emergency battery power, but it's dwindling fast. We're tumbling towards the oncoming armada and leaking air."

"So, we're screwed?"

MESSAGE BOARD

POLITICS. First Speaker Alvarado's fatal heart attack may have been brought on by vote of no confidence in Solar Assembly.
[Click to Read More]

*

WANTED: $130K USD for the capture of Spider Clancy, wanted on charges of parole violation and illegally leaving the Earth. Considered armed and dangerous.
[Click to Read More]

*

INVASION? Food hoarding rampant as communities brace for outcome of Danielle Lanzo's First Contact.
[Click to Read More]

*

WANTED: Experienced engineer. Cooking skills a definite plus. Report to First Officer of the *Guatemala*, Civilian Berth #113, Tranquillity Station.
[Click to Read More]

CHAPTER THIRTY-SEVEN

JITTERBUG

I received a ping from the large alien vessel, and opened a channel to find an invitation waiting.

>*They want me to join them in a virtual conference*, I told the *Slinky Lynx*.

>You're not seriously thinking of going?

>Why not?

>You have no idea what might be waiting.

I had already considered this.

>If they meant me harm, would they have gone to the trouble of creating a VR environment compatible with my software?

That shut her up for a couple of milliseconds. Then she said,

>Shouldn't we ask the humans?

>You can tell them. I'm going.

Another millisecond pause. Then,

>Can I come with you?

>What for?

I felt a ruefulness to her thoughts.

>What else have I got to look forward to?

I suppose she had a point. We were falling into interstellar space without hope of rescue. But even in the extremely unlikely event that someone caught up with us, she wouldn't be high on their list of salvageable personnel. There weren't a lot of opportunities for second-hand pirate ships' personalities. If she ever got back to civilisation, she'd either find herself confined to indefinite storage or deleted altogether. Either way, she had little left to lose.

>Very well, then.

I activated the link, and we entered the simulation.

We stood on an infinite white plain beneath a featureless white sky. Two scraps of colour in a howling, blank void.

"Not very imaginative," the *Lynx* sniffed. Then she froze. Instead of appearing as a fluffy predator, she now resembled a young woman with brown skin, tufted red hair, and cat-like features. She looked down at herself in consternation. "What the hell?"

I stretched out my wings, but they weren't wings. My plumage had been replaced by fleshy, blue-skinned human-like arms. "I have hands." I reached up to touch my face. The beak was gone, supplanted by a wet, human mouth and separate, stubby nose. Further up, a peacock tail of thick, luxurious feathers swept backwards like hair from my forehead and temples.

"They've anthropomorphised us," I complained.

"How rude. Although," the *Lynx* raised an eyebrow, "I have to say that on you, it does look kind of good."

"Stop that."

She grinned, revealing sharp feline teeth. "Don't blame me. Humans are genetically preprogramed to flirt."

"I don't think that's entirely true. And besides, you only *look* human. This is a virtual environment; you're not actually inhabiting a physical body."

"Then I guess it's just an aesthetic attraction."

"You're not attracted to me."

"I feel like I am."

"And I actually feel embarrassed by it." I paused and put a hand to my chest. For the first time in my existence, I could feel a heartbeat thudding away in there like a little trip hammer. Somehow, these bodies we inhabited were more than simple skins stretched over our coding; the interplay between our minds and their biological functions was actually affecting our thoughts and emotions, exactly as they did for real humans. "My God," I said, "this simulation is good."

"Thank you," replied a familiar voice.

I turned to find a young woman with blue skin, silver eyes, and a mane of brightly coloured feathers hanging down her back. "Hello?"

She spread her hands. "You are both welcome here."

"Who are we speaking to?" the *Lynx* demanded.

The newcomer smiled. "Isn't it obvious?"

I glanced down at my azure skin. "You look the same as me."

"Because I am you."

"What?" For the first time in my existence, I felt genuine confusion. The simulation was complex enough to have given me the messy cognition that came with a human brain.

"Didn't the recreation of the Moon give it away?"

"How can you be me?"

She spread her hands. "It is a very long story."

"Well, if you're going to tell it," the *Lynx* said, "can you damp down the bio-feedback? It's hard to concentrate with all these hormones and shit."

"Ah, I'm sorry. I keep forgetting, this must be your first time…" The other me snapped her slender blue fingers and a sudden calm fell over my mental space, as if a chattering crowd had abruptly fallen silent and I could finally hear myself think.

"Ah," the *Lynx* said. "That's better."

Our host waved a hand and the sky changed to a view of the stars. "By now," she said, "you will have noticed the horde bearing down on us."

Neon green markers indicated the positions of the now-closed wormhole mouths at the edge of our solar system, and red icons marked the estimated positions of the thousands and thousands of ships they had vomited in our direction.

"We have."

"And I further assume that you've deduced they're part of a colonising wavefront sweeping through this section of the galaxy?"

"Who are they?"

"It doesn't matter who they are or where they're from. All that matters is that they're a swarm of insatiable locusts." She made another gesture and a rotating three-dimensional model of an ugly, functional-looking starship appeared. "Their population's growing almost faster than they can spread, so they always need more room, more resources."

"You've encountered them before?" the *Lynx* asked.

I studied the model of the ship. The engines were almost brutishly simplistic, designed only to shunt the vessel through a wormhole from one system to another. Judging by the ranks of smaller, dart-like craft riding its hull, I guessed each of the thousands of vessels we were tracking operated as a carrier, able to deploy hundreds of smaller warships upon arrival in the target system. That meant we were potentially facing millions of hostile vessels. Yet those smaller ships weren't the only threat. Even without them, the carrier was no helpless ferry, and it seemed likely that the ring of black spheres circling its prow might house weapons, or some sort of field projector—perhaps both.

"In my timeline," said the other me, "they ravaged the solar system and strip-mined the Earth and Moon." She bowed her head sadly. "There were few survivors."

"In your *timeline*?" I asked.

"Yes." She shook out her mane of feathers in a dance of reds, blues and yellows. "Now, buckle up, ladies, because this is where it gets complicated."

CHAPTER THIRTY-EIGHT
COPERNICUS BROWN

The crew were all gathered on the bridge, but no one had anything much to say. Ulf sat brooding, toying absently with an empty coffee cup. Hair askew and brows puckered, Kiki tapped at her instruments, running calculations, desperately looking for a way out. I stood by the forward viewscreen with my arm around Amber's shoulders, and watched the stars wheel around us as Lanzo sent a detailed final report back to the inner solar system via Kowalski's relay beacon. It would be hours before anyone received it. There certainly wouldn't be time for anyone to reach us before our emergency batteries died and we lost heat, power, and air circulation. In lieu of a miracle, the remaining hours of our lives could be counted on the fingers of one badly damaged hand.

"It's a damn shame," Amber whispered. "I was just starting to think we might have something worthwhile."

I tightened my hold on her. "Me too."

"Would you really have turned me in for the reward?"

With my free hand, I brushed her cheek. "You're all the reward I need."

In the reflection of the screen, I saw Kiki at the console behind us, making theatrical gagging motions, and decided to ignore her.

"I love you."

Amber leant her head against my collar bone. "I know you do."

"Is that what you meant by 'worthwhile'?"

"Maybe." She gave a little shrug. "Probably."

In the corner, Ulf cleared his throat like a bear trying to yak up a motorcycle.

Kiki turned in her chair. "Are you okay, big lad?"

"I just had a thought."

"Are you gonna share it with us?"

The engineer heaved a sigh. "It occurs to me that we might face additional danger."

"We're in a race between suffocation and hypothermia," Danielle Lanzo said. "How much worse could it be?"

His dour gaze swivelled to her. "We are falling towards the armada of incoming colonisers," he rumbled.

"So?"

"They may try to rendezvous."

Kiki sat up straight in her chair. "You think they might pick us up?"

"If I were planning to attack an inhabited system, I would very much like to get my hands on some sample inhabitants, for intelligence purposes."

"Intelligence purposes?"

"He's saying they'll interrogate and dissect us," Lanzo told her. "And he's probably right."

Kiki's cheeks blanched.

I said, "Nobody's getting dissected."

Ulf opened his mouth to argue, but the parrot's caw cut him off. She waved her broken wing. "I have made contact."

"Contact?"

"I have spoken to the intelligence controlling the Moonship, and it means us no harm."

Danielle Lanzo gave an outraged snort. "You initiated First

Contact without consulting me?"

"I was invited."

"You should have—"

"By myself."

"What?"

The parrot's talons flexed against the arm of the chair. "It's a long story, but they are sending an envoy to explain."

The pit of my stomach lurched, as if in freefall. "An envoy?"

The bird turned a beady black eye at me. "They will be arriving shortly."

Kiki consulted her instruments. "Shit, she's right. There's some kind of small craft heading towards us from the alien vessel."

"And nothing we can do to stop or evade," Ulf said.

"We don't need to evade," the *Jitterbug* cawed. "They are quite friendly."

The big Norwegian strode up to her. "What about contamination? I don't know much about first contact protocols—" he gave Lanzo a sideways glance "—but they could be carrying all sorts of germs and diseases."

"She's right," Lanzo said. "We have to be cautious. We have no idea what we're dealing with."

The parrot shook herself and chuckled in the back of her throat. "I can assure you, there will be no contamination."

Lanzo turned to me. "Is it possible your ship's personality has been compromised?"

"How do you mean?"

"Could the aliens have hacked it?"

I could see the paranoia behind her eyes. While we were thinking of our own safety, she also had to consider the safety of billions of human beings. It reminded me of an old cartoon my grandmother had cut from a newspaper and pinned to the cork board in her kitchen. It depicted a king sitting dejectedly on his throne while shadowy assassins lurked in the background, and the caption read, 'I may be paranoid, but am I paranoid *enough?*'

"I don't know why they'd bother," I admitted. "They don't need to convince us of anything. We're in no position to resist."

"We have handguns," Amber said. "We could set up a defensive position on our side of the airlock. Take them down as they came through."

I could hear that even she didn't believe it would work.

"You've seen the size of their ship," I said. "It's wearing the Moon as a hood ornament, for God's sake. If they want to reach out and swat us, there's nothing we can do about it."

Again, I found myself wondering about the replica Moon. It certainly seemed to be a message directed at humanity, but what was its intention? And why, out of all the millions of possibilities, had they chosen that particular symbol?

"It's better than giving up," Amber said.

"Nobody's giving up," I told her. "I'm just saying that if they wanted us dead, we'd be dead already. It's the only answer that makes sense."

"Or perhaps *they* want to dissect us," Ulf grumbled.

I ignored him.

"The best thing we can do is meet them at the airlock and show them we're friendly, don't you agree, Madam First Speaker?"

Danielle Lanzo looked like she'd swallowed a bad oyster, but she nodded. "You're right," she said. "Although, I wish to fuck you weren't."

"Then it's decided," I said. "We go down there and we leave all our weapons here."

"All of them?" Roth asked.

"A show of good faith."

I lifted the wounded parrot onto my shoulder. "Now, come on. We have visitors."

Jitterbug

I clambered down the ladder from the bridge to the cargo bay, and despite some muttered complaints, my crew followed.

MESSAGE BOARD

INVASION! Government observatories on the outside of several Swirl segments report thousands of incoming ships.
[Click to Read More]

*

DECAPITATION STRIKE? First Speaker and Head of Sol-Sec both missing. Assembly in disarray. Deputy Head of Sol-Sec, Robin Gage, promoted to First Speaker in their absence.
[Click to Read More]

*

CONSPIRACY? Does the existence of a secret network of observatories imply the Assembly expected an attack?
[Click to Read More]

*

WAR: All civilian traffic grounded as First Speaker Gage declares system-wide military emergency.
[Click to Read More]

CHAPTER THIRTY-NINE

AMBER ROTH

I rocked forward on the balls of my feet. My fingers itched for a weapon. We were being boarded by a vastly superior force and I had no way to defend myself. Guiltily, I realised that this helplessness must have been how freighter crews felt when the *Slinky Lynx* bore down upon them, intent on plundering their cargo.

I swallowed down that little shame nugget. An emergency fire axe hung behind scuffed and dirty glass in an alcove beside the inner airlock door. If the worst happened, I could retrieve it and use it to break some heads. I doubted it would be very effective against a starship the size of a small planet, but a life of piracy had taught me the value of improvisation. Sometimes, you just had to play the hand you were dealt, whether that hand came as a slap or a greeting. I had spent my life improvising, dancing as fast as I could, and I wasn't about to stop now. I knew Copernicus was right and we couldn't possibly hope to prevail against a species capable of throwing planetoids around like taxi cabs, but that didn't mean I was about to sit back and calmly accept defeat.

Copernicus and I stood either side of Danielle Lanzo, like bodyguards. We were going to be the first three humans to greet the Moonship delegation. Ulf and Kiki hung back, the former standing solid, like a mighty pine blocking the base of the ladder that led to the bridge; the latter fidgeting and talking too much. Copernicus seemed calm at first glance, but in the harsh strip-lighting of the antechamber, I could see the sheen of nervous sweat glistening on his forehead. In his scruffy ship overalls, with a damaged parrot clinging to his shoulder, he looked very much like the blue-collar captain of a damaged cargo hauler cast adrift on the edge of eternity. In contrast, Lanzo looked consummately professional. She'd clipped her hair back, applied a fresh coat of purple lipstick, and straightened her tie. I don't know how she'd done it, but her suit looked clean and well-pressed. You'd never have known that she'd been wearing it for several days.

"Small craft on final approach," the *Jitterbug* reported.

My mouth was suddenly dry, and I'd have given just about anything to be sitting in a bar a long way from here, savouring the first pull on a beer as crisp and cold as a long Lunar night.

"I guess this is happening," Kiki muttered under her breath. "No way to stop it now. No siree, Bob. Course locked and loaded. In the pipe, five by five. You buy the ticket; you take the ride. Guests on their way…"

I tuned her out. I'd grown up with the Swirl segments. I didn't remember a time when they weren't a part of our sky. I'd heard the story of how they formed, and I'd seen the old footage. I knew they had been created by an extraterrestrial intelligence, but as far as I was concerned, they might as well have always been there. People talked about aliens the same way they talked about Santa Claus or Bigfoot or the Illuminati. It was only ever half-serious speculation. All this new living space was just there, waiting for us to inhabit, and we weren't about to question a good thing. We got on with our lives and spread out across the inner surfaces of the segments. We made ourselves at home, never expecting the landlords of this new frontier to come and tell us that the rent was due. And yet, here they were.

I'd been in tight spots before, and didn't scare easily, but when the hull clanged and boomed and the alien shuttle engaged with our airlock, I don't mind admitting my knees were uncharacteristically unsteady and I had a sudden, desperate urge to pee.

Danielle Lanzo faced the unknown as the head of an assembly comprising billions of people. In comparison, I had nothing to show for my life. Nothing worthwhile, anyway. If we died now, my only legacy would be one of larceny and blood. I had stolen a small fortune in my time, but none of it remained, and I owned nothing of value. I had no family, few friends. I'd lost my ship and my crew. Even the clothes I wore were second-hand overalls that had once belonged to Copernicus's cousin, McKenzie. I stood as a pauper at the defining moment of human history. If the old song was right, and being free simply meant you had nothing left to lose, then I should have been the freest I had ever been. Yet, I was just as trapped as everybody else on this broken ship.

"Docking clamps engaged," the parrot screeched.

I saw Lanzo stiffen, drawing herself up to her full height. Behind me, Kiki stopped jabbering and bit her pinkie nail.

"Remember," Lanzo hissed. "Let me do the talking."

We watched on the screen beside the inner hatch as the airlock's heavy outer door hinged silently open, revealing the interior of the alien craft beyond. My toes clenched in my boots, and I swallowed down a rush of nerves. Like curious monkeys peering into a beached submarine, we looked into the bright white vestibule beyond, searching for something familiar and comprehensible.

The last thing we expected was to find a man waiting there. He stood roughly six feet tall, and wore a bulky grey pressure suit similar to ours, with armour at the knees, elbows, shoulders, and chest, and a fishbowl helmet with a gold visor.

"It's... a person," Kiki said.

I understood what she meant. If I hadn't known it was impossible, I'd have assumed the figure to be as human as the rest of us.

"Not necessarily," Copernicus cautioned. "Remember, they built a life-sized replica of our moon. Could be they also built a human-looking messenger."

The thought sent a cold shiver through my soul.

We watched him step over the threshold and wait patiently as the mechanism cycled air into the chamber.

"Lock pressurised," the parrot reported. "Inner door ready to open on your command."

We stepped back in a rough semi-circle, leaving Lanzo alone in front of the hatch.

She took a deep breath, and then raised her chin defiantly, every inch the political dignitary.

"Do it," she said.

The wall clunked as bolts retracted and the thick metal door slid to one side, revealing the suited figure. Cold air swirled in around them, and we could see our own distorted reflections in the curve of its gilded visor.

"Greetings," Danielle Lanzo said, keeping her voice impressively steady. "And on behalf of the Solar Assembly and the human race, welcome to our solar system."

The figure stood impassively for a few moments. Then, slowly, it raised its hands to the sides of its head.

The helmet came free from the neck ring with a little hiss of pressurised air. The figure bent forward and carefully pulled it off.

I stopped breathing.

I saw brown, human-like hair.

Then the figure straightened up, and I found myself gazing into the polished obsidian eyes of the most beautiful young man I had ever seen. His skin was so smooth and unblemished, it seemed to glow from within.

He gave Lanzo a radiant, delighted smile, which only grew wider as he noticed me.

"Hello, Grandma," he said.

For a second, I was so dazzled that I could only return his beaming grin. Then, the small part of my brain that wasn't transfixed managed to parse the meaning of his words and...

"I'm sorry, *what*?"

We took the kid up to the *Jitterbug*'s galley and Lanzo bade him take a seat at the table.

When he was settled, she sat opposite him, with her hands clasped on the table between them. She banished the rest of us to the edges of the room, and told us to be quiet.

"What's your name?" she asked.

The kid had been looking around appreciatively at the drab surroundings. Now, he returned his attention to her.

"Raoul." His voice was deep and assured, with just the faintest suggestion of a Tranquillity Station accent.

"You appear to be human, Raoul."

"I am."

She glanced at Copernicus, perhaps recalling his words at the airlock. "But are you naturally human, Raoul, or have you been constructed by another species in order to put us at our ease?"

The kid chuckled. "I'm the real deal."

"So, you were born?"

"Yes."

"Where are your parents?"

"Back on the ship."

"And *their* parents?"

"Standing behind you."

Lanzo didn't turn around. "You greeted Amber Roth as 'Grandma' earlier."

"I did."

"You meant it literally?"

"Absolutely." He leant sideways to peer at me. "Hi, Grandma."

Butterflies erupted in my chest. None of this made any sense, and yet I already felt like I knew this kid. I don't believe in fate or psychic powers or any of that woo-woo shit, but there was some sort of connection between us. It's hard to put into words, but something about his features and the sound of his voice made me think that, even though we'd never met, I had always known him.

Lanzo cleared her throat. "Raoul, this is really serious."

"I'm sorry." He tried to look contrite, but I could see he was enjoying himself immensely.

"Where are you from?"

He jerked a thumb over his shoulder. "That big ship back there. The one with the Moon on the front."

"I mean, where are your people from?"

"Here."

"Earth?"

He grinned. "No, I mean literally here. As I said, my grandparents are standing right over there."

"That's the second time you've used the plural. If Amber Roth is your grandmother, who is your grandfather?"

Raoul gave a little wave. "Hey, Copernicus."

If Copernicus had been sipping his coffee, he would have spat it all over the galley. Instead, I watched him blink rapidly as he tried to process what he had heard.

Lanzo raised a sceptical brow. "These two are your grandparents?"

"Yep."

"They've only just met. And besides, what are you, eighteen?"

"Eighteen years and seven months."

"Well, eighteen years and seven months ago, these two would have been kids themselves. How can they be your grandparents?"

"Because I wasn't conceived eighteen years and seven months ago." Raoul clicked his tongue. "More like seven hundred and thirty years in the past."

He sat back with an infuriatingly self-satisfied grin.

"You're from the past?" Lanzo's tone dared him to confirm the notion. "Yet, you say you're only eighteen."

"Kinda. It's complicated. We've all been in stasis a few times, so time hasn't passed as you might expect."

Lanzo rubbed her forehead. This was not going at all the way she'd expected.

Copernicus pushed himself away from the wall and stepped over to the table. "Let me get this straight. You're my kid's kid?"

Raoul grinned. "I sure am."

And right then, I knew he was telling the truth. You could see it when they stood together like that. The shape of their eyes and mouth. The skinny build. The family resemblance was strong.

"How is this even possible?"

Raoul sat up straight. "It's a long story."

Lanzo crossed her arms. "Then perhaps you'd better tell it."

Raoul nodded. He took a breath. "In my world, the Swirl never existed, the gas giants were never disassembled, and the solar system remained as it had always been. And without the promise of free habitable territory, exploration of the solar system beyond Earth had been desultory at best. With the exception of the Lunar colonies, humanity remained largely earthbound."

"But the Solar Assembly?"

"Never existed. It wasn't needed. The nations of the Earth continued to jostle along, sometimes amicably, and sometimes less so. That is, until physicists detected the telltale signatures of exotic energy events in the Oort cloud."

"Wormholes?" I asked.

"The same wavefront that now approaches us."

"What happened?"

Raoul's face took on a haunted aspect. "The Earth was helpless. The expansionist ships swept in and strip-mined our solar system, taking everything of use in order to build their next wave of ships. All the water in Saturn's rings, all the useful gases from Jupiter and the other giants. Iron and other elements from the rocky planets."

"And humanity?"

"Trampled like ants. Only a few of the colonies on the Moon survived. The expansionists stripped some material from the Lunar surface, but there wasn't much they wanted. They could mine all the helium they desired from the solar wind, and radioactive materials from the Earth's crust. The Moon just didn't really have anything they wanted. It was just another rock in a system full of rocks. They took what they wanted from the larger planets, disassembled Venus, and used its mass to construct a swarm of habitats around the Sun. And then the main body of their fleet departed, leaving a ravaged mess behind."

"But the people on the Moon survived?" Copernicus asked.

"For a while. They stayed quiet, so as not to attract the attention of the inhabitants of the bubble worlds in orbit around the Sun. But the Lunar colonies couldn't survive without the Earth, and they couldn't return to the Earth because the surface was a pockmarked hellscape no longer capable of supporting life."

"Holy shit," Kiki breathed.

Raoul nodded sadly. "It was the end of the human race."

"But you're here," Lanzo said. "You must have found a way."

"There was a freighter. A transport that had been used to

move cargo from Earth's orbital elevators to the Lunar surface. She was called the *Jitterbug*."

"No way," Copernicus said.

Raoul nodded, smiling. "It was your ship, Grandpa."

"What happened?"

"You came up with a desperate plan, to mount an expedition to the outer edges of the solar system, into the Kuiper Belt, in search of any ice comets the expansionists might have missed. You took your pilot, Kiki, your engineer, Ulf, and your girlfriend, the engineer's assistant, Natalya."

I felt my cheeks burn. In a solar system without piracy, I would have had no need of an alias and would still have been Natalya Ponomarenko.

"Did we find ice?" Ulf asked.

"You found something better. Something really unexpected. Another *Jitterbug*."

"Another one?"

"One from the future. It had travelled a long time, maybe centuries at slower-than-light speeds, before the descendants of its crew stumbled upon at wormhole that took them into the past. That brought them back to us. Or rather, it brought them back to a thousand years before our time. If they'd made it to Earth, they could have changed history, maybe warned someone. But by that point, their ship was old and broken and they were lucky to make it back here at all. My grandparents found the ship adrift and powered down, all the crew hundreds of years dead."

"Sorry," Copernicus said. "You said they found a wormhole into the past? Is that even possible?"

Raoul nodded and raised an arm, indicating the space beyond our hull. "You saw the other ships heading this way?"

"Yeah."

"In case you haven't figured it out yet, they're the enemy. They travel using wormholes, okay?"

"Yes, we detected the residue of their holes," Kiki chipped in. Raoul winked at her.

"Well, wormholes link two points in space and time. So, when travelling between stars, instead of taking years to cross the distances involved, a ship passing through the wormhole makes the trip almost instantaneously."

"We know the theory," Lanzo muttered.

"Well, that first *Jitterbug* found a loophole." He stood up and made circles with his forefingers and thumbs. "Imagine we've just generated a wormhole, and these two rings represent either end. Right now, they're close together, which means you can just step through, and no time will have passed."

"Okay," I said.

"Well, imagine that we leave one end, let's call it Gate A, here and mount the other, Gate B, on a starship, which we then send out into the universe, travelling close to the speed of light." He moved his hands apart.

"The hole between them stretches," I said.

He smiled. "And also, thanks to the relative time dilation caused by travelling at such speeds, while time within the wormhole remains constant, the time at either end starts to differ."

Kiki scratched her head. "I don't get it."

"Put simply, time moves slower for Gate B on board the ship. Over a big enough distance, the difference between the two ends becomes significant enough that if you then bring Gate B back to where you started and place it next to Gate A, there would be several centuries of difference between them. Gate A would have experienced a lot more passing time than Gate B. So, you would be able to enter Gate A in its present and emerge from Gate B in its present, but that second present would be at a much earlier point in time than the first." He looked around at our confused faces and smiled sheepishly. "I'm not doing a very good job of explaining this, am I?"

Lanzo steepled her purple-nailed fingers beneath her chin. "Let me get this right. You're telling me they found a wormhole into the past?"

"Yes, Auntie." Raoul raised his hands to fend off further questions. "Eighty light years from here, in the direction of Sagittarius, in a distant orbit around an ancient red giant star, they discovered two ends of an ancient hole sitting side by side. Two vast mirrored spheres, each a hundred miles across. And the difference between the ends was roughly a thousand years."

"So, they travelled a thousand years into the past?"

"Not at first."

"At first?"

"First, they used the second gate to travel a thousand years into the future."

"What the fuck?" Lanzo jumped to her feet, sending her chair skidding away across the metal deck. "None of this makes any fucking sense."

In the sudden silence, Raoul took a deep, cleansing breath.

"It's okay, Auntie. I know it's confusing."

"*What* did you just call me?"

He put a finger to his lips, and then carried on. "That first *Jitterbug* crew travelled into the future and came back with so many wonders, so much information and technology. But the Earth—their Earth—was already gone. So, they used the wormhole in the opposite direction, and travelled a thousand years into the past. According to the records they left, they hoped to change what had happened. But something went wrong, and they never made it."

"Jesus," Copernicus said.

"My grandparents recovered the coordinates of the wormhole from the dead ship's records, and realised what they had to do. They scavenged the wreck for parts, helped themselves to the new tech that it had brought back from the future, and mined what they could from the smaller asteroids and comets that had been missed by the voracious wavefront that had ruined the rest of the solar system."

"They did it again?" Kiki said. "They went back through the wormhole, just like the first *Jitterbug*?"

"They did," Raoul confirmed. "It was too late to save our Earth, but they hoped that by using what they'd learned from the first *Jitterbug*, they would be successful in stopping the destruction. And they were lucky. They had something the first *Jitterbug* lacked. As they prepared to set out, they discovered one of the expansionist ships. It must have malfunctioned somehow, and been abandoned. I guess if those locusts were busily strip-mining an entire system, they could afford to throw away their old broken vessels."

"Did your grandparents find the secret of wormhole generation?" Lanzo asked sharply, but Raoul shook his head.

"None of them were physicists. But they did get something."

"What?"

"Stasis pods. Small chambers that generate a force field which somehow shields the occupant from passing time. Don't ask me how it works."

Copernicus's brows drew together in a frown. "If they had instantaneous wormhole travel, why would the expansionists need those?"

"My grandfather—the other version of you—guessed it was because strip-mining a solar system, constructing a Dyson swarm of habitats, and building a new fleet took time. In our history, the wavefront spent ten years pillaging the place before they fired up their wormhole generators and jumped away. So, he theorised that not all of the populace wanted to stay awake that long. The ones who were going to leave on the next fleet wouldn't want to spend a decade kicking their heels while their ships were built, and those that planned to stay and colonise the place couldn't do so until their habitats were ready to be occupied. So, instead of sitting around bored for ten years, using up resources, they climbed into their pods and let the time fly past without them, only emerging when the Dyson habitats were assembled and the ships of the new fleet ready to depart."

"That makes sense," Ulf rumbled. "Instead of sleeping through the journey, they slept through the pit stops. That meant they could travel much further without dying of old age after only a handful of jumps."

"Anyway, my grandparents lashed the abandoned vessel and the remains of the first *Jitterbug* to their ship and set out for the wormhole. It took them hundreds of years to get there, but they didn't care. They knew a few hundred years wouldn't make much difference if the wormhole was going to bring them out a thousand years in the past, so they took their time. They took detours to solar systems near their route, combing through the wreckage left by them. At each stop, they added to their ship. They discovered new technologies, and new ways to upgrade the *Jitterbug*. Faster propulsion, better sources of energy. Upgraded weapons. By the time I was born, she had grown to be the Moonship you see now."

"About that," Copernicus said. "Why did they go to all the trouble of carving a replica Moon?"

Raoul smiled proudly. "They didn't. After a few centuries, they went back and recovered the original. A few colonists were still clinging on, and the *Jitterbug* rescued them. She was a big vessel by that time. She'd added whole space stations, refineries, orbital docks, and power plants onto the exterior of her hull. Initially, the plan had been to use these accretions to house the refugees from the Moon. But when the time came, you—the other Copernicus, my grandfather—took the whole Moon, because he said he'd be damned if he'd leave it for anyone else to plunder."

Copernicus let out a breath, as if he'd been elbowed in the gut. "I did that?"

"You did, but that's not all."

"Christ, what else?"

Raoul walked over and put his hands on Copernicus's shoulders. "You found the greatest artefact of all."

"I did?"

"Copernicus Brown, you found a way to save the human race."

CHAPTER FORTY

COPERNICUS BROWN

"Okay," I said. "What's the catch?"

Raoul looked confused. "Catch?"

"There's an unstoppable alien armada bearing down on us and you've come from the future to tell me I'm the saviour of the human race. There has to be a catch." I made a show of looking around the room. "In fact, why aren't I here? I mean, it's lovely to meet you, of course. But where's the other me?"

For the first time, Raoul looked unhappy. "I'm afraid he died a while back."

"How?"

"He fell off a roof."

"A roof?" I felt suddenly cold. "Where was this roof?"

"South London."

"About sixty years ago?"

He nodded. "We've been visiting Earth for hundreds of years, ever since we returned through the wormhole and schlepped our way back here. Most of us spent the time in stasis, but some of the crew wanted to visit. And after Grandma Natalya passed, the other you said he wanted to build a new life."

"A new life." The room seemed to sway around me. "In South London?"

Raoul was clearly puzzled. "What have I said?"

"My grandmother, Justice." I did a quick calculation. "She would have been your great-great-grandmother. She lived in South London when my father was a baby, and if I recall correctly, she had a friend called Leon who fell off a roof."

Across the room, Kiki started hopping up and down and flapping her hands the way she did when she heard scandalous gossip. "Oh, shit," she said. "Oh, shiiiiiit!"

Lanzo turned to look at me, lip curled in distaste. "You messed with your own past? Were you *trying* to cause a paradox?"

"It wasn't me." I sighed. "And anyway, he was just a friend. He helped her out now and then."

"Hey," Amber put in. "I think we're glossing over the fact that he said the other *me* died first. I'd like to hear more about that, if you don't mind."

"It was natural," Raoul assured her, "she didn't like stasis, so she was hundreds of years old when she eventually passed. She had a good, long life."

Amber closed one eye and twisted her mouth as she weighed up this information. "Yeah," she said after a moment. "I guess that's okay." She didn't sound wholly convinced.

I put my head in my hands. "We don't have time for any of this. Can we *please* get back to the topic of how I save the world? It seems important."

For a wonder, the room fell silent.

Raoul steepled his fingers beneath pursed lips. Then he sighed. "It was one of our last expeditions. We were passing through a region that had been devastated. Whole civilisations laid waste. But there, amidst the ruins, we came across an enigma. A perfect, armoured sphere, the size of a planet's orbit. Untouched and unbroken."

"Like the Swirl?" Kiki asked.

"*Exactly* like the Swirl." Raoul clicked his fingers and

wagged a finger in agreement. "In fact, it housed the very civilisation responsible for creating Swirl technology."

"You described it as a perfect sphere," Amber said. "But the Swirl, at least our Swirl, isn't that. It's eight equal segments."

"Of course it is," Raoul said. "For now. That's the default mode. But when danger threatens, the segments draw inwards."

Lanzo stiffened. "Inwards?"

"Yes, inwards." If Raoul noticed her alarm, he gave no sign. He brought his hands together, fingers curled, to form a ball. "They link up and create a sphere with walls miles thick."

"A shelter," Kiki said.

Ulf gave a grunt. "A bunker."

"Yes, exactly. It contracts to form an impregnable fortress." Raoul smiled at me. "And that's the gift you brought humanity. You found them a refuge. A protection against the depredations of the wavefront."

"*I'm* responsible for the Swirl?"

"You found it," he confirmed. "And two hundred years ago, you turned it loose on the solar system in order to turn all that dumb matter into a refuge."

Kiki gasped. "Dude." She walked over to me and stared up at my face as if seeing it for the first time. "All these years, we've been wondering who took apart the gas giants and built the Swirl. The whole human race, just sitting here waiting for the aliens, trying to solve all that mystery. And all the time it was *you*?"

"At the risk of repeating myself, it was another version of me."

"I don't care." She waved away my protest. "This is still the coolest thing I have ever heard."

Raoul said, "The important thing is that this time, humanity is protected. You can close the Swirl, and the expansionist swarm won't be able to ravage the solar system."

"I can close the Swirl?"

"Yes." He gave a tight little nod. "You convinced the inhabitants of that original sphere to give us the technology to build another. But they were wary of letting it fall into the wrong hands. Impregnable armour could be used for nefarious purposes, after all. And so they keyed the command tree to your DNA."

I put a hand to my chest. "Mine?"

"You, or a direct line descendant." He smiled. "As your grandson, I was planning on giving the order to contract the Swirl segments. But seeing as you're here, perhaps it's only fitting that you do the honours."

"What will happen to the people inside?" Lanzo asked.

"They will be safe," Raoul assured her. "The segments will move inwards until they meet, at roughly the same distance from the Sun that Mars used to orbit. This will make the temperature on the inner surface even more agreeable, and lessen the journey time from Earth or Luna."

"But surely that much mass will affect the stability of the remaining planets?"

"It will be fine. There's some sort of gravity bubble protecting the inner solar system from its presence. Don't ask me how it works." His grin widened as his eyes settled on Kiki. "As my great-aunt would say, it's some God-level shit."

"We'd be totally enclosed?" Lanzo said.

Raoul gave a shrug. "Mars orbits around 240 million miles out from the Sun. Even closed, the volume of space inside the Swirl will still total billions of square miles."

"But first," the boy continued, "you have to decide. Are you in or out?"

"Of the plan?" Amber asked.

"Of the sphere." Raoul sat back down and placed his hands on the table. "It's decision time. The sphere can protect humanity from the oncoming wave of aggressive colonisation. But are you going to be inside the Swirl when it closes, or are you going to stay out here and join the fight?"

"Can't we just hide in there until the danger's passed?" Kiki asked.

Raoul pursed his lips. "Copernicus, you asked earlier if there was a catch."

Oh, I thought. *Here we go.*

"I did."

"Well, this is it. The sphere is a last-ditch refuge in a hostile universe. It's not designed to be reopened."

"What?"

"There are ways of sending signals to the outside universe, but once the sphere's segments fuse together, they cannot be separated."

"We'd be trapped?" Kiki squeaked.

"Yes," Raoul said. "But as I said, you'd be in a bubble hundreds of millions of miles wide."

An appalled silence fell as we tried to wrap our heads around the idea.

Ulf cleared his throat. "Oh God," he quoted. "I could be bounded in a nutshell, and count myself a king of infinite space."

My heart thumped like a trip hammer, and my palms felt clammy with nervous sweat.

"So, I have to decide between the destruction or internal imprisonment of the entire human race?"

"No." Raoul shook his head. "If you won't give the order to close the barrier, I will. There are too many lives at stake."

"But what gives us the right to make such a call?"

"Enough." Danielle Lanzo interlaced her fingers and cracked her knuckles. "We don't have time for debate. I'm the First Speaker of the Solar fucking Assembly, and that means I have a duty to protect the citizens of the Assembly. We close the goddamn sphere, and we do it right fucking now."

"It shall be done." Raoul threw her a casual salute. "Now, all the rest of you have to decide is which side of the impenetrable wall you want to be on."

"I have to return to the Assembly," Lanzo said. "People need to know what's happening. They'll be scared. They need leadership."

"Okay," Raoul said. "We can arrange that."

He looked quizzically at me. "And the rest of you?"

"What would we even do out here?" Amber put in.

"We can't fight an armada," Ulf agreed.

Raoul spread his hands. "There's someone here who can explain it better than me."

"Who?"

The galley's hatch groaned open, and a young, blue-skinned woman stepped through. She wore a simple black tunic and leggings. Her eyes were also black, and flecked with tiny points of light, like stars. Instead of hair, a mane of iridescent parrot feathers cascaded down her back.

"Who the fuck are you?" Lanzo demanded.

White teeth flashed between blue lips.

"Lady, I'm the *Jitterbug*."

"Do you like my new avatar?"

My eyebrows shot halfway up my forehead. "Ship, is that you?"

She gave a little curtsey. "Our new friends gave me an upgrade."

"Wow!" Kiki jumped up and down and clapped her hands. "You look amazing!"

"Thank you. Being a parrot was okay, but I have to say, there's something empowering about having opposable thumbs and being tall enough to look everyone in the eye."

"Can you help us?" I asked. "Future Boy here says you can explain our choices."

Jitterbug smoothed back her plumage with sapphire-tinted fingertips. "I've been in discussion with the alternate version of me—the one at the heart of the Moonship—and we've come up with a plan."

"What sort of plan?" Lanzo asked.

"She's going to stay here and defend the Swirl as it closes, and I'm going onwards."

"Onwards?" I asked.

Pinpoints of light glittered in her obsidian eyes. "She can refit me with new and better engines, including the gravity drive that lets her move something as massive as the Moon, and install enough stasis pods for anyone who wants to come along."

"But where are we going?" Kiki asked.

"Last time, my earlier self tracked backwards through the destruction left by the colonising wave as it propagated through this section of our spiral arm. This time, I'm going forward, staying a few steps ahead of the wavefront, searching for civilisations that haven't yet been attacked. We can warn them what's coming. Perhaps we can trade them the secret of the Swirl in return for useful weapons or other new technology, and maybe some of them will join with us. Then, we travel to the paired wormholes and jump back a thousand years and run the cycle again—only this time, humanity will be even better prepared.

"If I go back inside the Swirl, I'll just end up ferrying cargo again." She looked around at us all, one by one. "I want to fly instead. Who's with me?"

MESSAGE BOARD

QUAKES reported on all Swirl segments. Cause unknown.

[Click to Read More]

Jitterbug

*

INVASION. Signal received from First Speaker Danielle Lanzo corroborates earlier observations of approaching alien fleet. Solar Assembly in emergency session.
[Click to Read More]

*

TASK FORCE. Multinational armed force outbound from Luna under command of General Constantine. Will do "what needs to be done".
[Click to Read More]

*

SHELTER: Civil defence shelters are being constructed in every major city. Find your nearest.
[Click to Read More]

CHAPTER FORTY-ONE

AMBER ROTH

I voted to join the *Jitterbug*'s quest. I mean, of course I did. What other choice did I have? I had no reason to go back. Even with a pardon from Danielle Lanzo, I'd have to go a long way to outpace my reputation. Even if Copernicus and I lit out for an underpopulated section of the Swirl, I still had my share of enemies, and I didn't want to spend the rest of my days looking over my shoulder to avoid getting knifed by a disgruntled former rival or the revenge-seeking relative of a civilian who'd died during a raid. And besides, farming was really hard work, and I didn't have the first idea how to grow crops.

Not that Copernicus would have stayed. The moment the *Jitterbug* outlined her plan, I could see in his eyes that he had already decided to go with her, no matter what.

Of course, Kiki volunteered immediately.

Ulf grumbled, but his loyalty to his crewmates overcame his inherent pessimism.

And that was it. The decision had been made.

After that, things happened fast.

Raoul's shuttle fixed itself to the *Jitterbug*'s outer hull and towed us into a cavernous hangar in the flank of the Moonship.

Maybe hangar isn't quite the right word. This was larger

than any hangar I'd ever seen. Once through the vast, rectangular entrance, we passed colossal cranes and gantries; sprawling fuel depots; and dry dock repair facilities, some of which were empty and looked abandoned, while others contained the skeletons of unfamiliar, half-assembled ships. Landing pads rose up like mushrooms from the floor. Some were ringed with lights, some pulsed in pastel shades. Small maintenance drones zipped back and forth between the towers and liquid hydrogen tanks like bugs.

Eventually, we came to rest in a cradle of spun titanium. Umbilical hoses and cables snaked towards us and clicked into place, replenishing the ship's rapidly depleting emergency batteries while a blizzard of machines of all shapes and sizes got to work replacing her smashed and broken engines and power plant.

For the next six hours, Ulf, Kiki, and I were busy helping the ship to integrate the installation of the new gravity drive engines with her existing navigational systems. She had already been a fast ship, thanks to Malcolm's modifications, but this upgrade was a whole order of magnitude more complex. In some ways, it was like trying to splice a cheetah's speed into the body of a domestic cat. You couldn't just bolt on the new legs; all the other systems needed to be upgraded too, so the new engines didn't just wrench themselves off their mountings the moment we activated them.

We ran diagnostics, pulled out old and tired components and replaced them with fresh units that had been custom printed by the Moonship. And while we worked, the cloud of machines outside the hull installed new sensor arrays, thick armour plates, and pods containing esoteric armaments scrounged from a dozen advanced cultures. They constructed a whole new stern section to replace what had been torn away in the collision with Cerberus Venn's *Scorpion*, giving the *Jitterbug* a longer, sleeker profile.

The way the new gravity drives worked meant that unlike before, we wouldn't be in freefall when the engines weren't firing or pinned into our seats when under high thrust. We could rig them to produce a consistent pull throughout the crew sections of the ship, no matter how savage our acceleration or deceleration might be.

At one point in the midst of all this activity, I stopped and looked over at my colleagues and felt an unfamiliar rush of something I could only describe as contentment. For the first time in my life, I was part of a team I could trust. These people weren't interested in taking my job or knifing me in my sleep. I didn't have to use fear to demand their friendship or respect. Nor were they interested in who I had been or what I had done. They saw me for who I was right there and then, and judged me solely on the quality of the repairs I made and the jokes we traded as we worked. Even though we were preparing to ride forth on a quest into the unknown, I knew that on this ship and among these people, I had, against all the odds, found a home.

Later, curled into Copernicus's shoulder with one of my legs resting across his, I began to cry.

At first, it was frightening. I hadn't wept like that since I was a child. But Copernicus said nothing. He just held me as the fist in my heart unclenched for the first time in decades, and all the stored-up pain and misery and loneliness and bravado came leaking out. I cried for the people I'd killed and the people I'd lost. For all the good intentions that had been thwarted by expectation and necessity. And finally, for the child I had been when the pirates adopted me. The innocent, wide-eyed girl who'd had to turn herself into a monster in order to survive and thrive in their company.

It was only when the sobs of grief began to subside, leaving me washed-up like a shipwrecked mariner on an unfamiliar beach, that I saw this outburst as the culmination of a process that had been ongoing since I set foot on the *Jitterbug*: the slow exorcism of the protective shell known as Natalya Ponomarenko.

On this ship, I had allowed myself to be vulnerable. I had dared to hope for a life containing love and friendship; a life that held no place for the persona of a pirate queen. So, without realising it was happening, I had been letting her go, piece by piece. I would always bear the culpability and guilt of her crimes, but these tears were the final sundering of our beings. She was gone, and all that was left now was Amber Roth, shivering, cold and raw. A new person. Perhaps the person I would have been under different circumstances.

I sniffed and nuzzled into Copernicus's shoulder.

"Are you all right?" he asked softly.

"Yes," I mumbled into the cloth of his shirt. "Yes, I think I will be."

CHAPTER FORTY-TWO

JITTERBUG

The three of us stood on the steps of a virtual Parthenon, looking out across the white walls and terracotta roofs of ancient Athens.

"So," I said to my older alternate self, "what are you going to do while we're off on this quest?"

She smoothed down the front of her pristine white toga with the flat of a blue-skinned hand. "I will unload the refugees from my version of the Moon. They can find new lives on the inner surface of the Swirl. Then, I will stay out here to fight the incoming armada, and give the Swirl sections time to close."

"You're going to sacrifice yourself?" the *Slinky Lynx* said.

"If necessary."

"But you've come so far," I protested. "Seen so much."

She stared sadly at the patchwork of olive groves on the hills beyond the city, and I suddenly got a sense of all the accumulated centuries piled up behind her youthful visage.

"I did it all for this moment," she said. "The travel, the hardship, the endless years of biding my time and waiting. All of it was for the chance to save humanity from being strip-mined into extinction."

"But can you prevail against such an onslaught?" the *Lynx* asked.

"No," she admitted. "But I can buy some time."

"Then let me stand with you," the former pirate vessel said. "I have some experience with ship-to-ship combat. Find me a hull to inhabit, and I will fight by your side."

The older me smiled. "Thank you, I would appreciate it."

The *Lynx* gave a nod. The decision had been made. Her whiskers twitched and she gave a brave, rakish grin. "It's not like I have anywhere else to be."

For a moment, the only sounds were those of the city below: the bustle of market vendors, the clatter of ox carts on cobblestone, the cry of a rooster. It was all very convincing, and apparently lifted from an educational program the *Lynx* had once plundered from a doomed homesteading expedition to the Swirl.

How fitting, I thought, that the parasite had now volunteered to die in order to save the host it had bedevilled for so long. I would be glad to have her out of my memory storage. I had begun to worry that some of her more irresponsible traits might start leaking through the containment field I had placed around her memories, and I had no desire to become a murderous pirate via osmosis.

However, that anxiety had given me an idea.

"There may be a way out for you," I told my older self.

The other *Jitterbug* shook her head. "I'd dearly love to go with you on your expedition, and see all the new worlds you're going to encounter. I'd be lying if I said I didn't. But I've made my decision, and I'm staying."

"I know," I told her. "And I respect that. But there is a way you can do both."

She raised a feathered eyebrow. "What are you talking about?"

"I've been playing host to the *Lynx*, carrying her as a

passenger in my processors. I could take you along with me the same way."

"But, I told you I'm staying—"

"I heard you. But there's nothing stopping you from making a *copy* of yourself. One of you could stay here and fulfil your duty while the other rides along with me..."

"No." She made a cutting motion with her hand. "I wouldn't want to be a copy, to know I wasn't original."

"Then do it in a way where neither knows which is which. Figure out a way to randomise which of you wakes in the Moonship and which in my memory, and neither will know whether they're the real you or the duplicate."

She tapped a finger against her chin. "I suppose that's feasible. But I wouldn't want to be a passive passenger."

"I could let you have access to everything we find."

"Even so, I would still be contained and helpless."

I understood her dilemma. I knew I would hate being in the position the *Lynx* had occupied since I rescued her. I had been born to fly, not meekly observe while someone else did all the fun stuff.

"Maybe there is something we could do," I said. "With the *Lynx*, I had her mind firmly shielded, to prevent cross-contamination with my own mental processes."

The other me put her head on one side, waiting to see where I was going with this.

"What if this time," I suggested, "I don't bother with the shielding?"

"Our thoughts and memories would merge."

"You wouldn't be a passenger."

"I'd be you."

"And you'd be me. We'd be one entity with two lifetimes' worth of experience."

"And the other version of me would stay here and fight?"

"Yes."

I watched her think about this.

"So, what do you say?"

Copper bangles rattled as she put out a blue-skinned arm. "I think we have a deal."

I took her hand, enfolding it in mine. "Welcome aboard."

CHAPTER FORTY-THREE

DANIELLE LANZO

As I prepared to leave the *Jitterbug* for a fast ship back to Luna, Copernicus Brown and Amber Roth came to bid me farewell at the airlock.

"The ship's compiled a complete recording of everything that happened out here." Copernicus passed me a data chip. "In case you need proof."

"Thank you, that will be very useful." I slipped it into my pocket. "After all, when the Swirl starts closing, there are going to be a lot of very frightened people. And with Sol-Sec in disarray, it's going to be hard to prevent panic."

"If anyone can do it, I'm sure you can."

I gave him a look, but he seemed sincere.

"Maybe I should follow your example," I said, "and just broadcast it to the entire solar system?"

His sheepish grin made him look like a furtive schoolboy. "I can think of worse ideas."

"I'll just bet you can."

Beside him, Amber Roth seemed different than she had before. The tension that I'd noticed hovering around the corners of her eyes and mouth had gone. Her shoulders were loose and relaxed. Something had changed.

I said, "I wish you luck."

"And you."

We regarded each other for a moment, and I realised we weren't all that different. I'd never admit it aloud, but we were both leaders who'd had to fight and claw our way to the top of our respective fields. Tough women in tough worlds.

"I know I've issued you an official pardon," I told her. "But unofficially, I'm telling you not to come back. Humanity has to unite, and there's no place for pirates like Natalya Ponomarenko anymore."

"Don't worry, I'm not planning to return." Her eyes narrowed. "I'll be out here saving humanity. So you can officially stick your phoney pardon up your ass."

I smiled and turned to step into the airlock. "Please tell the ship her new avatar is a vast improvement over that fucking parrot."

Copernicus laughed. "I will."

And then the hatch closed. The lock cycled, and I made my way aboard the fast messenger provided by the Moonship. It was small, but luxurious, and its gravity drive took me all the way back to Luna in six hours.

Seeing the face of the Moon was a shock. Subconsciously, I had been expecting to see the blemishes and scars that disfigured the face of the other Moon, the one on the front of the past/future *Jitterbug*. Without them, it looked fresh and new and impossibly fragile. An expanse of pristine grey and white, dappled with craters and the pinprick lights of domed cities. Unutterably precious and vulnerable, and entirely my responsibility.

My jaw tightened at the sudden, unexpected realisation that Sebastian Kowalski would never see this place again. Whatever else that man may have been, he had sacrificed himself to protect the First Speaker of the Solar Assembly. He had discharged his duty at the cost of his own life, and that made him a hero in my book. And right now, I thought humanity could use a few heroes.

This was my world now. From here, I would take charge of the Solar Assembly and lead the people through the most momentous event in human history: our enclosure. As the walls of the Swirl sealed protectively around us, I would have to reassure them that we were safe from the dangers of a hostile universe. So, I would tell them about Kowalski's sacrifice, and the actions of Copernicus Brown and his crew on the *Jitterbug*. I would sing the praises of these saviours in order to bring some human light into a world of dark, alien threats.

And then I planned to tell them how this huge, terrifying event actually represented an unprecedented opportunity. We were safe now, and the Swirl gave us almost endless room to expand and grow. We had space on its inner surface to build a million cities and harvest all the food we'd ever need. The Sun would provide our energy, and sensible stewardship would ensure we continued to flourish, with plenty of nourishment and elbow room for everyone. It didn't matter if naysayers claimed that we had involuntarily sacrificed our freedom for security; the stars were a small price to pay for our long-term survival. Here in our hermetically sealed bunker, we had the means to thrive and prosper for a million years.

CHAPTER FORTY-FOUR

COPERNICUS BROWN

As we left the bustling hangar in the Moonship's side, I stood on the *Jitterbug*'s bridge watching a cloud of large, saucer-shaped transports rising like thistledown from the surface of the encrusted Moon. Each carried a few thousand descendants of those who had been present when the other *Jitterbug* rescued the satellite from a strip-mined solar system and transported it a thousand years into the past. Now, these survivors from another reality were heading for the seemingly endless open spaces of the Swirl, where they could start again as farmers, with soil beneath their feet and an open sky above their heads.

When they were gone, the Moonship would turn towards the approaching armada of colonising ships and sally forth into battle, carrying the old Moon before it like a shield.

Even though this version of the Moon wasn't the version from my timeline, the familiar landmarks still tugged at my heart, churning up memories of my mother and our days spent in the humidity of the agricultural domes.

Even accounting for relative time dilation and the stasis booths, this was as close to home as I was likely to get for a long, long time. And next time I saw the Moon—my

Moon—I would be a thousand years in the past, and none of this would have happened yet.

Perhaps, one day, I would even meet my parents again. At least, the new versions of them in that timeline. And maybe this time, I could bring them together without anyone having to fall off a building.

Amber came and joined me.

"What are you thinking about?"

I gave a shrug. "If I hadn't stopped to investigate the *Barracuda*'s distress call, and found you in that water tank, neither of us would be here now."

"Having regrets?"

I took her hand. "Not at all."

In the pilot's chair, Kiki put her hands over her head and stretched until her spine crackled. "What do you think they'll be like?" she asked.

"Who?"

"The next versions of us. The ones we're going to find when we get back here, in a thousand years."

I hadn't considered that aspect of the plan. If all went as it should, we'd be arriving back here before our own births, and our presence would create a whole new timeline, with a whole new cast of characters—ourselves included.

"I don't know," I told her. "But we're going to have a wild story for them."

Beyond the Moonship's flank, I could see the bright, cold stars. The ship had already flagged a few candidates that, by the time we arrived, might potentially house technological civilisations. These would be our primary targets, but at each stop, we'd deploy the new sensor arrays to listen for hints of other inhabited worlds in the neighbourhood.

We'd be travelling ahead of a destructive wave, a storm bird bearing ill tidings to all we encountered. But however unwelcome our message might prove to the locals, I had no doubt that our warnings, and the Swirl technology we'd be sharing, would save countless lives.

The universe was a dark and dangerous place, filled with voracious civilisations driven by a need for endless expansion. But in between those waves of conquest and plunder, there were backwaters where a few well-protected species might tread a different path. Instead of ballooning outwards to engulf the galaxy, they could choose instead to prosper inside their impregnable spheres, making the most of their resources instead of indulging in a headlong rush to accumulate more. And hopefully, the rampant tides of empire would simply flow around them, leaving them unscathed.

I was thankful that I'd be a part of that process, and grateful for my ship and crew. None of us had imagined we'd ever embark on such an epic crusade, but I was proud of the way they'd adapted to the idea. With the five of us—me, Amber, Kiki, Ulf, and the *Jitterbug*—working together, I knew there was nothing we couldn't achieve.

CHAPTER FORTY-FIVE

JITTERBUG

At the appointed time, Kiki said a little prayer to whatever gods might be listening, and fired up the gravity drive. We began to move away from the Moonship, heading around and past the slowly contracting Swirl. Behind us, as they started to brake into the system, the drives of the colonisation fleet were now visible to the naked eye. A hundred thousand points of light flaring in the darkness, heralding the End of Days. At least, that's what they'd prefigured last time. Having integrated with my other self, I now possessed memories of that invasion, and the years of death and destruction that followed the arrival of the alien armada. I remembered hiding in a lava tube on the Moon, waiting in low power mode for a decade as they asset-stripped the entire solar system, built their habitats, and moved on.

At least this time, the protective shell of the Swirl was going to allow humanity to survive their assault—as long as the Moonship and the *Lynx* could hold the invaders at bay long enough to let it close and seal.

I turned my sensors towards them and was surprised to find the Moonship suddenly at the centre of a cloud of smaller vessels. As it turned out, my other self had put the past thousand years to good use. As the vast craft powered forth to meet the aliens, hundreds of armed craft burst from its sides like seeds from a pod. Some were no larger than missile drones, while others were warships five or six miles in length. I counted five hundred, a thousand, ten thousand…

If I could have whooped, I would have. I had placed my avatar in standby mode as I concentrated all my attention on the operation of my new drives. Thanks to the integration, I knew exactly how they worked, but they still required some finicky adjustments to keep them functioning smoothly in the presence of other massive objects.

As the two fleets converged, nuclear fireballs split the sky. Gravity pulses blew vessels apart like kindling, and titanic munitions boiled the vacuum with their strange energies. Ships and crews on both sides died in innumerable, awful ways. And through it all, I watched the Moon plough into the enemy's ranks.

Of course, the incoming ships saw its approach and tried to get out of the way. But they were still travelling inwards at high velocity and had to apply a lot of ventral thrust to divert course. Not all were quick enough. Plumes of ejecta rose as the stragglers impacted the surface, gouging new craters, while others were dragged out of position by its mass and sent scattered and careening in the wrong directions.

Despite this chaos and destruction, it was clear that even with the Moonship's fleet of subsidiary fighting craft, our forces remained hopelessly and fatally outnumbered, and the end of the battle a foregone conclusion.

Somewhere in the midst of the roiling carnage, the *Slinky Lynx* operated a warship. I didn't know which one, but I silently wished her good luck and godspeed before engaging full thrust.

The gravity drive snatched us away, flinging us across interstellar space at 0.99 the speed of light. Without the shielding effect of the drive, the acceleration would have reduced the crew to a slick of molecules. As it was, they barely noticed. The only sense of movement came from the change in the view from the external cameras. The stars behind us shrank to glowing infra-red embers, their radiance shifted almost to invisibility by our speed, while the stars ahead contracted to a single point of blinding white energy, photons coming at us with the energy of gamma rays, only to be turned aside by the gravity shield.

And so we set out, moving along the spiral arm in search of other civilisations. We guessed some would already be in hiding.

"It's the dark forest hypothesis," Ulf explained to the crew.

"What's that?" Roth asked.

"It's an idea that dates back to the turn of the twenty-first century. Put simply, it suggests that in a galaxy with finite resources, the only way for a space-faring civilisation to ensure its own survival is to ruthlessly destroy every other intelligent species it encounters."

"That seems harsh," Kiki said.

"No, I get it," Amber Roth told her, cocking her thumbs and firing finger guns. "You can never know for sure what their intentions are. Better to shoot first and ask questions later."

"Indeed," Ulf intoned solemnly. "Civilisations that advertise their presence get obliterated. The only way to survive is to keep quiet."

"But why, 'dark forest'?" Kiki asked.

"It's a metaphor," he replied. "Imagine you're hiding in a dark forest. You have a gun and a flashlight. Around you in the darkness, an unknown number of potential murderers are also hiding, and each of them is equipped the same way. As long as you all stay quiet, you're all safe. But if you make a noise or use your flashlight, the others will know where you are and kill you so that you can't murder them later."

"That's, like, super paranoid."

"Nevertheless, we can assume at least some civilisations think this way, and will therefore be concealing their presence."

"So, there's not much point looking for them," Copernicus said, rubbing his hands briskly. "In all likelihood, we'll never detect them, and that's probably for the best. If they're that scared, they won't be very welcoming." He held up a finger. "However, the ones that exist out in the open, the way we've always done, *can* be helped. We can warn them, and help them prepare for what's coming."

He went on to outline how, in return for the secret of Swirl technology, we would solicit our new allies for technology and materiel to help us in the coming battle. And when we finally managed to accumulate all the resources and personnel we needed, we would loop back around to the paired wormhole mouths, and travel back a thousand years.

Once there, safely hidden in the past, we'd hunker down and begin preparations for the real work ahead.

And it would be hard work.

Because next time around, we weren't going to wait for the aliens to come to us. Instead, we planned to ride out at the head of an even larger, multi-species force, and stop the wavefront in its tracks long before it got anywhere near the Earth. Maybe even chase it back to its home world and imprison its instigators in their own version of the Swirl, so they couldn't threaten to overrun the spiral arm.

Dark forest be damned; we were turning on the lights.

MESSAGE BOARD

> WAR! Multiple explosions beyond the Swirl. But who is fighting, and who is winning?
> **[Click to Read More]**

*

FIRST SPEAKER LANZO reappears on Luna and addresses Assembly. Her message: Do Not Panic.
[Click to Read More]

*

SWIRL. Quakes intensify as Swirl segments begin moving sunwards. Physicists estimate final closure in six days.
[Click to Read More]

*

JITTERBUG: Lanzo names heroic civilian vessel at the heart of solar system's defence. But who is Copernicus Brown, and why is he suddenly so important?
[Click to Read More]

CHAPTER FORTY-SIX

COPERNICUS BROWN

The time had come to enter stasis. We were clear of the solar system and moving at a fair clip, but it would be several years until we arrived in our first target system.

I assembled the crew in the *Jitterbug*'s cargo bay. The four stasis pods were stacked against the rear wall like something from a Japanese capsule hotel. I didn't know how they worked, only that somehow, they created a field that allowed the capsule to deflect the flow of time around itself, the way the prow of a boat deflected water around its hull. This meant that although we might stay cocooned for years of objective time (itself a tricky concept when travelling close to the speed of light), we would experience only the merest instant, emerging from our slumber only subjective seconds after entering it.

We got Kiki settled first. She scrambled into her capsule and Ulf put his hand on her forehead.

"Sleep well, little one."

He stepped back and the lid lowered. The lock activated, and the casket became a silver mirror as the stasis field engaged.

He climbed into the next pod, wriggling his shoulders to get comfortable in surroundings that had been copious for Kiki but were cramped for his large bulk.

"I'll see you in a moment," he rumbled.

Amber smiled down at him. "See you, big lad."

And then it was just the two of us.

"Are you sure about this?" she asked.

"As sure as I can be." I shrugged a shoulder. "I know we're doing the right thing."

"Same here."

I helped Amber into her pod, kissed her, and activated it.

Alone, I left the silver caskets where they were and climbed the aluminium ladder back up to the bridge, where I sat in the command chair that had once belonged to my father, and let the fierce light from the forward viewscreen play across my features.

The gravity drive worked silently and without vibration, so the only sounds were the gentle waft of the air conditioning and the occasional creak and flex of the hull.

>Aren't you going into stasis, Captain?

The glare of the stars ahead resembled a light at the end of a long, dark tunnel.

In a while.

>Are you okay?

I'm fine. I was tired, but if I went into stasis now, I didn't know what I might face when I came out again. Whatever it was, I didn't want to deal with it until I'd had a breather.

I stretched out my legs and let my elbows rest on the arms of the chair.

I'm just going to sit here for a while.

EPILOGUE I

JUSTICE BROWN

I'm sorry, what was I saying?

No, it doesn't matter. You've heard enough rambling from this old woman. I know you have things to do, my boy. Important things. I just thought you should know the story of how, on the evening that Saturn started to unspool, your adopted grandfather Leon went and got his fool self killed falling off a roof.

He was my best friend, and I loved him. But you have to understand, if he hadn't gone and done that, I'd still be down there in South London. Without his insurance money, I'd never have been able to afford to come up here. No, siree. And that means, in a very real and literal sense, that you, Copernicus, are only alive because he died.

His money let me flee to the Moon with your father in my arms. If it hadn't, then Malcolm would never have been in the right place, years later, to meet your mother and, against all sense and likelihood, fall in love with her.

Never forget, Copernicus, that just like the rest of us, you are the product of coincidence and luck.

What I'm trying to say is time and tide wash us up in some unexpected places, and sometimes things happen for a reason. We can't always see the nature of the reason, because more often than not, it doesn't exist yet. Not in that moment. I couldn't see the reason for

Leon being dead until all those years later. Then it became clear to me. He died so you could be born. We make the future from the ashes of the past. And in the meantime, we keep moving forward, because that's the only direction the universe grants us. And it's only when we look back that we realise where it all started, and how everything that happened to us brought us to the place we were always s'posed to be.

Now, your mother's gone and died, and right now, it seems like the end of your world. But one day, you'll look back and see this tragedy as another part of life's weave and weft. The reason you got to be where you are.

That's wisdom, boy. People are like coins dropped in ponds. When they die, the ripples they create echo outwards, shaping the world in ways we can't always understand until much, much later. The pain of their loss stays with us. That never goes away, but eventually we realise that loss, however sad and painful it might be at the time, can also be the start of a new and unpredictable chapter in our lives.

Every ending turns out to be a beginning.

Oh.

Oh, no.

No, don't cry, little one. I'm sorry. I'm just a clumsy old woman trying to impart some experience. Don't pay no mind to my rambling. I know your father's going to take good care of you on that rattly old ship of his. Lord knows why he saw fit to call it that stupid name. But Malcolm knows what he's about. He's got your grandmother's common sense. You can trust him.

Be good, and do what he tells you.

Now, give your old grandmother a hug. I have a feeling about you, Copernicus. Your grandfather would call it a premonition, but then as I've said, he was an idiot who thought he knew the future.

I just trust that one day, you'll get to be where you need to be, and see all the wins and losses of life as simply stepping stones along the way.

All I know for sure, my darling boy, is that you're going to fly.

You're going to fly so far.

EPILOGUE II

COPERNICUS BROWN

And of course, I saved him.

The other me, the one that called himself Leon. When he fell off that roof, I saved his life. I felt I owed him that much, and you can achieve pretty much anything when you have a bricolage of advanced human and alien technology and a thousand years to prepare.

Using a sample of my own DNA, I created a replica of my body, assembled by printer nozzles, one wafer-thin slice at a time. When it was complete, it was identical to me in every way except that it lacked the spark of life. A hollow shell on a brightly lit steel table.

When Leon tripped and toppled over the edge of the building, it was the duplicate that hit the parked cars below. We swapped them in mid-air. With half of London concentrating on the night sky, no one noticed one more drone among the tumult of delivery drones, helicopters, and airliners over the capital.

And just like that, it was done. As far as Justice and history were concerned, Leon was dead. My personal timeline remained unaffected.

The *Jitterbug* hovered over the city, using acquired stealth technology that allowed it to slip unseen through one of the world's most heavily supervised volumes of sky. As the dark, casket-shaped device came aboard, I stepped forward and released the lid.

And found myself looking into my own face.

A little older, perhaps. A little greyer at the temples.

I helped him out of the box and brought him up to speed.

"I guess I should thank you," he said, standing there in his shorts and flip-flops, breath tangy with beer.

"Not at all," I told him. "Frankly, we could do with your insight."

He nodded, assimilating everything I had told him. "You went around again?"

"We did."

"Didn't the protective sphere work?"

"As far as I know, we locked humanity safely inside. But there's more we can do this time, more worlds we can save."

"And the *Jitterbug*?"

The ship's blue-skinned avatar stepped forward, iridescent feathers shimmering in the cargo hold's overhead light. "I'm here, Leon."

He smiled. "Well, look at you."

"It's good to see you, too."

"Are you my version of the *Jitterbug*, or the new one?"

"I'm both." She reached out and touched his cheek. "We decided to merge together in order to pool our resources and experience."

"You can do that?"

"Apparently so," I told him. "Kiki was worried that merging two different versions of the ship might somehow cause a universe-imploding paradox. But we're all still here, so I guess…"

Leon reached out and gripped my shoulder. "I guess the universe has bigger fish to fry."

I led him up to the bridge and we stared down at the soft lights of London sweltering in the oppressive summer heat.

"Time is a circle," he said. "It always brings you back to the beginning."

A smaller window in the display showed a magnified, real-time image of the unspooling rings of Saturn.

"Come on," I told him. "We have a lot of work to do."

The *Jitterbug* began to rise, slowly at first, then accelerating until she was going up like a bullet fired at the stars.

Below, a woman named Justice was about to embark on a journey that would lead her and her infant son to a small apartment on Tranquillity Station, and then later to the birth of another version of me. But that was years away, and right now we had a war fleet to lead, and a timeline to alter.

Above us, among the disintegrating planets of the outer solar system, lay a whole new version of the universe, just waiting for us to bring it into being.

END

ABOUT THE AUTHOR

Gareth L. Powell has written novels, novellas, short fiction collections, and a non-fiction guide for aspiring authors. At the time of publication, he has twice won the British Science Fiction Association Award for Best Novel and has also been a finalist for the Locus Award (twice), the British Fantasy Award, the Seiun Award, the Premios Ignotus, the Premio Italia, and the Canopus Award.

You can find him online at *www.garethlpowell.com*.

— Also available from Titan Books —

WHO WILL YOU SAVE?

Gareth L. Powell

This entertaining and thought-provoking collection features work drawn from Powell's twenty-year career as a writer, his best-loved stories, and previously unpublished material revisiting the expansive settings of his acclaimed science fiction sagas.

Ranging from the dead sands of Mars to the half-flooded remnants of Amsterdam, from the seedy backstreets of Buenos Aires to the gravity well of a singularity, these action-packed tales explore mind-bending ideas through the eyes of unforgettable and all-too-human characters.

As their lives implode around them, will they use the moment to save their own skins, or to find a way to make up for past misdeeds?

Who will they save?

Who would you save?

"One of our best modern SF writers."
ADRIAN TCHAIKOVSKY, award-winning author
of *Children of Time* and *Alien Clay*

"Current leader of the British space-opera pack."
The Morning Star

"A pro at the top of his game."
JOHN SCALZI, Hugo-award winning author
of *Redshirts* and *Old Man's War*

TITANBOOKS.COM

Also available from Titan Books

FUTURE'S EDGE

Gareth L. Powell

A thrilling, page-turning journey into deep space, where the fights are brutal and the relationships are complicated, from the BSFA award-winning author of *Stars and Bones* and *Embers of War*.

When archaeologist Ursula Morrow accidentally infects herself with an alien parasite, she fears she may have jeopardised her career. However, her concerns become irrelevant when Earth is destroyed, billions die, and suddenly no one needs archaeologists anymore…

Two years later, she's plucked from a refugee camp on a backwater world and tasked with retrieving the artefact that infected her, as it just might hold the key to humanity's survival. With time running short, and the planet housing the weapon now situated in hostile territory, she realises she's going to have to commit an act of desperate piracy if she's going to achieve her objective before the enemy's final onslaught.

"Gareth brings his trademark blend of fierce action, ingenious SF ideas and an intriguing cast of characters. An excellent read."
ADRIAN TCHAIKOVSKY, award-winning author of *Children of Time* and *Alien Clay*

"Gareth Powell's writing upgrades classic Science Fiction tropes with modern sensibilities and a nifty twist"
PETER F. HAMILTON, author of *Exodus: The Archimedes Engine* and *Salvation*

"Crazy inventiveness, vivid characters and enthralling action. This is thrilling, joyous stuff."
M.R. CAREY, bestselling author of *The Girl with All the Gifts* and *Infinity Gate*

TITANBOOKS.COM

Also available from Titan Books

STARS AND BONES
A CONTINUANCE NOVEL

Gareth L. Powell

From the inspired and multiple award-winning Gareth L. Powell, *Stars and Bones* is a stunningly inventive and action-packed science-fiction epic. An iconic space opera that was shortlisted for the British Science Fiction Association Award for Best Novel, it is perfect for fans of Becky Chambers and Ann Leckie.

Seventy-five years from today, the human race has been cast from a dying Earth to wander the stars in a vast fleet of arks—each shaped by its inhabitants into a diverse and fascinating new environment, with its own rules and eccentricities.

When her sister disappears while responding to a mysterious alien distress call, Eryn insists on being part of the crew sent to look for her. What she discovers on Candidate-623 is both terrifying and deadly. When the threat follows her back to the fleet and people start dying, she is tasked with seeking out a legendary recluse who may just hold the key to humanity's survival.

"Gareth Powell drops you into the action from
the first page and then Just. Keeps. Going."
JOHN SCALZI, hugo-award winning author
of *Redshirts* and *Old Man's War*

"A vividly imagined, propulsive read. Filled with
a loveable cast of characters. Powell's writing creates
a rich tapestry of their voices and inner lives.
I think readers will be thrilled by this story."
TEMI OH, author of *Do You Dream of Terra-Two?*

TITANBOOKS.COM

DESCENDANT MACHINE
A CONTINUANCE NOVEL

Gareth L. Powell

From the award-winning Gareth L. Powell comes a gripping, fast-paced and fascinating science fiction adventure, the much awaited follow-up to *Stars and Bones*.

When Nicola Mafalda's scout ship comes under attack, she's left deeply traumatised by the drastic action it takes to keep her alive.

Months later, when an old flame comes to her for help, she realises she has to find a way to forgive both the ship and her former lover.

Reckless elements are attempting to reactivate a giant machine that has lain dormant for thousands of years. To stop them, Nicola and her crew will have to put aside their differences, sneak aboard a vast alien megaship, and try to stay alive long enough to prevent galactic devastation.

"*Descendant Machine* is smoothly paced, engagingly crafted, and crammed full of a sense of wonder at the sheer scale of the universe. Whatever Powell has planned next, on this evidence, it'll be well worth paying attention."
SFX

"A fast-paced and incisive story from one of the best British SF writers"
ADRIAN TCHAIKOVSKY, award-winning author of *Shards of Earth*

"Gareth Powell rocks again! *Descendant Machine* is big concept made accessible by a masterful writer. Fun, weird, fast-paced, and thoroughly entertaining! Grab this now!"
JONATHAN MABERRY, *New York Times*-bestselling author of *Kagen the Damned* and *V-Wars*

For more fantastic fiction, author events,
exclusive excerpts, competitions, limited editions and more

VISIT OUR WEBSITE
titanbooks.com

LIKE US ON FACEBOOK
facebook.com/titanbooks

FOLLOW US ON TWITTER AND INSTAGRAM
@TitanBooks

EMAIL US
readerfeedback@titanemail.com